Printed in the United States 2010
By BookMasters, Inc.
30 Amberwood Parkway
Ashland, OH 44805

Ascent of the Immortal
ISBN: 978-0-9828248-0-1
vampires, fiction

US $12.95
CA $14.95

ASCENT OF THE IMMORTAL

ANN MARIE KNAPP

For Mom and Dad,
The two greatest people I've ever known.
I love you.

ACKNOWLEDGEMENTS

First and foremost, I am truly grateful to Patricia Dannenberg, for her extreme generosity, emotional support, and editorial advice. She played a significant role in making this book happen and I owe her my eternal gratitude. I'd also like to thank Barbara Morvay for her kindness, support, and wealth of information that helped me quickly move forward in the publishing process. A very special thank you to Pamela Holland for countless hours of editing and advice regarding this story. Her passion for my story served as an inspiration to keep writing. I am also grateful to my friend, Pamela Sostheim, for supporting my efforts to write this book and for sound advice regarding details of the story and landscape of the area. Cindy Bacot has my appreciation for spending numerous hours on the phone listening to me obsess over Gwenevere and Connor's story and for her support of my ideas. I am indebted to Marilyn and Robert Hauser for their incredible editorial advice and assistance. You are amazing and I am so appreciative of your help. A special thanks goes to Russell Kinslow for his incredible graphic artistry on the cover and formatting expertise. I'd like to thank Antonio Capulera, the face of Connor Blake, for providing the face of such a special character as well as Beverly Taylor Capulera for her incredible support and enthusiasm for the book. A final thank you to my parents, family, friends, and colleagues for helping make this book come to fruition.

Chapter 1

When Dr. Gwenevere Ryan arrived at *The Immortal,* she wondered if she was making a mistake. Already she could see a block-long line had formed at the front of the solid steel doors. A six-foot-nine-inch barrel-chested Caucasian male with dark sunglasses and pallid skin stood with his arms folded surveying the crowd. Gwen had been right in assuming the club theme was based on vampires as several of the individuals waiting in line were wearing black with some sporting fake fangs. Gwen felt her face flush when several men smiled in her direction. She waited for over thirty minutes before she started to walk away. Just then the tall bouncer approached Gwen asking for her identification. He grabbed a small flashlight from the back pocket of his pants and with it examined her license carefully. Towering over her, the pale-skinned man stood unusually close to Gwen with his nose near her face.

"AB positive. Very nice," he whispered before his lips curled into a twisted smile.

Gwen stared at him bewildered, before he motioned for her to present her right hand with the palm facing down so that he could stamp the back of her skin. The stamp was a small black rosebud with several prickly thorns that appeared to be dripping something wet, possibly blood. The tall man escorted Gwen to the front of the line, where the doors to the club opened automatically. Gwen reflexively showed her license to another young man standing just inside the club doors. He barely noticed the ID she handed him.

"Is there a cover charge?" she asked. The young man gently took Gwen's hand in his and looked carefully at the stamp.

"No, you have a rosebud. Entrance is free for you," he replied with a glint in his eye. Gwen was about to ask the man why entrance was free for people with rosebud stamps, but refrained. She figured the money she saved on the cover charge would pay for her drinks. Gwen moved through the turn style of the booth and passed red posh drapes that hung from the wall allowing full access to the club.

The interior design of *The Immortal* reminded Gwen of a gothic horror movie set. Most of the walls were painted flat black, while the doors leading to smaller rooms and the restrooms were painted blood red. Several massive crystal chandeliers were hung prominently from the ceiling and gas lamps lined the walls providing an eerie, surreal atmosphere. Torches hung on the walls on either side of the stainless steel bar that was also illuminated from behind with bright red lights. A grand fireplace with a white marble mantle lined the wall opposite the bar. Silver candelabras with long red-lit candles adorned the mantle, while the wooden floors were lined with expensive oriental rugs.

Gwen walked over to the bar and asked the bartender for a top-shelf margarita.

"When is the band playing?" she asked as the bartender placed her drink in front of her.

"They're due to play in twenty minutes upstairs." The bartender, pale like the previous employees, pointed to the spiral staircase that led to the second floor of the club.

"Thanks," she replied as she grabbed her drink and walked over to the fireplace.

Gwen noticed a young couple sitting on a plush red couch on one side of a dark wood ornate coffee table that was beside the fireplace.

Gwen sat down with her drink on the empty couch opposite the pair. The couple barely noticed her and kept talking in muffled tones as the man ran his fingers along the young woman's delicate neck, whispering in her ear. Gwen noticed the young woman had a far away look to her like she was drugged or in a trance. As if detecting her thoughts, the man looked at Gwen with a look of admonition and then quickly motioned for the young woman to rise from the couch and leave with him. As the young girl walked away hand-in-hand with the man, Gwen noticed she, too, had a black rosebud stamp.

A steady flow of patrons moved about the club, most climbing the stairs to get to the second floor where the band would be playing. Gwen noticed as people walked close by, that most of them sported one of three types of stamps on their hands. A few patrons, like her, had black rosebuds and a handful of others had what looked like a drop of blood. However, the majority of the crowd simply had, "*The Immortal*" written in Old-English script stamped on their skin. Gwen wondered what the distinction was among these three types of stamps and why hers differed from the other two. Rising from the couch, she finished her drink, placed her empty glass on the coffee table, and walked upstairs.

Gwen found a seat across the stage that would allow her a great view of the entire band, dressed in black jeans and tattered t-shirts bearing the band's name, "Scarlet Lines" in bright bold red lettering. All members of the band had dark spiky hair, save for the drummer who wore her long platinum blonde hair swept up into two side pigtails. She was pretty with delicate features, but the black leather choker with chains surrounding her neck and metal rings that pierced her upper lip severely sharpened her look. The band played multiple cover songs from a variety of time periods, demonstrating their incredible range and talent.

After an hour of playing, the band took a well-deserved break. Gwen quickly got up to use the restroom hoping that when she returned she'd still have a seat at her table, but the seats had rapidly filled in her absence. She scanned the room for another seat that would have a decent view of the stage and found only one near a table already occupied. She didn't see any other open chairs and hoped the people at the table wouldn't mind her asking for the vacant seat. As she walked towards them, she was struck by how strikingly beautiful these four individuals appeared to be. Comprised of three men and a woman, the four had flawless translucent skin and delicate features. It wasn't until Gwen was in close proximity to the table, that she could see they all possessed the same luminescent ice-blue eyes, a color that appeared too radiant to be real. Before she could even ask them about the chair, they all turned to stare at her as she approached. It was as if they could read her thoughts and Gwen suddenly felt vulnerable and insecure. She noticed the pupils in each of those glowing pairs of eyes dilated as she moved closer.

Gwen mustered her courage and blurted out what she wanted to say. "I'm sorry to impose, but may I ask if that vacant seat is taken?"

"No, that seat is not taken and you are quite welcome to join us if you would like," one of the young men said as his gaze drifted from her eyes down the slope of her neck to the neckline of her black corset blouse before returning back to her eyes. I am Derrick Cole, nice to meet you," he said, as he held out his hand to shake Gwen's.

She placed her hand in Derrick's and was immediately taken aback by both the coolness and hardness of his skin. Gwen instantly experienced a chill, but halfheartedly smiled in an effort to conceal her momentary discomfort. Her unease was clearly apparent to Derrick who smiled sardonically back at her. Gwen guessed he was about twenty-five years old with medium length dark blonde hair that curled around his ears. Derrick was physically stunning and clearly this information wasn't lost on him. While Gwen didn't particularly care for Derrick's obvious narcissism, something about him was both appealing and enigmatic. In fact, she felt all the strangers at this table oozed an appeal that was palpable, yet indescribable. Gwen sat down in the empty chair beside Derrick.

Gwen forced another smile as she introduced herself to the group. "I'm Gwen Ryan. Thank you for letting me join you tonight."

The younger male next to Derrick stood up to shake her hand. "Pleased to make your acquaintance, I am Aidan Cole, Derrick's younger brother," Aidan said.

Gwen noticed that Aidan averted his gaze, suggesting he was shy compared with his more outspoken sibling. Aidan also had dark blonde hair that was cropped short, and he looked like he could be no older than twenty-one. The female introduced herself as Lucinda Blackmore, cousin to the Cole brothers. Lucinda had long brown hair that cascaded in big soft curls down her back. She looked to be in her mid twenties with a heart-shaped face, a tiny upturned nose, and intelligent looking eyes. Gwen felt a coldness emitting from Lucinda that made her anxious. She sensed the woman didn't care much for her presence or the meaningless pleasantries of introductions, but nevertheless was going through the motions.

Gwen looked toward the last member of the quartet. The most striking of the group, the man had thick wavy black hair that fell just above his shoulders, a square-jaw line, long black eyelashes that framed his sparkling eyes, and a perfectly shaped nose. In short, he looked like he could easily have stepped out of a Ralph Lauren catalog. Gwen guessed he was about twenty-eight or so.

"Connor Blake, nice to meet you Gwenevere," the man said, as he briefly glanced at her. Gwen's eyes opened wide and she felt her heart race.

"Pardon me, but I don't remember saying my full name when I introduced myself. How did you know Gwen was short for Gwenevere?" she asked, incredulously. Gwen had never run across another person named Gwenevere in her life and most people thought Gwen was short for Gwendolyn or Gwenyth. A look of alarm was noticeable in each pair of those luminous eyes. Connor's gaze shifted away from Gwen toward Derrick, Aidan, and Lucinda at various times, as if he were in a silent conversation with each of them.

After what seemed like several minutes, Connor glanced back at her. "Lucky guess, I suppose." There was another moment of uncomfortable silence at the table before Derrick spoke.

"So Gwen, what do you do, if you don't mind my asking?" Derrick's gleaming eyes furtively danced about the room before returning his gaze to her face.

"I'm a college professor at Emerald Coast University."

"Interesting, what do you teach?" Derrick asked.

"Psychology," Gwen said, matter-of-factly.

"Intriguing. What's your specialty?" Derrick asked.

Gwen was about to answer when Lucinda interrupted her conversation with Derrick. "So *Gwen* what brings you to the club tonight?"

"I came to hear the band," Gwen said.

"Really, is that the *only* reason you came tonight?" Lucinda asked, as she moved closer to Gwen's face. Her mouth forming a smirk as Lucinda took Gwen's hand in her own examining the rosebud stamp. Lucinda's fingers, like Derrick's, were ice cold and smooth like marble. Lucinda used her index finger to trace the rosebud pattern on Gwen's skin.

Gwen suddenly felt light-headed and a bit nauseous. "I—don't know what you mean. Is there some other reason I'd come here?" Gwen stammered as she pulled her hand away from Lucinda's firm grip.

Lucinda smiled wider at Gwen fascinated by her response.

"I see this one is strong-willed. Nice—I like someone with a bit of fight. It makes things so much more interesting wouldn't you say—" Lucinda said to the three men observing the strange exchange between the two women.

"Lucinda, can't you tell you are making our guest feel uncomfortable? We do not want the poor girl to run off before we have even had an opportunity to have any fun," Derrick said, flashing Lucinda a dirty look.

"Perhaps, she doesn't know—" Aidan, said.

"She does have a rosebud stamp on her hand, Aidan. Surely, she has some idea. Or does she?" Lucinda asked, her brows knitted.

"I don't have any idea what the rosebud stamp means. I see that very few people have them here tonight and for that matter, why don't any of you have a stamp?" Gwen asked hoping they'd answer her questions for a change.

The group stared at one another again in yet another moment of prolonged awkward silence before Derrick spoke.

"The rosebud means you possess something rare and special that is coveted by some individuals in this place. Specifically, it means that you—"

"Derrick, perhaps it's best if we leave this conversation for another time," Connor said, firmness in his tone. "Gwenevere, the stamps aren't important, pay no attention to my cousins. They are bored and toying with you."

"I don't *appreciate* your tone, Connor," Lucinda retorted.

"Forgive me, dear Lucinda. I meant no harm," Connor said.

"Honestly cousin, you can be quite insufferable at times. Fine, we'll discuss this matter with Gwen another time," Lucinda said as she turned her attention from Connor back to Gwen.

Gwen wasn't sure what was going on among the cousins, but she didn't care for their games or being trifled with. She was about to leave, when Derrick asked her to dance.

"I don't think that would be such a good idea. It's getting late and I should be getting home. Besides, the band is still on break."

Just then, Gwen noticed the band was back on stage and had resumed playing. She had spoken too soon.

"Please forgive me for my poor behavior. All I ask is one dance so you'll see I am actually a nice guy," Derrick insisted, as he looked at Gwen. His expression seemed to soften and the mocking tone apparent only moments before was gone. His eyes conveyed a sincerity Gwen hadn't observed before.

"Okay, one dance," she sighed. "But, no funny stuff or you'll be sorry," she said with a forced smile. The truth was that Derrick made Gwen uncomfortable, but she didn't think much harm could come from one dance.

Derrick stood up and pulled out Gwen's chair so that she could easily rise. It appeared that Derrick had manners after all. He escorted her to the dance floor and he put his arms around her waist pulling her close to him. Gwen wasn't used to being this close to a stranger and intentionally put some physical distance between her body and his. She thought she heard Derrick chuckle as she did this, but when she looked up at him, his face was serious again. Gwen didn't recognize the song, but it had a hypnotic beat and she soon felt herself relax and sway in time with the music. It was curious, but she noticed she felt light-headed as they danced. It had been quite some time since she had her margarita and she knew she wasn't intoxicated. She wondered why she felt this way, but soon the music and mood of the club overtook her and she just decided to enjoy the moment.

Although Gwen had only promised Derrick one song, over thirty minutes had passed since they started dancing. He started pulling her closer to him and she didn't feel the need to resist this time. The intoxicating feeling Gwen experienced was intensifying and she was so close to letting him kiss her. This was unlike her, her emotions in conflict with her rational thought. However, Gwen's emotions and desires soon won over and when he pulled her even closer to him, she was ready to kiss him. Just then, she felt someone tug at her arm.

"Mind if I cut in?" Connor asked, pulling Gwen from Derrick's grasp and into his arms before Derrick could protest.

Gwen saw a flash of anger in Derrick's luminous blue eyes, but it soon extinguished as he quickly regained his composure.

"Sure cousin, no reason for me to be greedy. Thank you Gwen, and have a good evening." With that Derrick smiled and quickly departed from view.

Gwen noticed Connor was several inches taller than Derrick and a better dancer as well. Yet, he seemed to be more guarded than Derrick as he intentionally kept her at a greater distance from his body. They danced like this for nearly an hour. Gwen noticed the band started playing one of her favorite songs, "How Soon is Now," by The Smiths. She was amazed by how much the lead singer sounded like Morrissey. She found herself moving instinctively closer to Connor as she swayed to the beat of the haunting and sensual melody. The familiar feeling of intoxication returned with a vengeance and Gwen wondered whether she would need a cab to go home that evening.

Although she sensed an internal struggle within him, she observed Connor's body drifting closer to hers. She felt quite giddy and noticed the every sensation seemed to be heightened. She could detect each note of the music, each pulse of light that flashed from above, the intoxicating sweetness of Connor's scent. It was wonderful and she felt drawn to it. Gwen desperately wanted him to kiss her and as if reading her thoughts, his lips soon found hers. They were cold, but smooth and amazingly soft as they delicately brushed up against hers. His lips played with hers briefly, before he pulled away and gently kissed her face moving down towards her neck. She could no longer hear the music, just the beating of her own heart as she felt his lips make contact with her skin. Suddenly, she felt something sharp lightly move across the skin at the base of her throat before Connor abruptly pulled away from her.

"You really shouldn't be here, Gwenevere. This place isn't safe for you," he whispered to her as he held her to him.

Gwen looked into Connor's eyes surprised by his comment and sudden change of behavior.

"What do you mean?" she asked.

"Just what I said, you are in danger here." He looked intently into her eyes.

"From what?"

"From people here who would take advantage of your innocence."

Gwen thought Connor's comment a ridiculous cliché. "I'm a big girl. I can handle myself. I'm not a young, naïve woman who doesn't have a clue about men and the way they operate. I can take care of myself just fine, thank you," she said, as she attempted to pull away from him, but Connor held her close.

"I'm not insulting you Gwenevere, just giving you a friendly warning. There are people here who would harm you if given the opportunity. I don't want to see you get hurt."

"I don't understand how you could go from kissing me one moment to warning me about looming dangers the next" she said, rolling her eyes. "Your lack of confidence in me is condescending." Connor looked away from her, his expression now one of embarrassment.

"I'm sorry, forgive me for making an ass out of myself. I guess I'm being a bit melodramatic."

"Yes, I would say so!" At that moment, Gwen saw Connor's mortified expression. She surmised he was reacting out of embarrassment over their kiss more than anything else.

"I guess I was just embarrassed by my actions on the dance floor. I don't usually kiss women I've just met," he whispered to Gwen confirming her perception of his actions.

"Well, I certainly don't kiss strange men I've just met either," Gwen said, relenting. "That's completely uncharacteristic of me. If anything, I'm generally considered standoffish when I first meet people."

"Well, no harm done then right?" Connor asked.

"No, no harm done," Gwen replied, noting how tired she unexpectedly felt.

"May I walk you to your car? Connor asked, as he pulled his arms away from her and put them in the pockets of his black slacks.

"That would be kind," Gwen stated, observing how uncanny it was that his thoughts seemed to be in step with hers.

Gwen noticed that the feelings of intoxication she had experienced during the time she danced with both Derrick and Connor had completely vanished. She was bewildered by her interactions with this family and the two men, in particular. While Connor accompanied Gwen down the staircase and out of the club, it seemed like he was intentionally avoiding touching her as he escorted her to her car.

"I hope you have a good night, Gwenevere,"

"Thank you, you too Connor."

Connor smiled one last time at her before he walked back towards the club. Gwen watched his retreating figure until he was at the club entrance before she turned to face her car. She was opening her car door when a strange man unexpectedly approached her. Catching her off guard, she dropped her car keys to the ground and the man swooped down to pick them up.

"Sorry to bother you, but would you happen to know the time?" he asked as he was in the process of handing Gwen her keys.

Gwen was about to reply when without warning, he grabbed her arm wrenching her body close to his and buried his face in her neck. She was frightened and tried to pull away from the stranger, but his grip was powerful. Gwen suddenly felt weak and faint. She made an attempt to scream, but couldn't get her vocal chords to cooperate. It was as if she were paralyzed. The man seemed to enjoy her struggle, evident by his gruff laughter at her unsuccessful attempts to break free of his hold. Gwen knew he was going to kill her. Although she couldn't see the weapons, she felt him press two sharp knife-like objects against the skin of her throat. Terrified she closed her eyes bracing herself for the painful death she was certain would follow.

Suddenly, Connor appeared by her side growling at the man in an inhuman voice as he forcibly jerked Gwen from the stranger's grasp. She thought she heard the man mumble something apologetic to Connor regarding a human familiar, but she could not grasp his meaning. The stranger sped off before Gwen could scan his face. Connor asked Gwen if she was okay, but she only nodded, unable to speak. She would have collapsed to the ground, had Connor not swiftly swept her up in his arms. He carefully placed her into the passenger seat of her car and fastened the seat belt around her body. Still in a haze, Gwen watched Connor sprint to the driver's seat, and crank the ignition.

"Gwenevere, look at me," Connor commanded.

Gwen slowly rolled her head towards him. Her body felt leaden as she struggled to maintain consciousness.

Connor gentled stroked the left side of her face as he whispered to her. "Go to sleep Gwenevere, you are safe now."

Gwen struggled vainly to remain awake, but darkness overtook her and she slept. Hours later, she would wake up to find herself in her own bed, her car in the driveway, her house locked, and the keys sitting on the kitchen table, having no memory how she got home or what had happened to Connor Blake.

Chapter 2

The following morning, a line of storm clouds that stretched from Texas to the Florida Panhandle brought intense rainfall to the region. Gwen sat at her kitchen table sipping coffee as she watched the onslaught of heavy showers whip across her backyard soaking everything in its path. Puddles of rain were collecting in the valleys in her grass and she noticed a few yellow finches huddled closely seeking refuge under her awning. Her mind raced as she reviewed the events of the previous night.

Upon first awakening Gwen was convinced it was all a dream or some wild fantasy she had contrived. However, when she went out that morning to check her car shortly before the storms arrived, she noticed her front seat had been moved farther back than her typical setting. She would not have been able to drive the car comfortably with the seat in that position. In fact, its current setting would be considered outright dangerous for Gwen if she were the driver. The only logical conclusion was that someone much taller than she had driven her car home last night. *Connor!*

She remembered the outline of Connor's face, the way she felt when he held her hand, his scent, their brief kiss, and his saving her from harm. Gwen shuddered when she thought of how the strange man easily overpowered her in the parking lot. Had it not been for Connor's swift arrival, Gwen wasn't sure she'd be alive now. Connor was right. It wasn't as safe at *The Immortal* as she had thought. Nevertheless, his admonition angered her. Gwen was used to being strong and capable of defending herself, but the strange man caught her off-guard and that's all it took. This thought frightened Gwen. She was grateful for Connor's help, but hated acknowledging that vulnerability. It had taken Gwen years to feel strong and secure in her ability to shape the events in her life following her divorce and in one quick night her confidence had been shaken.

Another thought plagued Gwen. *How had Connor managed to get to her so quickly when he was so far away from her car?* She specifically remembered watching him walk from her car to the entrance doors of the club. The distance was considerable and it just didn't seem possible that he could span such a large distance in mere seconds. For that matter, Gwen wasn't able to scream and the parking lot was fairly dark. She didn't remember seeing anyone except the stranger who seized her, so who had alerted Connor to her distress? It made no sense and it troubled her that she couldn't produce a rational explanation for Connor's phenomenal timing.

Gwen also wondered how Connor had managed to lock her front door from the inside. She had a deadbolt mounted on the front door that could only be locked from the outside with a key. The only other way to secure the lock was for someone to slide the deadbolt on the door from the inside. Gwen had no memory of locking her door last night. In fact, there was no evidence that Connor had even been at her house, save for the seat setting change in her car. Things just weren't adding up.

Gwen sat mesmerized staring out the window. She wanted to put thoughts of Connor Blake out of her mind. But, this was proving to be a difficult task and hours disappeared as Gwen replayed the events of the previous night. At some point, the phone rang, breaking Gwen's concentration.

Gwen jumped up to grab the cordless phone from its cradle off the kitchen countertop. She recognized the number instantly. It was her friend, Cindy Sinclaire.

"Hey Gwen, how was last night?"

"It was bizarre."

"Bizarre? How so?" Cindy asked.

"Long story—"

"Please, I need a break from my three kids, they're driving me crazy. Come on, spill—"

"I'd rather tell you in person. How about we meet at Java Jake's in an hour?" Gwen asked.

"Yeah, I think my husband can handle the kids for awhile. I'll meet you for coffee before I hit the grocery store."

That settled, Gwen quickly showered and left her house in her 2008 dark blue Infiniti G37 coupe. The morning's heavy downpours were replaced with a light mist. She pulled into one of the many open parking spaces near Java Jake's, a swanky little coffee shop in the old downtown area of Panama City. During the workweek, finding a parking space would have been nearly impossible. Cindy was already inside the shop sipping coffee when Gwen walked inside.

"Hey, Gwen how are you?" Cindy asked, as she reached over to give Gwen a hug.

"I'm good," Gwen said. "I'll go order my coffee and be right back."

"Okay, sounds good," Cindy said.

Gwen walked over to the counter and ordered her usual, a vanilla latte. She waited patiently as the young woman behind the coffee fountain brewed her coffee and steamed the milk. The young woman smiled at Gwen as she placed the coffee on the counter and took the five-dollar bill Gwen had placed on the counter over to the register. Handing back Gwen's change, the young woman walked back over to the coffee stand to put fresh coffee in the machine. Gwen stared at her a moment, trying to figure out where she'd seen the woman before.

"Gwen, you coming over any time soon?" Cindy asked.

"Sorry Cindy, I was just trying to figure out where I've seen that woman before. Something about her seems vaguely familiar, but I can't place it."

"Maybe she was a former student?"

"No, I don't think so—anyway she just seems familiar somehow."

"You okay Gwen, you look distracted."

"Yeah, I'm okay; it just kills me every time I have to leave Andy in Georgia. Feels like I'm missing part of my self when he's gone."

"I know it must be awful, but it's just for eight weeks. At least you know that Andy looks forward to summers with his Dad. That should help, right?"

Gwen sighed. "I suppose so, but it doesn't make the house feel any less empty."

Cindy placed her hand on top of Gwen's and smiled at her. "I'm sorry Gwen, I know you miss him."

Gwen nodded. Andy was Gwen's only child and greatest blessing in life, but being a divorced single parent posed challenges for Gwen, that were hard to deal with, such as Andy's annual summer visitation with his father. She knew it was good for Andy to spend time with his dad, but every year she dreaded his absence from home.

"Lucky for you, I've got three kids who would be happy to spend time with Aunt Gwen, if you'd like," Cindy joked.

"One night soon, I'll come over and watch your three little hellions so you and James can have a night to yourselves," Gwen said as she winked at Cindy. "God knows you need it."

"Hmm, you have no idea."

The two women had been very close for a couple of years now and Cindy was like the sister Gwen never had. Born just five days apart near the end of April, Gwen used to joke that she and Cindy could have been in the nursery at the hospital together. As similar as the women were in personality, they differed in physical attributes. Gwen was tall with long wavy dark blonde hair, an oval-shaped face, pale skin, and grayish-blue doe-shaped eyes. In contrast, Cindy was tan, petite, and brunette. Cindy's deep green eyes reminded Gwen of the green waters of the gulf and with her perfect complexion and round full lips, she was simply gorgeous.

"So tell me about last night and don't leave out any details," Cindy said, her sparking green eyes squarely focused on Gwen.

Gwen recounted the entire story for Cindy. When she had finished there was a moment of silence while Cindy just stared at her wide-eyed.

"Cindy?"

"I don't know what to say. I'm just glad you are okay. You could have been hurt or even killed by that nut. As for Connor, I am speechless. If he *is* real, thank God he showed up when he did to scare the guy off," Cindy said.

"Cindy I'm not crazy, the seat adjustment in my car proves I didn't imagine him."

"I know Gwen, but you have to admit the whole story does sounds kind of surreal."

"Yeah, I suppose if someone told me that story I'd be dubious too. *You* believe me though, don't you?"

"Yes, I do—So what are you going to do now?"

"I don't know. I'd like to put Connor Blake out of my mind, but so far no luck. In fact, he's all I can think about today. I guess I need a distraction."

"So I take it you are going to go back to *The Immortal*?"

"I don't know. Maybe—we'll see!" Gwen replied, looking into her coffee cup that was now half empty.

"Well, I'd be extra careful next time, certainly park somewhere better lit and take a weapon in case you need one."

"That's not a bad idea—anyway, I just want to forget about the attack last night, among other things."

"Give it a few days. You're kind of freaked out right now, but things will improve with some time. And—remember not to be so hard on yourself; you have more than your fair share of stress compared to most. Focus some of that nervous energy on projects you want to get done, that should help," Cindy said.

"Yes, you're right. I have a number of papers I've been planning to tackle this summer break. But, I need some down time. Okay if I come by tomorrow night to see you and the gang? I miss the kids."

"Sure. Come for dinner. We're having lasagna. Why don't you bring some dessert?"

"Sounds great. I'll bring a chocolate cheese cake," Gwen said smiling.

"Perfect!" Cindy exclaimed.

"Okay, we'll I'll see you tomorrow."

Cindy got up to give Gwen a hug before tossing her empty coffee cup as she left. Gwen looked over at the woman who had served her coffee, noticing a small tattoo of a black rosebud on her lower back, when the young woman leaned over to pick up a box behind the counter. Gwen's eyebrows rose. The tattoo matched the stamp that was now fading on the back of Gwen's hand. The young woman looked over at her and Gwen quickly diverted her gaze. Gwen thought it an interesting coincidence.

On the drive home Gwen mulled over her conversation with Cindy. Cindy was right; she needed a distraction. When Gwen arrived home she changed into her workout clothes and jumped on the elliptical rider for an hour before hitting the shower and making herself some dinner. Then she called Andy to check in with him. She missed him so much.

"Hi Baby, what did you do today?" Gwen asked.

"Dad took me to the Atlanta aquarium. Mom, it was so cool we saw sharks, whales, and dolphins. You would have loved it."

"That's great Andy, I'm glad you're having a good time. What you'd have for dinner?" Gwen asked making sure Dan was feeding Andy properly.

"We had hamburgers on the grill with corn-on-the-cob and salad. Dad insisted I eat the salad and corn, but I preferred the burgers."

Gwen smiled, relieved that Dan was making an effort to abide by her demands for balancing meals for Andy.

"Good. I'm glad you're having a great time with Dad. Have any fun plans for tomorrow?"

"Dad mentioned having a picnic in a nearby park or something like that," Andy said, in a less than enthusiastic tone.

Gwen got the feeling Andy was leaving something out of the conversation from his voice inflections, but didn't press him. She figured whatever it was; it would come out sooner or later. "Okay Sweetie, well I just wanted to let you know I was thinking about you. Remember, you can call me anytime you want."

"I know Mom and I miss you too. I should go, I promised Dad I'd play a video game with him before going to bed tonight."

"Well, goodnight Sweetie. I'll talk with you soon. Love you."

"Love you too Mom," Andy said before hanging up the phone.

After Gwen hung up the phone, she decided to call it an early night and get some rest before heading into the university in the morning. Two minutes after Gwen's head rested on her pillow she was out cold.

The next morning Gwen woke up feeling rejuvenated and ready to write. She went through her usual morning routine brewing coffee and eating breakfast while she watched "Good Morning America." A quick shower and a thirty-minute commute later she was in her office writing. Gwen worked on a paper until five-thirty that evening, making good use of the large chunk of uninterrupted time. During a regular semester, she would have to advise several students during a typical day. Having the summer off to write was pure luxury.

Gwen left the university and picked up a cheesecake from the grocery store before having dinner with Cindy and her family that night. The rest of the week she concentrated on writing to distract her from thoughts of Andy and Connor and it had worked. Gwen finished editing two manuscripts that she was submitting for publication, with plans to work on a third paper the following week.

Gwen left the university late Friday night and went straight home to bed. She was wiped out, but felt good about her productivity. Somehow the bizarre events of the previous weekend were long gone from her mind. Or so Gwen thought.

Sleep escaped Gwen for most of Friday night, but close to dawn she finally fell asleep and had an intensely vivid dream. She was standing on the beach feeling the warmth of the humid breeze. Surrounding her were the sounds of waves cresting and falling along the shoreline. She noticed a figure approaching her beneath the light of a full moon. He was tall with a slim build and his black hair was blowing wildly in the wind. Gwen couldn't make out the details of his face, until he was closer and then she saw his brilliant blue eyes. It was Connor. He held out his hand for her to join him. Gwen didn't hesitate running to him and placing her hand in his. They walked along the beach coming to a blanket several feet in front of them. The beach was secluded and they knew they'd be safe from view here. Connor pulled her down to the blanket so that she was lying next to him. He stroked her hair, moving a few stray strands out of her eyes.

"Are you sure this is really what you want?" Connor whispered.

"Yes," Gwen said.

"There's no way I can talk you out of it, is there?" he sighed.

"No."

"This will change everything between us."

"I understand, but I have to know——"

He looked into her eyes one last time before pulling her to him. He ran his fingers through her hair as his lips reached for hers. Gwen felt the smooth coolness of his lips as they lightly touched hers. The kisses were soft at first, but soon became more urgent as his mouth and tongue greedily tasted hers. Connor started kissing her face working his way across her cheek and down to the base of her neck. Gwen responded by running her hands up and down his back pulling his torso closer to hers. She tried to relax, but adrenaline was coursing through her body. There was no way to prepare for what was coming, but she couldn't wait any longer—and then it happened.

Gwen felt something razor-sharp and needle-like pierce the delicate skin of her neck. Initially, she felt acute pain that made her gasp, but the pain quickly dissipated into one of the most intensely pleasurable sensations she'd experienced. Her body suddenly felt light and weightless, as if she were floating. Her mind was free of anxiety and wandered unreservedly as if there were no boundaries or limits to what she could observe. Her senses were dramatically heightened. Gwen noticed blemishes on the moon's surface she had been unable to see with the naked eye and detected the subtlest of nuisances in the scents and sounds surrounding her. It was like she was viewing the world for the first time and seeing details she never knew existed. Gwen felt overwhelming peacefulness and contentment. As she felt her blood being drained from her veins it occurred to her that she might die. Although she trusted Connor would stop in time, she knew it was a distinct possibility and, amazingly enough, she was not afraid. Gwen detected a new sound that was both steady and hypnotic. The pulsing sound captivated her and she wondered where it was coming from. It was only after Connor pulled away that she realized the pulsing sound was the rhythm of her own heartbeat. She heard him whisper to her that she would be fine and just needed some rest, but something inside her had changed. When he looked into her eyes, she knew he had been right all along. Things between them would never be the same. *He would hold an undeniable power over her, until she became like him.*

Gwen woke with a start. She lay there going over the details of the dream and how very real it seemed. Of course, vampires didn't exist and it was comical to even consider it. It wasn't the content of her dream that bothered her, but the fact that a week's worth of work-related distractions hadn't erased Connor from her mind. Gwen had the answer to Cindy's question. She was going back to *The Immortal*, if nothing else to thank him. But, she hoped for much more.

The Immortal was packed by the time Gwen arrived at the club Saturday night. She observed the line of club hopefuls was twice as long as last week's reflecting the club's growing popularity. Gwen didn't have to wait long to gain entrance; as soon as the tall bouncer saw her walk up to the line he immediately marked her hand with a rosebud stamp and escorted her inside. She looked for one of the red doors leading to a restroom. Inside Gwen was relieved to see her teeth were lipstick-free and she brushed a loose eyelash away from her cheek. Gwen left the bathroom and went upstairs looking for Connor Blake. Wearing a flattering rose-colored blouse that revealed a hint of breast, low-riser designer jeans with a bootleg cut, and her favorite black-strapped sandals, Gwen felt confident. Her long blonde hair bouncing as she climbed the stairs.

Gwen didn't see any evidence of Connor on the top floor of the club near the band arena. An inspection of the first floor didn't reveal any evidence of his presence either. Disappointed, Gwen walked over to the bar and ordered a drink. The bartender poured Gwen's vodka and cranberry juice cocktail in a frosted glass tumbler and handed it to her without saying a word. *Weird how the people who worked at this club had so little to say, she thought.* She sat at the bar sipping her drink feeling defeated. All she could do all day was think about *him* certain that she'd find him here tonight. Gwen could have simply looked for Connor in the phonebook, but where was the fun in that? And—for that matter not everyone had a phone number listed in the white pages. Most of her friends owned cell phones these days since they were cheaper and more convenient than a landline. Gwen sighed as she finished her drink. She entertained staying at the club, but just wasn't in the mood to be in a crowd. She had only come here for one reason and clearly it wasn't panning out. Images of the beach from her dream were still fresh in her mind and she thought that sounded like the place she wanted to be right now. Placing the bartender's tip on the bar, Gwen was grabbing her purse to leave when someone tapped her on the shoulder. Startled, Gwen turned to see Derrick standing next to her.

"Hi Gwen, I thought that was you, care to join us?" Derrick said, smiling at Gwen, his eyes drifting from her face to the contours of her bust line.

"Oh hi, Derrick. I didn't know you were here. Is Connor with you?" Gwen asked, hopeful.

"I see you favor my dear cousin, do you? Well, sorry to say I haven't seen the old boy, tonight."

"Oh, that's too bad. I wanted to discuss something with him."

"Really?"

"Uh-huh," Gwen nodded.

"Well, since Connor isn't here tonight would you like to join me and some close friends?"

"I don't know, I was actually on my way out to go to Panama City Beach," Gwen said.

Before Gwen could protest, Derrick took her hand in his caressing her fingers. Gwen instantly felt light-headed and dizzy.

"Are you sure you won't join us Gwen? I'd love to buy you a drink before you leave," Derrick pressed, with a roguish grin on his face.

Derrick's gaze made Gwen feel uneasy. She couldn't put her finger on it, but he was staring at her like she was a gourmet meal. Derrick's grip on her hand tightened and attempted to draw her closer to him. Gwen fought the mental fog she was experiencing to answer him.

"Thanks Derrick—perhaps another time—but right now I'm not feeling so well and I just want to get some fresh air. I hope you don't mind, but I'd appreciate it if you'd pass along the message to Connor that I was looking for him. He can reach me at the university. Thanks again," Gwen said, hoping Derrick wouldn't be angry and would carry out her wish. He begrudgingly released his grip on her hand and smiled.

"Of course, Love—enjoy the beach."

Derrick smiled once more before he disappeared into the crowd. Gwen thought it curious that she immediately felt better now that Derrick was gone. She noted that every time he touched her she felt dizzy and intoxicated. As she walked out of the club doors she removed a can of pepper spray from her purse before walking to her car. Better safe than sorry. Within a few minutes Gwen found her car and was exiting the parking lot.

She drove to Highway 98 and crossed the Hathaway Bridge into Panama City Beach before continuing on Back Beach Road. Gwen was happily cruising along when she realized the car behind her had been following her since Highway 98. She was in the left lane and decided to quickly move over to the right lane to see what the other car would do. She noticed the car reflexively slowed its pace to keep in time with hers. When they came to a red light, she seized the opportunity to get a good look at the car idling beside her. It was a 2009 black Porsche 911 with windows tinted so dark it was impossible to see the driver inside the vehicle. The Porsche revved its engine clearly sending Gwen an invitation to race. She sighed to herself, because she was pretty sure she couldn't beat the Porsche. Still, being that she was intrigued by the Porsche's boldness she figured she'd go for it.

When the light turned green Gwen slammed on the accelerator and held on for dear life. Initially, she was ahead and up to 90 mph in the blink of an eye, but the Porsche dropped down a gear and then punched it, sailing right by her. She giggled to herself, that she had been foolish to let the Porsche owner entice her to behave like a child. But, it wasn't her first time to behave recklessly speeding and racing and she doubted it would be her last. Just a few months ago, Gwen had chased a Dodge Viper on a road with heavy traffic because the driver had cut her off. The Porsche turned off Back Beach Road and Gwen lost site of the car. She slowed down to drive the speed limit and turned onto Claire Avenue. Within a few minutes, she made her last turn on Front Beach Road to one of the public entrances to the beach.

Gwen pulled into a parking space in the lot adjacent to the public beach entrance. She turned off the ignition, noticing a car pulling into the space alongside her. As she got out of the G, she quickly glanced at the car beside her and noticed it was the black Porsche that had just raced her. Her heart fluttered as she walked over to the Porsche's front door waiting for the mysterious driver to reveal himself. The driver's side window lowered just enough for Gwen to see a pair of radiant light blue eyes staring back at her.

"Hello, Gwenevere."

Gwen stood frozen for a moment unable to say or do anything. She couldn't believe her eyes.

"Connor?"

He smiled at her as got out of the car and closed the door. "In the flesh," he said, as he shrugged his shoulders and produced a playful smirk.

"Did you follow me from the club?" Gwen asked.

"Kind of—"

"What do you mean, kind of?"

"Well, I ran into Derrick and he said you were looking for me. He mentioned that you were going to the beach. I figured you'd come this way. It's the closest beach to the city," he said with his arms folded across his chest, leaning against the Porsche.

"Oh—okay."

"So are you mad I won?" he asked with an impish grin.

"Won what?"

"The race. You know—the one where I left you in my trail of dust back there?" Connor said, gloating.

"Oh—yeah—*that*—race. Hmm, yeah you did kick my ass back there didn't you? But, at least my car has a backseat." Gwen wished she had a snappier comeback, but came up empty.

"Well, you've got me there. But, somehow I'm not devastated by that news."

Connor wore faded jeans, a dark blue button down shirt, and leather boots. Standing there against his car he exuded a confidence that Gwen found extremely attractive. He possessed a quality Gwen rarely ran across; *he had swagger*. He stood there smiling at her as if waiting for her to say something, but he was the one to break the awkward silence.

"So what did you want to talk about?"

"I wanted to thank you for saving me from that strange guy who grabbed me by my car last week," she stated, nervously.

"Oh, *that*," he said. "Well, you are quite welcome. That place can be dangerous. Especially, for someone like yourself."

"What exactly does that mean—you know—that it would be dangerous for someone like me?" she asked, irritation evident in her voice.

Connor's relaxed expression changed, as he suddenly seemed uncomfortable with the tone of her question. He frowned as he shifted his position, moving slightly away from her.

"Well—I would guess that an attractive woman like you is susceptible to unwanted advances from all kinds of unsavory characters," he said, a bit defensive.

"Oh—thanks, I guess. So does that mean if I was large and beastly I wouldn't have to worry about being attacked?"

"No, of course not. I guess I didn't make my point very well. I seem to be good at sticking my foot in my mouth around you don't I?"

Gwen laughed nervously. He wasn't really answering her question, just feeding her a line that was meant to flatter her, while simultaneously being evasive. *What was he hiding that he didn't want her to know?*

"I know what you meant, I think. Anyway, I'm sort of curious about something."

"I'm listening," he said.

"Well, I'm trying to figure out how you got all the way from the club entrance to my car so quickly. It just seems unbelievable that someone could move that fast."

"I run four times a week and keep pretty good time. I guess I'm just quicker than most," he said with a sly grin. "You know in certain situations, people are capable of doing things that would seem impossible under normal conditions. Maybe, for your sake, I just got lucky that evening and rapidly scaled the distance. Anyway, does it really matter? The important thing is I got to you right?"

"Yeah, I suppose so—I just don't understand how that was humanly possible," she said.

"Is that all?"

"No—I also don't know how you managed to lock my front door from the outside. I mean it's not possible without a key to lock the deadbolt from outside."

"Well, Gwenevere that's because *you* locked the door."

"What are you talking about? I don't have any memories beyond the parking lot. The only thing I remember is waking up in my bed with no recollection as to how I got there."

"Maybe you had too much to drink and you don't remember, but you said goodnight to me and locked the door when I left."

"Connor, I only had one drink that night and it was several hours before I left the club. I wasn't intoxicated from alcohol I promise you." Gwen didn't want to mention to Connor that she had felt drugged that evening because she couldn't explain how or if she had been exposed to something. The only occasions in which she felt like she was under the influence ironically enough were when she was dancing with Derrick and Connor, when Lucinda held her hand, and later that evening when the strange man grabbed her near her car. It was only when physical contact diminished with each of these individuals that she felt like herself.

"Well, I don't know what to tell you Gwenevere. You locked the door the night I brought you home. Can't you just be grateful I got you home safely?" he huffed.

"Thanks," she whispered right away bowing her head as a sign of deference. "I just wanted to understand what had happened, it bothers me that I can't remember the details."

"Can we change the topic, please?" Connor asked.

"Yes—absolutely," she said, while holding her fingers crossed behind her back. She'd drop the topic for the moment, but she wasn't satisfied with his answers.

Connor stood silently a moment appraising her with a look of amusement.

"What?" she asked.

He smiled at her, his radiant eyes boring into hers. "Why do I have a feeling this conversation isn't over?"

Gwen smiled confidently. "It is. For *now*."

Connor glanced away, a wide smile spread across his face. "Would you like to walk on the beach with me? It's beautiful out here tonight."

"I'd love to."

The pair walked on the boardwalk path that led to the beach. When they got to the sand, Gwen stopped to take off her sandals and she noted Connor did the same with his boots. She thought he was going to hold her hand, but he kept a slight distance refraining from touching her. A soft gentle breeze glided across the waters of the Gulf providing them with relief from the oppressive humidity. She observed a few teenagers lying on beach blankets giggling and chatting with one another, while an older couple was sitting holding hands in two Adirondack chairs. Connor and Gwen walked for a few more minutes until they came across a patch of unoccupied beach.

Chapter 3

Connor spotted two vacant chaise lounge chairs on a patch of sand close to the surf. He tugged on Gwen's blouse indicating that she should follow him to the chairs. She wondered why he didn't just take her hand. They both sat down in the lounge chairs leaning their backs against the wooden slatted frames so that they could stare at the waves coming ashore.

"It's so beautiful here. I sometimes forget just how amazing the Gulf can be. Ironic that I live here and rarely get a chance to visit the beach," Gwen said.

"I've spent many years traveling the world, and the beach is always the place I feel most at home. Of course, I'm really partial to New England beaches."

"Are you from New England"?

"I was born in Manchester, England, but my parents immigrated to the states when I was an infant. I spent my childhood on the shores of Massachusetts learning how to sail, dig for clams, and fish. The beaches in New England are very rocky and there are fewer sunbathers there compared to the beaches down here. Unlike the booming tourism industry in Florida, New England's coastal economy predominantly relies on fishing, trading, and other forms of commerce. "

Gwen thought it interesting that Connor didn't have much of a New England accent. "What brought you to Panama City?" she asked.

"My cousins wanted to open *The Immortal* and asked if I'd be a shareholder in the club. Basically, they wanted my help getting the place started. So, I agreed to move down here for awhile until they felt confident they wouldn't need my services any longer."

"What do you do, if may ask?"

"I'm involved in real estate and investment properties. I've been around long enough to get a feel for what investments and businesses will work and which will fail. My specialty is finance and raising capital. Because I have a very high success rate, I live very comfortably. I'm lucky, I guess. I've managed to do well in even some of the worst economic times," he replied matter-of-factly.

"What about you Gwenevere? What brought you here, clearly you aren't from the South,"

"How'd you know that?"

"The moment I saw you in the club, I knew immediately that you were different from the people in this town. Your style of dress, mannerisms, gestures—the way you speak. You are a classy and educated woman. Honestly, Gwenevere when you walk into a room, it's hard for people not to notice you," he said, grinning at her.

"You seemed a bit wary of me when I met your family at the club. I thought you didn't care much for me."

"You remind me of someone from my past and it's a bit unsettling I suppose. I'll get used to the idea though," Connor said

"Please tell me I don't remind you of an ex-wife or former lover?"

"You remind me of my late wife, Elizabeth, who died many years ago."

"Oh—I'm so sorry for your loss." Gwen noted the sudden awkwardness of the moment.

"Thank you," Connor replied.

"Do I resemble her?"

"No, that's the strange part. Your appearance couldn't be more dissimilar from hers. Elizabeth was petite with dark russet hair and brown eyes. You remind me of Elizabeth because like her you are strong willed, confident, and unafraid to take chances. I've never met anyone as stubborn as Elizabeth—till now," Connor said, his brilliant white teeth gleaming in the moonlight.

Gwen ignored the subtle jab, which was meant as a compliment. "I can't understand what that must have been like for you." She wished she could think of something more consoling to say.

"That's okay. Most people don't know what to say when they hear I'm a widower. I guess the topic is too uncomfortable for them," Connor said with a sigh. "The truth is—losing Elizabeth was like losing a part of my soul and I have quite successfully avoided having another serious relationship since the day she died."

Gwen wanted to ask when Elizabeth died, curious to know how long he had been mourning her loss. But, she felt it inappropriate to ask him right now. She thought of changing the topic since she could see the obvious pain in his expression. Luckily, Connor beat her to the punch.

"So, what do you do when you aren't visiting the beach or coming to my family's nightclub?"

"I teach at Emerald Coast University."

"Oh that's right, I remember your speaking of that at the club. Psychology right?"

"Yes. I'm interested in the biological basis underlying behavior and perception," Gwen said thinking how incredibly nerdy that must sound to someone outside the field.

Connor laughed as he glanced in Gwen's direction.

"Are you laughing at me?"

"No, not really—okay, yes I am," he said.

"Hey—what I do isn't funny," Gwen said, her posture defensive.

"No, what you do is wonderful and I take it very seriously, just think it's funny that you think of yourself as a nerd. Nerdy is not the word that comes to mind when I think about you, Gwenevere."

"Well, I never referred to myself as a nerd. I was sort of thinking it, but I didn't say it," Gwen said, amazed at Connor perceptiveness.

"I guess I just picked up on a vibe from your tone or something.

Anyway, was I right?" Connor glanced over at her with a playful expression.

"Yeah, you were—*dammit!*" She giggled looking back at him.

"Do you have any family here?"

"My folks are up in Southern New Jersey, and extended family are in central Florida. I'm very close to my parents, but I don't get to see them that often. It's tough sometimes and I wish I could find a job closer to home, but academic jobs are difficult to find and I'm just grateful to have my job here. What about you? Any family here besides your cousins?"

"No, my cousins and I are the last of our family I'm afraid to say. We've outlived everybody and for that reason are very close to one another. But, they have a different philosophy than I do about a number of things that occasionally creates conflict. Anyway, that's it. Do you have any children?" Connor inquired.

Gwen smiled as she answered, "Yes, I have a ten year-old son. Andy's beautiful, bright, and the best thing to ever happen to me."

Connor glanced at Gwen with a look of admiration on his face.

"You are lucky. I never had children," he whispered, wistfully staring straight ahead looking at the white caps.

"You're young, you have plenty of time—" Gwen examined his beautiful profile. She saw a flash of what looked like regret on his face.

"If only it were that easy," he said, continuing to look off into the distance.

Gwen decided not to broach this subject, at least not for the moment. The two engaged in small talk for a time, until Gwen felt sleepy. Connor suggested he walk her to her car and she head home for the evening. Gwen cursed her biological need for sleep, not wanting the night to end. When they got to their cars, his radiant eyes looked into hers once more.

"Will I see you again?" she asked.

"Absolutely."

Then unexpectedly, Connor leaned over briefly allowing his lips to lightly brush against hers. Before Gwen could register what had just happened, she was watching Connor's black Porsche drive away from her towards the city.

The following Thursday Gwen sat in her office staring at the computer screen in a futile effort to be productive. She wasn't sure how long she'd been reading the same paragraph repeatedly, but she noted that several hours had passed since she opened the manuscript on her computer. Gwen had managed to be fairly industrious earlier in the week, but as the days passed with no word from Connor she began to wonder if she'd ever hear from him. "This is ridiculous," she thought. "I'm acting more like an infatuated lovesick schoolgirl, than a tenured college professor." But, her self-imposed insults did little to diminish thoughts of Connor.

Frustrated, Gwen sighed as she shut down her computer and left the office for the day. She decided since she wasn't getting any work done, why torture herself. Gwen left the university, stopping to pick up a lasagna entree for dinner from one of her favorite Italian restaurants on her way home. Placing her take-out on the countertop, Gwen listened to her answering machine messages while she searched for a wine glass from the hutch in her kitchen. She had one message from her mother and another from her friend, Pam Holloway. As she listened to her messages Gwen opened a bottle of Chardonnay pouring herself a small glass. She figured if she had to be dining alone why not do it in style, so she placed the lasagna on a piece of her finest Lennox china before sitting down on her sofa to eat dinner while watching the evening news.

Gwen devoured the lasagna and drank two full glasses of wine before calling her mother. She was extremely close to her mother and appreciated her mother's unique wit and ability to provide comfort and love when she really needed it. She talked with her mother for over an hour about everything occurring in her life, apart from Connor. Gwen didn't see the point in mentioning him since he hadn't called or contacted her. After Gwen hung up with her mother, she called Pam, but only got Pam's voicemail, so she left a message before putting the phone back on its cradle.

Her inhibitions diminishing, Gwen decided to do something she'd wanted to do for some time, but had refrained. She was a researcher, so why shouldn't she research the person who was occupying her thoughts? Gwen booted up the computer in her office and searched for information on Connor in several search engines. Tons of hits came up, most of which had nothing to do with "her" Connor Blake, but various men with that name living throughout the United States and abroad. She narrowed her search to Panama City and only found a brief mention of him associated with the club. Gwen couldn't find a local address or phone number for him.

Remembering Connor had said he was from Massachusetts, Gwen altered her search options accordingly. This proved to be more fruitful as she found several hits for Connor Blake in Massachusetts. Gwen read that Connor owned a profitable fund company headquartered in Boston that invested in small start-up companies and businesses. She also learned that he was quite the philanthropist donating hundreds of thousands of dollars annually to various charities. Photos of Connor in expensive business suits at parties with Boston socialites and other wealthy Bostonians were widely available on the net. However, despite Gwen's thorough search efforts, she still couldn't find a home address or phone number for him in Massachusetts. He was obviously careful to keep his private residence concealed from the public. She did see a business address, but she wasn't going to call him. It was still up to him to contact her.

Gwen noticed a couple of links with Connor's name that were associated with organizations in other parts of Massachusetts. Some of the links described businesses run by men with Connor's name dating back as early as the late 1600s and as recent as the mid 1900s. *Connor Blake must have been a common name.* Then something caught Gwen's eye that struck her as unusual. She found a link displaying old photographs from the late 1800s of well-known trading merchants in Salem. One of the photos displayed a room full of men at a business function. Towards the back of the room of about forty faces, she saw a tall man with dark wavy hair and bright luminous eyes in period dress smiling mischievously for the camera. She had seen that look before. This man looked exactly like Connor. It was really quite uncanny and Gwen wondered if this was a distant relative who was Connor's namesake.

Taking things one step further, Gwen decided to search for Elizabeth Blake. Immediately, Gwen knew something was wrong with her search parameters as she could only find one marriage record for a "Connor and Elizabeth Blake" that apparently took place in Salem in 1683. Gwen stared at the computer screen puzzled. She decided to search the death records for women named Elizabeth Blake in Massachusetts and found several recent death notices, but only one that was also listed as being the late wife of a man named Connor and that occurred in 1693. She surmised that Connor and Elizabeth must have married in another state or country. Connor mentioned he traveled a lot; he and Elizabeth must have lived elsewhere until her death. She tried a nationwide search next, but the hits were in the thousands, and she didn't see a direct link between the names, Elizabeth and Connor Blake anywhere else.

Gwen realized she had more questions about Connor than she did answers. She clicked on the photo of the Salem merchants' again, staring at the man who could be Connor's doppelganger. The man's features were so striking and similar he must have been related to Connor; that was the only rational explanation. In fact, Gwen convinced herself that there were rational explanations for everything she had viewed this evening. If she ever got the chance to speak with Connor again, she'd eventually ask him about his past. Of course, that was the important key element here wasn't it? *If she ever heard from him again—*

That night Gwen thrashed about in bed, plagued with bizarre dreams. She saw Connor beckoning her to join him on the beach, but this wasn't a beach in the Gulf. This beach was littered with thousands of small round rocks that covered the sand. It was bitter cold and Gwen wrapped a thick handmade quilt around her body to keep warm. She noticed that Connor was skipping rocks along the shore smiling as he ran up and down the sand. She had never seen him this animated and was amazed at how quickly he could run. As she looked around the shoreline she noticed the few houses she could see were dark or dimly lit and they looked primitive in architecture. If it weren't for the moonlight, Gwen would barely be able to see anything at all. Connor kept calling to her, but she couldn't make out what he was saying over the howling wind. She tried walking towards him, but her feet kept slipping on the slick wet rocks and she was afraid she'd fall into the frigid water. Frustrated she gave up and simply waited for him to come towards her. Gwen knew he was saying her name over and over again, but she couldn't hear him. Finally, he approached her. Gwen looked into his gleaming blue eyes as she grabbed his hands in hers. He pulled her close to him and whispered "Elizabeth."

Gwen screamed as she woke with a start. She was drenched in sweat and her heart was pounding thunderously in her chest. Gwen grabbed the water bottle that was on the nightstand, vigorously sucking its contents down her throat in an attempt to quench her monstrous thirst. After a few moments had passed her respiration slowed and she wiped her brow with her hand, removing strands of wet-hair that were clinging to her eyes. Gwen looked at the alarm clock. Five-thirty. She sighed to herself in frustration as she got up to use the bathroom; briefly stopping by the mirror to examine her reflection. Dark purple circles lined the bottom of her eyes and her nightgown clung to her clammy skin. Gwen let out a heavy sigh as she turned the knob of the bathtub faucet. As she showered she thought about the images of her dream. They had seemed amazingly real. Gwen convinced herself the dream was simply the result of too much wine and an overactive imagination fueled by her computer search. Yet, this information did little to console her. Afterwards, she changed her bed sheets and tried to go back to sleep, but it was no use. Gwen couldn't relax and decided to go into work early.

The university was fairly quiet around six-thirty, with just a few staff members pruning and cleaning the grounds of the campus. Gwen used her swipe key card to open the building and enter her office. She had picked up a hot cup of coffee on the way in and was ready to focus her attention on some work. The dream, like the one before it, had been unsettling, but she was a rational and logical person who knew dreams weren't prophetic or recollections of past memories. Dreams were patterns of random neural activity that often didn't make sense. It was the fact that she kept dreaming about Connor that really bothered her. Gwen promised herself that she would push him from her mind today, even if it killed her.

Gwen opened her email and spent the next hour answering messages from journal editors, students, and colleagues. She then spent several hours editing a manuscript that needed some final touches before submission. Gwen briefly spoke with colleagues stopping by to say hello, before they went to their offices. Around noon, she left her office for a few minutes to grab a tuna salad sandwich from the cafeteria downstairs. She ran into a few colleagues she hadn't seen for a while and caught up on some local news related to the university and union before returning to her office. Gwen was in the middle of eating her sandwich when she heard someone lightly knocking on her door. She looked up to see a tall man with wavy black hair tucked beneath a black baseball cap, wearing dark sunglasses, a faded light blue t-shirt, blue jeans, and black Nike sneakers. She recognized the impish grin immediately.

"Am I catching you at a bad time?" Connor asked, as he took off his sunglasses and sat down in one of her office chairs.

Gwen chewed quickly so she could clear her throat to speak.

"Oh—no—come in," she stammered. Gwen quickly grabbed a napkin off her desk and anxiously wiped her lips clean.

"I'm sorry I haven't been able to drop by sooner, but I've been tied up this week."

"Oh—sure. I understand," Gwen said, trying hard to suppress her excitement.

"Well, there were some issues with the personnel I left in charge of my fund company up North, so I was out of town for most of the week straightening things out. I was going to call you, but felt it more chivalrous to come in person. Guess I'm kind of old-fashioned that way," he said.

Gwen felt like a heel. She had assumed he was blowing her off, but he was in the middle of a personnel crisis. "I completely understand. I hope the trip was worth it and you worked things out."

"I had to make some changes at the company, but all in all I think it will be in better hands. A dear old friend of mine whom I trust implicitly will be running things for me until I decide to move back home."

"Are you thinking of moving soon?" Gwen asked using her best matter-of-fact tone, hoping Connor wouldn't detect her obvious concern.

"No, my plans are indefinite at the moment. I want to see how things pan out here," he said, smirking.

Gwen didn't say anything. She hated that he got to her the way he did. And—what was more important, he knew it. But, she would do her best to play it cool. Still, she was glad he wasn't leaving. That had happened to her a couple of times before. She'd meet someone she really liked and he would suddenly be deployed as most interesting men in the area were in the military or simply moved to a different location for their jobs. She hadn't been involved with anyone in almost three years, because she didn't want the misery of disappointment when the relationship would ultimately end for one reason or another. In fact, before meeting Connor she wasn't interested in a relationship at all. This whole situation took her by surprise.

"Gwenevere, unfortunately I have to meet my cousins for a business meeting shortly so I'll have to go. But, before I leave I wanted to ask you if I could take you to dinner tomorrow night? I'll pick you up at six if that's okay?" Connor asked.

"Yeah, dinner would be great." Gwen flashed him a brief smile.

"Well, then I'll see you at six tomorrow."

"What's the dress code? I mean are we going somewhere formal?" she inquired.

"Dress casual, we'll be walking outside at some point," he pointed out, as he turned to get up and leave. "Oh—and one last thing. I picked you up a little souvenir from home last night before flying in this morning. I know how much you love the beach," Connor said as he placed a small gift bag on her desk.

"Oh—thanks," Gwen said, surprise in her tone.

"Well, gotta run—Sweet dreams."

Gwen watched him walk out of the office before she grabbed the gift bag and pulled out something small and heavy that was wrapped in white tissue paper. She eagerly removed the tissue paper revealing a small round rock. Her heart raced, she knew in an instant that it was a stone from the New England Coast.

Chapter 4

Sitting on the sofa in her living room, Gwen examined the rock Connor brought back from the Massachusetts coastline. It was fairly heavy, round, and incredibly smooth from years of being pounded by the relentless waters of the Atlantic. As she held the rock in her hand, she thought of the vivid images she had experienced in her dream. She could almost feel the slippery surface of the rocks beneath her feet as she approached the beach. Connor had walked on a beach very similar to the one in her dream only the night before. Gwen thought that a strange coincidence. Moreover, his bringing the stone to her as a souvenir seemed even more remarkable. It was almost as if he was there last night. Realizing she was obsessing over the rock, Gwen put the stone down on the coffee table. She noticed how quiet the house was. The ubiquitous chaos she had grown accustomed to in Andy's presence was painfully absent. Gwen missed the noise. Weary from the week, she went into her bedroom, changed into her nightgown, climbed into bed, and turned off the light. Sleep would bring a welcome respite from a strange day. Besides, tomorrow she was having dinner with Connor and she had the feeling she'd need all the sleep she could get.

The next morning Gwen woke to the sound of mockingbirds and

cardinals chirping outside her window. She lay there with her eyes closed in the hope of obtaining some additional sleep, but her mind had other plans. She was going out with Connor tonight and as soon as that thought registered in her brain, her eyes shot wide open. Rays of sunlight filtered through the vertical blinds in her room casting light and dark shadows across her bedspread. Gwen watched the light dance playfully across her comforter, moving in her direction. She wondered what he had planned. It was hard to predict with Connor. The truth was Gwen really didn't know him. On the one hand, she could easily envision him taking her for dinner at some swanky restaurant on Panama City Beach or a hip jazz club further down the road. There was no telling what the night would be like. Then another thought hit her. What was she going to wear? She groaned as she pulled the pillow over her face. Damn, she hated thinking about this. It was like he had power over her already.

Gwen spent the day taking care of some minor errands like shopping for groceries and banking to keep her mind occupied. It had worked briefly, but time wasn't on her side. Before she realized it, it was close to five o'clock and she needed to shower. She decided to wear a light pink cotton summer dress that would be comfortable in the sticky heat. Wearing her hair in long cascading curls, Gwen applied light makeup to her eyes and face. She was in the processing of putting on her pink topaz earrings when the doorbell rang. Gwen quickly exited her bedroom and observed Connor's silhouette through the stained glass window of her front door. Taking a deep breath, Gwen unlocked the deadbolt and pulled the door open. Connor stood before her dressed in black slacks, a light blue dress shirt, black suit Jacket, and black leather shoes. His hair was still a bit unruly, but it gave him the casual chic look that was so popular these days. Connor surveyed Gwen quickly and produced a smile that showed off his obscenely perfect white teeth.

"You look beautiful," he said, walking into the foyer of her house.

"Oh—thanks. You look great yourself," Gwen stammered, while trying not to trip in her black high-heeled sandals.

"Nice dress," he mentioned as he moved closer to her. His eyes locked onto hers.

Gwen tried to think of what she wanted to say, but his eyes disarmed her. Something about them was inviting and she had to suppress the urge to blurt out what she was thinking for fear of sounding like an idiot.

Connor snickered as if he was in on some private joke.

"What?" Gwen asked with a puzzled expression on her face.

"Oh—nothing—just thinking of something I heard the other day," he muttered, looking amused. "So you ready to go?"

"Yes. Are you going to give me a hint as to where we're going?"

"Sure. We're going to a restaurant where they serve seafood,"

"Well that really narrows it down. Think you could be a bit more specific?"

"Well, I could—but I'm not going to." Connor smiled playfully at her.

"Why?"

"Because, you'll spoil the surprise."

"Do you like surprising people?"

"Depends."

"Depends on what?"

Connor smirked as he placed her hand in his. "Depends on who I'm surprising."

Gwen noticed she felt slightly faint. She surmised it was just her excitement and the anticipation of the evening. She locked the house and the couple drove off in Connor's black Porsche.

Gwen had no idea where they were going, but noticed Connor took local roads until he got on interstate 10 heading west. It was dusk and there were surprisingly few cars on the road. Gwen's feeling of dizziness had abated when they got into the car. She noticed the sensation waned when Connor started driving and needed his right hand to shift gears. The dark outline of trees raced past them as they zoomed towards their destination. Wherever that might be.

"Are you comfortable?" Connor asked. "I can turn the air down further if you'd like."

"Actually—it's freezing in here. Do you mind if we turn the air off?" Gwen asked, as she leaned over to hug her body with her arms.

"Oh—sorry, I didn't realize it was so chilly in here. The cold doesn't bother me much. Guess it comes from growing up in New England. You kind of get used to it up there."

"Not me, I think my blood has thinned since I've moved down here. I freeze if the temperature drops below 75," Gwen giggled. "So are you going to give me a hint where we're going, now that we're on the road?"

"Nope."

"You're really enjoying this aren't you?"

"You have no idea," he replied glancing briefly at Gwen with a wicked grin.

Gwen cleared her throat a moment. She had so many questions; she thought she'd ask a few to see if she could crack his polished exterior. This seemed as good a time as any.

"Connor, I'm curious. Where in Massachusetts did you grow up?"

"I grew up in Boston. Why?"

"Oh—just wondering."

"Uh-huh." Connor nodded.

"Have you ever been to Salem?" she asked.

Connor momentarily looked wary; a glance of apprehension noticeable in his expression. "Yes, a *long* time ago."

"When?"

"I don't remember; it's been several years. I used to visit the place as a kid."

"I see."

"What makes you ask about Salem?" he asked.

"I don't know, I wondered if you had relatives there." Gwen thought she noticed Connor visibly flinch, but it was so fast she couldn't be sure if it was a real response. He hesitated a moment before answering.

"Yes, I did have extended family there, but they are all deceased. How did you know I had relatives in Salem?"

"Lucky guess I suppose," Gwen replied flatly.

"Why do I find that hard to believe?"

Gwen shrugged her shoulders, giving him her best naïve look.

"Is there something you aren't telling me?" he asked.

Gwen bit her lip nervously. "Not really."

"Gwenevere?" he asked, concern apparent in his voice.

Gwen hesitated. "Well, I'll tell you if you promise you won't get ticked off at me."

Connor sighed— "Okay—I won't get angry with you."

"I searched for information about you online."

"And?" Connor asked, failing to disguise the slight agitation and alarm that was evident in his tone. She noticed his inflections wavered more than normal.

"I found a picture from the 1800s of Salem trading merchants and a man appeared in the photo who could be your twin. I wondered if this was a distant relative of yours. The resemblance was rather *uncanny*," she remarked.

Connor reflexively gripped the steering wheel tighter, a slight hesitation before he spoke; yet his voice was calm. "Well, that's interesting. I know my great grandfather moved to the Boston area from Salem, but that's as much as I know about the old family tree. I suppose the man in the picture could be a relative. So, what else did you find out about me?"

"Well, I also found information about your fund company and saw all the charity work you do. All positive stuff—very impressive."

"Good. Anything else?" he probed.

Gwen desperately wanted to ask him about Elizabeth, but felt it better to ask another time.

"You don't list your home address or phone number."

"I like my privacy." His lips were drawn into a tight line.

"Are you annoyed I searched for information on you?"

"No, I'm not annoyed."

"You seem annoyed."

"I'm frustrated that one's personal life is so easily available to the public. Guess that's the price we pay for technology and so called, *progress*," he retorted.

"I didn't mean to pry—I was just curious to know more about you. You're a bit of an enigma," she confessed looking over at him trying to smooth things over.

Connor smiled at Gwen. "Well, you are a psychologist, that makes you one of the nosiest people on the planet."

Gwen laughed. "Okay, I guess I deserve that."

"I'm not quite ready to divulge all my dark secrets yet. Give me some time," he whispered looking over at her with a serious expression.

"Oh, so you do admit that you have some skeletons in the closet?"

"Doesn't everyone?" The roguish grin reappeared.

"Good. I was beginning to think you were perfect," she stated before smiling at him. "So I suppose trying to guess any of your secrets is out of the question?

Connor looked over at Gwen fleetingly. "Maybe I'll make an exception just this one time. I'm curious to know how that brain of yours works. Go ahead, fire away."

"Okay—have you robbed any banks?"

"No."

"Done lots of drugs?"

"No."

"Cheated on your taxes?"

"I may be a bit liberal with my deductions, but no, I have not committed tax fraud—at least, not to my knowledge. If anything happens my accountant will have some explaining to do."

"Had an affair?"

"No, wouldn't have even considered it."

"You're not making this easy, you know?" Gwen said, sensing how much he was enjoying this.

"Give up?" he asked.

"Nope, " she mentioned, mocking his tendency to be blunt and terse. "Gambling?"

"No, it's too boring."

"Gambling is boring? Are you serious? I've only done it a couple of times, but I was ecstatic when I won three hundreds bucks on the slots, once."

"Sorry to disappoint you, but we're not on our way to Biloxi," he said, "Want to give up now?"

"No, but I'm running out of ideas," Gwen commented, noting how disappointed she sounded. "Oh—the mafia. Are you in the mafia?"

"What?" Connor laughed so hard Gwen thought he was going to crack a rib.

"Hey, I'm from New Jersey. That's a completely reasonable question to ask," she said, laughing.

"Oh yeah, you gotta watch out for that Boston mafia," Connor retorted, shaking his head.

"Okay, okay—one last question before I give up. Have you ever killed anyone?" Gwen asked, thinking how absurd the question sounded as soon as she'd said it.

"*Definitely.*" Connor whispered looking into Gwen's eyes, before he swiftly grabbed her hand and held it tightly in his.

A surge of nausea hit Gwen hard and her thoughts became temporarily jumbled; she couldn't remember what Connor had just said.

"You okay?" he asked, as he released her hand and looked straightforward towards the road.

"I guess so—just feel a little dizzy that's all. That was so weird. What were we talking about? I can't remember."

"You asked if I was in the mafia."

"Oh- okay—I thought I asked you something else, but I'm blanking now."

Gwen leaned her head back against the seat rest noticing she was starting to feel more lucid. Connor was quiet and seemed preoccupied by something. He had a strange emotional expression she couldn't place. Gwen stared at his delicate facial features struggling to figure out what he was thinking and then it registered. *Guilt.* He looked like he felt guilty about something.

"Connor, are you okay?" Gwen asked, wondering what was bothering him. They had been laughing only a few moments ago. She wondered what had happened to change his mood?

Connor looked over at Gwen. "I'm fine Gwenevere—just looking for our exit off the interstate." Although he looked calm, his arms and body appeared rigid and tense.

"You sure?"

"Yes," he whispered, sounding more like himself. "There it is." Connor pointed the road out in front of them.

The Porsche pulled off the interstate onto a small service road. They drove in silence for a few minutes, before Gwen noticed they turned onto a private road that lead to a small home on the beach. Connor pulled into the driveway of the home and parked.

"We're here," he said, as he smiled at Gwen.

"Where are we?" Gwen asked.

"We're in Destin."

"I thought we were going to a restaurant?"

"I thought it would be nice to have dinner in a more intimate setting than a restaurant. Come with me. I think you'll like what I have planned."

Connor got out of the car and walked over to open Gwen's door. When she climbed out of the car, she noticed the charming Cape Cod home was located high up on a bluff and protected by twelve-foot iron gates in the front entrance. The home wasn't as small as Gwen originally thought. It fact, it wasn't small at all.

"What is the square footage of this place?" Gwen inquired.

"About four thousand—It's modest, but I like it," Connor said, matter-of-factly like everyone could afford to live in such a lovely home in one of the world's most coveted beach communities.

The house was predominantly white, with gray trim; clearly different from the typical stucco or brick homes that most people bought in Northwest Florida.

"Did you have this place built?" she asked.

"Yes. I actually had it built two years ago as a getaway from the craziness of the city. I love Boston, but like any big city, it can be overwhelming. I could hop a plane and be here for a weekend giving me a chance to breathe and have some much needed privacy. It's nice."

"Is this your primary residence here in Florida?"

"No, with the club being in Panama City, I have a small house in Panama City Beach where I stay during the week," he stated.

Connor gestured for Gwen to follow him towards the house. When he opened the door Gwen was immediately overcome with the most wonderful scents from the kitchen. A chef, two assistants, and a butler were in the process of preparing dinner in a kitchen the size of Gwen's entire house. The beauty of the kitchen, the rich dark wood cabinets, the stainless steel appliances, and the large island in the center of the kitchen where the chef was preparing a dish, impressed her. Although Gwen wasn't much of a cook, she appreciated the culinary arts and recognized that this was a state-of-the-art kitchen. The staff quickly turned to greet Gwen and Connor and then returned to their preparations. Among, other things, Gwen noticed a platter with a large red lobster sitting on the countertop. Lobster was Gwen's favorite seafood.

Connor led Gwen to a table set outside on a large screen-enclosed porch overlooking the Gulf. You couldn't see another house or soul for miles. Connor opened one of the wine bottles that had been chilling in a silver ice bucket beside the table. He poured Gwen a glass of Chardonnay, her favorite white wine, and placed it in front of her before sitting down on the opposite side of the small round table. She noticed there was already a glass of red wine in front of him.

"Cheers," he said as he held up his glass to tap with hers.

They both took a large sip from their respective glasses.

"Wow, this wine is spectacular. What is it?" Gwen asked.

"It's from some small winery in France. Glad you like it. I'll have to ask the chef later for the details."

"How did you know I liked Chardonnay?"

"Well, I read your mind of course." Connor mentioned, his lips forming a sardonic smirk.

"Oh—right—you seem to be able to do that a lot," Gwen said, only partially kidding.

"So I hope you like lobster, shrimp, and filet mignon. I figured I couldn't go wrong with surf-and-turf."

"That sounds great."

They spoke for a few minutes before two servers dressed in tuxedos came out holding two entrees covered in silver trays. The servers placed both entrees in front of Gwen before leaving the table and porch. Gwen was befuddled.

"Connor, you're not eating?"

"Actually, I'm not that hungry. I had something earlier today. Anyway, enjoy yourself," he said motioning for her to start eating.

Initially, Gwen felt guilty eating alone, but she surmised that Connor probably ate like this all the time and it wasn't a big deal to him. There was broiled Maine lobster, shrimp scaloppini, and a perfectly grilled tender cut of filet mignon. Gwen couldn't help herself and she devoured most of the meal.

"Wow, that was amazing! Please give my compliments to your chef. Everything was wonderful. I don't think I've ever had lobster or steak that tender. Thank you so much," Gwen gushed.

"I'm glad you enjoyed it." Connor smiled at her as he lifted his glass to her again.

"How's your wine?" Gwen asked.

"Excellent."

"Can I try some?"

"No! I mean—*sorry*—this is the last of the bottle and I'm out of red wine," Connor snapped, noticeably flustered and uncomfortable.

Gwen was taken aback by Connor's abrupt response to her question, but she kept her composure. "Oh—it's okay. I was just curious what it tasted like. I noticed you're really enjoying it. No worries, I'm very happy with my white wine," Gwen assured him. There was a moment of awkward silence between them and she noticed Connor looked embarrassed.

"Would you care for some dessert? I believe the chef has made chocolate silk pie." His face lit up in a genuine smile, as he looked at her.

"Connor, you're going to have to remove me from your house on a stretcher. I won't be able to walk if I eat much more," Gwen joked, intentionally lightening the mood between them.

"That's okay, I'll have all the leftovers and the pie wrapped up so you can take them home later."

"Thanks. But, that's not really fair to you—I mean you didn't eat any of this meal. You should, in the very least, enjoy the pie."

"I insist," he said as he stood up and held out his hand to hers, an invitation for her to join him. "Would you like to take a walk on the beach?"

"Certainly." She placed her hand inside of his.

Gwen felt a sudden chill as the cool skin of his hand enveloped hers. The dizziness she had experienced earlier in the evening returned, but this time it wasn't an unpleasant sensation. *"No doubt, the result of the wine she had with dinner," she thought.* Connor led Gwen down the stairs of the porch to the beach. She instinctively stopped and removed her black sandals and left them on the last step of the stairs. Connor followed suit, placing his shoes next to her sandals. They walked hand-in-hand towards the wet sand of the beach. A gentle breeze blew across the Gulf waters. Connor and Gwen walked quietly for several minutes before he spoke.

"I'm happy you're here with me."

Gwen smiled. "I'm happy to be here with you too."

Connor stopped walking and turned to face Gwen. His shimmering blue eyes searched hers. She sensed he wanted to tell her something, but was conflicted. "Gwenevere, you and I—we're *different*. And—well, you'll have to be patient with me as I figure things out. I haven't done anything like this before, but I want to with you," he said, looking intently into her grayish-blue eyes.

"Connor, what do you mean? How are we different? I don't understand." Gwen wondered why he was being so cryptic.

"Gwen—I can't talk about this right now. I just need you to trust what I'm saying."

"It's not fair for you to mention our differences and keep me in the dark. What are you talking about?" Gwen said, keeping her voice calm so he wouldn't mistake her tone for anger. "Is this about our age difference?"

He looked at her perplexed.

"Is it because I'm older than you?" Gwen clarified.

Connor laughed. "First of all, you are assuming that you're older than I and secondly, no, it wouldn't matter even if you were."

"Connor, I'm thirty-nine—and you look like you're barely thirty."

"You don't look anywhere near thirty-nine. But your age isn't important to me. Besides—I'm older than I look." Connor stroked the side of Gwen's face sending sensations down her skin and body; resulting in a subtle heaviness in her limbs. Gwen repositioned her feet to maintain her footing.

"How old are you?" she asked.

"My license says twenty-eight."

"So you *are* younger than I am."

"I told you what my license says."

"What is you real age?" she asked, frustrated by his evasiveness. She wondered why he just wouldn't tell her the truth.

"I'm older than I look—is all I am willing to admit at the moment."

"When will you tell me?" Gwen asked, her facial expressions displaying her impatience.

"Soon—I promise," he whispered softly as he pulled Gwen close to him, his arms wrapped tightly around her. Gwen's annoyance with Connor's evasiveness abruptly vanished. She felt the coolness of his skin through his clothes, and it sent chills down her body. However, the momentary coolness gave way to feelings of warmth and contentment. Gwen was in a languid state and she felt it difficult to move her limbs. Without warning, Connor picked her up like she was a feather and carried her down the beach. He walked for what seemed like an hour with her in his arms. Gwen wondered how he did this without appearing the least bit weary. She managed to turn her head and look up into his face. She noticed he had a slight smile on his lips. Connor returned Gwen's gaze and she saw a gentleness in his expression, the likes of which she had never seen before. He stopped walking for a moment to lightly kiss her forehead, before he continued walking with her in his arms. Gwen leaned her head back against his chest and closed her eyes.

Gwen woke to find Connor lying next to her on a blanket on the sand. She was lying with her head nestled near the base of his neck and her arm draped across his chest. She breathed in his magnificent scent as she lifted her head to look at him. Connor appeared to be staring straight up into the sky.

"Hi, did I fall asleep?" she asked.

"Yes." He turned to look at her, grinning.

"Sorry. I don't know what happened. I just felt an overwhelming sense of fatigue and I couldn't keep my eyes open—I guess it must have been the French wine," she replied.

"Oh sure, blame it on the wine. Admit it, I was just boring you."

"Connor, trust me, you are anything but boring. What are you looking at?" Gwen mumbled, as she smiled at him.

"The constellations. Orion's belt is so easy to view out here. Near the city you can't see the stars very well," he said.

"You like to star gaze?"

"Very much, actually. You?"

"I don't know much about them, but yes, I like to take a look now and then."

"I've got a great telescope at home in Mass. It's quite impressive. You'll have to come up and see it sometime."

"I'd like that."

"I should be getting you home soon."

"Why? I'm so happy here. Do we have to leave?"

Connor laughed as his hand stroked her back. "Well, a gentleman should return a lady home before the morning, don't you think?"

"I feel so content right now, why spoil things."

Connor rolled over to face Gwen directly, using his finger to stroke her lips. "Gwenevere, humor me. I want to do this right."

"Why do you always call me by my full name, when everyone else uses Gwen?" she asked, her brow furrowed.

"I love your name, it means *smooth, fair one*. It describes you so well," he whispered into her ear, before leaning over to briefly kiss her lips.

Gwen didn't think it possible to feel this happy and when Connor kissed her, the feelings only intensified.

"You still didn't answer my question."

"I don't think Gwen does your name justice. I told you I'm old-fashioned about *some* things. Speaking of which, it's four in the morning and I should take you home."

Gwen sat up alarmed. "It's four in the morning? Are you kidding?"

"No I'm not joking. You've been asleep for a few hours."

"Why didn't you wake me?"

"You looked so peaceful I didn't have the heart to wake you," Connor said.

"Oh my God—I'm so *embarrassed*. I can't believe I fell asleep on you. I'm so sorry, " she said, heat rising in the skin of her face that would soon be bright red.

"Don't be. I'm just glad you feel so comfortable around me."

"You know—I *really* do," she replied.

"Good," he whispered.

Connor jumped up, rather spry for someone at four AM and helped Gwen get up from the blanket. They walked the short distance back to the stairs where they retrieved their shoes before leaving. During the drive home, Gwen noticed that Connor broke every speed limit set by the roads. At one point he was up to one hundred miles per hour. She also noticed he was quiet on the drive home and seemed lost in thought. Occasionally, Connor would look over at Gwen and smile before returning his eyes to stare at the road. In record time, they were at Gwen's. Connor opened the car door for her and escorted her to the house.

"Thank you for an incredible evening," she said.

"This was one of the nicest nights I've spent in what seems like centuries," he whispered with a twinkle in his radiant eyes.

Connor kissed Gwen lightly before walking away. "Goodnight."

"Goodnight," she mumbled.

Gwen listened to the sound of the Porsche driving away as she closed her front door.

Chapter 5

Late Sunday morning, the phone rang startling Gwen out of a dead sleep. She dragged herself out of bed, stumbling over one of Andy's toy cars in the hallway as she raced to grab the phone. She managed to pick up the phone just before the call went to voicemail. It was her friend, Pam Holloway.

"Hello?" Gwen muttered, sleepiness apparent in her voice.

"Gwen, how are you? I'm sorry I missed your call the other night. Did I wake you?" Pam asked.

"That's okay, it's getting late and I need to get up anyway. How are you?" Gwen asked, as she struggled to pour ground coffee into the filter of her coffee pot.

"I'm doing well Honey, but I haven't talked with you in ages. We need to catch up. What's your day looking like?"

Gwen and Pam exchanged additional pleasantries, before Gwen agreed to meet with Pam at Java Jake's two-thirty that afternoon. Gwen finished pouring water into the coffee pot and hit the start button eager to get the coffee brewing. Although she was in a great mood, she was still sleepy and craved the energy caffeine would bring her. As if on cue, Gwen detected the familiar arrival of hunger pangs and opened the pantry door to retrieve a loaf of rye bread. She toasted two pieces of the bread and fried an egg, before eating breakfast. The protests of her two cats reminded her to place fresh food in their bowls.

After finishing breakfast, Gwen cleaned the house before showering. She yanked a pale yellow sundress with little rosebuds off a hanger from her closet and quickly dressed. She could have worn shorts, but the weather was so oppressive she surmised the dress would be cooler. Summers in Florida meant daily record temperatures over ninety degrees with high humidity. Gwen dreaded this time of year. Every day within minutes of taking a fresh shower, she'd exit the house on route to her car only to break out into an instant sweat that would cling to her skin until she showered later that evening. Gwen grabbed a pair of yellow sandals that matched her dress from the bottom of her closet and pulled her hair back into a ponytail. She selected a sheer white scarf that she wrapped around her hair. Satisfied with her appearance, Gwen left the house and headed downtown.

The coffee shop was busier than usual, with fewer vacant parking spaces available. Gwen managed to find an empty space a block down the street from Java Jake's. As she walked towards the coffee shop, she noticed a large number of police and other law enforcement officers canvassing the sidewalk. Gwen also observed several news teams with cameras and reporters scouting various individuals for quick interviews. She wondered what had happened to elicit such a response from the authorities and the media. When she got to the coffee shop, she found several patrons crowded around a television set with breaking news of a horrific murder that had occurred earlier in the morning. Evidently, a man had been decapitated and severely burned with the charred remains dumped near the bay behind the Marina Civic Center. In a live press conference that followed the news report, a spokesperson from the Panama City medical examiner's office reported that the body was so badly burnt, the use of dental records to positively identify the body was questionable. They were hoping someone might come forward who witnessed the crime, or at least noticed something out of the ordinary. Gwen shuddered as she thought of the brutality of the man's murder.

She couldn't believe it had happened here of all places.

Gwen was standing in line to order her coffee when Pam tapped her on her shoulder. Gwen jumped with a start.

"Hi there, stranger," Pam said, as she gave Gwen a warm hug. "How are you Miss?"

"I'm so happy to see you. I've got so much to tell you, you won't believe it," Gwen said, with a big smile on her face.

"You want to order the coffee and I'll grab us a seat at the table in the corner away from the crowd?" Pam asked.

"Yes—that would be great."

Gwen watched Pam walk over to the table securing two seats for them. Pam had a natural beauty that emanated from within. Her heritage, predominantly a mixture of African and Native American descent, resulted in Pam's flawless light brown skin, sculpted high cheek bones, alluring almond shaped brown eyes, and perfect lips. Like with all Gwen's friends Pam's outward beauty paled in comparison to her inward light.

Gwen was thinking about her friend, when she heard the young woman behind the coffee counter asking her for her order. She turned to look at the woman and noticed it was the same young woman who had served her coffee a couple of weeks ago when she was here with her friend, Cindy.

"Sorry, I must have been distracted. May I have two large vanilla lattes please?" Gwen asked, smiling at the young woman.

Gwen saw the outline of a nametag on the young woman's shirt and waited patiently for the girl to finish making her coffee. As the woman turned, Gwen got a good look at the nametag. *Jasmine.*

"Will that be all?" Jasmine asked, placing the two coffees in front of Gwen.

"Yes, that's it. How much?"

"Nine dollars, please."

Gwen handed Jasmine a crisp ten-dollar bill and spied the remnants of a black stamp on the back of the young woman's hand. It was badly faded from hand washing, but Gwen could make out the outline of a rosebud. *Jasmine had been to The Immortal.* Jasmine glanced at Gwen's eyes for a moment before taking the money from her hand.

Gwen was sure Jasmine knew what she was looking at, but didn't say anything. As the young woman opened the cash register to retrieve Gwen's change, she noticed how pale Jasmine appeared compared to the last time she'd seen her. There were dark circles under the young woman's eyes and her bones were more visible through the thin skin of her face. She also thought it interesting that on such a hot day, the young woman wore a scarf tied around her neck.

"Thanks, keep the change." Gwen grabbed the coffees and walked away from the counter. Gwen handed Pam her latte and then placed her own on the table in front of her chair. Sitting down, Gwen surveyed the coffee shop and was relieved to see the crowds had thinned. A sigh of relief escaped her lips. They'd be able to hear each other now.

"Did you hear about that gruesome murder, Gwen?"

"Yes, I did. What a horrible way to die," Gwen said feeling a chill run down her spine.

"I know it's incredible. It scares me that people are capable of such violence. I hope the police get some leads soon. Anyway let's change the topic to something positive. What's new in your life?" Pam inquired.

Gwen smiled at Pam and took one last sip of her coffee before speaking. "A lot—actually."

"Would this have anything to do with a guy? You look positively radiant. What's happening? Fill me in on all the details and don't leave anything out."

"Well, yes, there is someone. His name is Connor Blake and we met at *The Immortal*. I know what you're thinking, no one ever meets a nice guy in a club, but there is definitely something special about Connor."

"*The Immortal*? Is that the new club in town everyone's talking about?" Pam asked.

"Yes, it's a pretty cool place. I've never seen anything like it in my life. You'll have to go sometime."

"Gwen, you know me. I'd rather stay at home and curl up with a good book than do anything."

"I understand. It's not everyone's favorite pastime, but there is something rather—I don't know—kind of mysterious about that place."

"Well, anyway, tell me about Mr. Connor Blake," Pam pressed in her genteel southern accent, her pupils flaring in the light.

Gwen recounted all the events that occurred at the club, the night she ran into Connor at the beach after their race, and their date. Pam's eyes grew wide as she listened. When Gwen had finished, she waited for Pam's reaction.

Pam hesitated, sitting there quietly before she finally spoke. "Girl, I don't know what to say. He sounds impressive, but at the same time he's got a bit of a dangerous streak. He's definitely hiding something big from you."

"You think?"

"Well—sure, he intimated as much, right?" Pam asked.

"Yes—he did," Gwen said, begrudgingly.

"Gwen, you look happy. Just be careful and keep your emotions in check.

Don't tell him or let him know what you're thinking. At least not just yet."

"You're right I need to play it cool for awhile even though that's hard for me to do." Gwen giggled. "So what's new in your life?"

Pam filled Gwen in on the months' activities about her kids, her job as a schoolteacher working with developmentally disabled children, and her son's proud accomplishments in the military. Gwen enjoyed hearing all of Pam's good news and was happy to see she was doing so well. The two of them decided to get together for dinner in a couple of weeks.

"Gwen, I've got to run. I've got a church function tonight. Be careful and keep me posted on your progress with Mr. Blake."

"I will," was all Gwen could say. She hugged Pam goodbye and watched her run out the door.

As Gwen was watching Pam walk to her car, Gwen's cell phone rang. She glanced at the number and it was one she didn't recognize. Normally, Gwen wouldn't answer the call, but she was curious, so she picked up the phone.

"Hello?"

"Good evening Gwenevere. How are you?" Connor asked.

Gwen smiled at the sound of his silky smooth voice, "Great—how about you?"

Connor laughed a moment. "I'm wonderful. Do you mind if I meet up with you shortly? I've got leftovers from last night's dinner I forgot to grab this morning before I drove you home."

The corners of Gwen's mouth curved into a large smile. "Yes—that would be great. When are you coming over?"

"Actually, I've got to meet with my cousins tonight. It's kind of a family thing. But, I was hoping I could meet up with you now and we could spend some time together before I leave for Lucinda's house."

"Oh—okay—I'm actually at a coffee shop on Harrison Avenue. It's Java Jake's. You want to meet me here? They will be open for another hour," Gwen said, hopeful.

"Sure, see you in a few."

"Okay. I look forward to seeing you, again!"

After they hung up the phone, Gwen looked up his number on caller ID and recorded it with his name as a new contact on her speed dial. At least now she had a number, although she didn't know if it was his mobile or home line. Looking around she noted that she was one of two people left in the coffee shop. She watched Jasmine who was busy busing a table, pick up dirty coffee cups and saucers and place them into a brown plastic bin. Gwen was half paying attention; half caught up in her own thoughts, when she noticed something that unexpectedly caught her interest. In Jasmine's vigorous efforts to grab the dishes from the nearby tables, the scarf she wore around her neck had become dislodged, revealing two small puncture wounds that were scabbed over. The wounds were at the base of the young woman's throat and were fairly sizeable. Jasmine stood up and instinctively pulled the scarf down concealing the wounds. She glanced over at Gwen who was watching her and smiled nervously, before she turned to lift the heavy bin full of dishes to the back of the shop. Gwen wondered what had caused the puncture marks, as she watched Jasmine walk away.

Gwen spied a used copy of the morning newspaper lying on the table next to hers. She picked it up and started reading the story highlighting the murder she'd heard about on the local news only a couple of hours earlier. She was just becoming engrossed in the story, when something cold touched the back of her neck, startling her. Gwen jerked as she turned to face Connor who was looking over her shoulder at the article she was reading. His expression momentarily reflected concern, before morphing into a genuine smile when his eyes met hers. He quickly sat down next to Gwen placing a package on the table beside her. She detected the faint smell of shrimp and meat. Among other things, she smiled knowing the leftovers would be her dinner this evening. Connor placed Gwen's hand in his as he spoke; the coolness sending minor chills down her arm.

"Did you sleep well this morning?" He stared down at her hand, using his thumb to trace circles in the center of her palm.

"Yes—you?" she asked.

Connor nodded.

Gwen searched Connor's face, noting the circles beneath his eyes were darker than usual and something in his expression concerned her. She got the impression he was worried about something when she noticed him glancing down at the newspaper article again.

"Connor what is it?"

He shook his head a moment. "It's nothing. Just have a lot on my mind I guess," he whispered, glancing away from her.

"You know if there is ever anything bothering you, you can always tell me about it. It won't go any farther than this table," Gwen said.

Connor squeezed her hand a bit tighter as his smile brightened. "I know and the time will come when I will open up to you. Don't worry about me right now. I'm okay—just have some things to work out with the family."

"Oh, I see. Say no more. Family disputes can be a real nightmare."

"It's not what you think. But, yes we do have some differences of opinion on how to handle the business right now. I'm starting to regret some of my decisions—"

Gwen saw another flash of worry in Connor's face. She wished she could say, or do something to assuage his fears, whatever they might be, but she didn't know how. As if sensing her concern he pulled her closer to him, draping his arm across her shoulder. She turned to face him and he lightly kissed her lips. She felt that familiar sense of peacefulness she always seemed to feel whenever he touched her. His gleaming blue eyes stared into hers while they sat there in silence. Gwen felt herself becoming lost in his expression when a voice interrupted her thoughts.

"Connor, is that you?"

Connor and Gwen turned to see Jasmine running excitedly towards them. To Gwen's surprise, Connor smiled at the young woman and got up to give her a hug. A twinge of jealousy overcame Gwen and her face flushed. Gwen quickly tried to mask her reaction.

"Hi Jasmine, nice to see you again," Connor said, as he hugged Jasmine and kept his eyes locked firmly on Gwen's. Her momentary brush with envy was extinguished when Gwen saw Connor smile and wink at her over Jasmine's shoulder.

Jasmine turned to face Connor smiling, as she spoke. "Haven't seen you in over a week. Derrick said you were out of town on business and preoccupied with other things." Gwen noticed Jasmine turned to glance her way.

"Yes, I was in Boston last week, but I've got things under control there. Is my cousin treating you well?" Connor asked, his gaze resting on the dark circles under the young woman's eyes.

"Well, you know Derrick. He likes to keep his options *open*."

"Yes, he does. Jasmine you should not waste your time on Derrick. He's a non-committal type and I don't imagine he ever will be any different," Connor replied, feeling sorry for the young woman.

"I know—but you can't choose who you love," Jasmine said, looking at Gwen again.

Connor noticed Gwen looking uncomfortable. "Where are my manners today? Gwenevere, this is Jasmine, a very good friend of Derrick's."

Jasmine faced Gwen and held out her hand. "Nice to meet you Gwen. I've heard a lot about you."

"Really?" Gwen asked, pleasantly surprised that she had been the topic of conversation. She shook the young woman's hand in hers.

"Yes, Connor's told me you're a college professor, what do you teach?" Jasmine asked, genuinely interested.

"Psychology. Are you a student?"

"Yes, but my major is in criminology. However, I'd love to double major. Maybe I can stop by your office sometime?"

"Sure—I'd be happy to help," Gwen said, noting she finally knew why Jasmine seemed familiar to her. She had likely seen the young woman walking the halls of the university.

"Well, I should be going. I have to lock up and get the dishes done before closing. It was nice meeting you, Gwen. Connor, don't be a stranger. Derrick and the gang missed you last week," Jasmine said, as she walked towards the back of the shop.

Connor waved to Jasmine. "Take care of yourself."

Connor looked at Gwen who was still and quiet. He pulled her to him for a close embrace.

"She seems like a nice girl," Gwen said, looking into Connor's eyes.

"She's a sweetheart and Derrick doesn't deserve her. It's always bothered me the way he uses women, but he'll never change. He's always out for himself. It's a shame Jasmine didn't choose someone like Aidan, who would appreciate her the way she deserves. She's right though, you can't choose who you love! Just hope she doesn't get hurt," Connor said.

Gwen didn't know what to say. She hadn't realized there was so much animosity between Connor and Derrick. She stood there waiting for something to break the awkward silence.

"Gwen, I've got to run myself. But, I'm happy I had the chance to see you today."

"Me too. It was a very nice surprise."

"Well, I'd like to see you again this week. May I call you?" His brilliant smile caught her off-guard for a moment.

"Of course." Gwen wanted to ask when, but remembered what her friend Pam had warned her about earlier. She heard an auditory caricature of her friend, Pam's voice inside her head warning her to play it cool.

Connor suddenly broke out in laughter as he hugged Gwen goodbye and kissed her on the forehead. He started walking towards the glass door of the coffee shop.

"What's so funny?" Gwen asked.

He turned to look at her one last time, his roguish grin in place, before he waved goodbye to her closing the door behind him. Just as he reached his car, he stopped and turned to face the coffee shop and mouthed the word, *soon* before he turned and quickly got into his car. Gwen watched him drive away before she grabbed the leftovers from

Chapter 6

The remainder of Gwen's Sunday evening was spent on the phone catching up with friends and family she hadn't spoken with in a few days. Gwen checked in with Andy first and much to her relief, realized that Dan was keeping up with Andy's typical eating and sleeping schedule. She also learned that Dan had been busy the past few weeks taking Andy to every zoo and animal related activity in the Atlanta metro area. Dan had bought Andy a few new video games that he was enthralled with so things were going well with their visit. Of course, it would be a rough transition for Andy when he returned home to the more mundane events surrounding life than he experienced on his vacations away, but that couldn't be helped. At least for the time being, Andy was happy.

Gwen also checked in with her mother. She told her Mom about the typical items related to work, her productivity on papers and so forth, before finally mentioning Connor. To Gwen's complete surprise, her mother was extremely positive about the news. Usually, her mother was wary of the men Gwen dated, but Gwen couldn't blame her since she didn't have the best track record. Her mother seemed to like Connor's old-fashioned ways more than anything else. It also didn't hurt that he had money. Gwen's mother wasn't materialistic, but nevertheless liked knowing that Connor wouldn't be asking Gwen for money like some of her previous boyfriends had. Gwen could not care less about Connor's wealth, she liked the way he treated her and that she was genuinely intrigued by him. Still, it didn't hurt to have her mother's approval. Her mother was her ultimate best friend in life and had never been wrong about a man before. Gwen hoped she was right this time as well.

Shortly after Gwen finished speaking with her mother the phone rang again. Gwen looked at the caller ID and saw it was her friend, Bridget McIntyre, whom she hadn't talked with in a few weeks. Bridget had been away in the North Carolina Mountains vacationing with her family. Of all Gwen's friends, Bridget had the most difficulty dealing with the Florida heat and humidity and would escape the high temperatures by staying in her cottage in the Appalachian Mountains at least twice during the summer months. In her early fifties, Bridget was strikingly beautiful, with fair skin, light red hair, and a few freckles that dotted her face and torso. Unfortunately, Bridget also suffered from an autoimmune arthritic condition that left her in chronic pain and discomfort much of the time. Gwen and Bridget tried to get together at least every other week when possible. Like Cindy, Bridget was married, and often busy with her family, but she and Gwen were very close and they kept tabs on one another as frequently as possible. It was also easier for Gwen to physically go out with Bridget than Cindy, because Bridget's kids were grown and out of the house. Among Cindy's brood, she had five-year old twins, which made private time for Cindy close to impossible.

"Gwen, do you have a moment to speak?" Bridget asked.

"Sure, I'm just getting ready for bed, but I can spare some time. How are things in North Carolina?"

"Heavenly. Guess what temperature it is here?"

"I don't know—let me see—seventy-four degrees," Gwen said, a bit jealous as it was ninety-five in the shade in Florida.

"Sixty-two!" Bridget squealed with delight in her voice. Gwen could tell she was feeling well from the exuberance in her tone.

"You lucky girl—I'm sweating my ass off here," Gwen said, as she giggled. "I had to peel my dress off when I got home today, even though I was in and out of air conditioning most of the time."

"You need to come visit me up here sometime. I know you're busy at the university, but you could use the break. How's Andy doing with his dad?"

"I spoke with Andy tonight, and he seems to be happy enjoying time with his dad. Dan's taken him to every animal exhibit they have and a baseball game. Andy thinks he's died and gone to heaven! It's going to suck when he returns home and he has to go back to his school routine. It's so unfair; Dan gets to play with him during the summer, while I get to be the taskmaster doing all the hard parenting. I'll bet at the first sign of illness, Dan would freak out and call for me to come get Andy. You know what I mean."

"Well Gwen, that's why you divorced Dan. He thinks he's God's gift to the world and everything revolves around him. He never helped you with Andy and he wasn't there for you when you needed him; he was too busy having an affair. But, look at it this way. You really do need some time for yourself and this is your chance to let Dan take some of the responsibility for a change."

"You're right. At least Andy is happy. Besides, I've met someone so I'm taking advantage of the little bit of freedom I have right now."

"Oh—so who is the new guy? Anyone I know?"

"His name is Connor Blake. I don't know if you've heard of him," Gwen explained.

"No—that name doesn't ring any bells. What does he do?"

"He's into finance. Raising capital and stuff like that. You know me; I have no idea how the business world works. I've been safely ensconced in academia most of my life, shielded from the real world of economics and commerce. I just know he's successful."

"How'd you guys meet?"

"Do I have to tell you?" Gwen asked, her voice wavering a bit. She was a little embarrassed by the circumstances of her first meeting with Connor.

"Come on, Gwen, it's me, Bridget, I won't judge you. Was it online?"

Gwen cringed, as she said it. "No, we didn't meet on the computer. We met at a club."

"Oh—that's okay. Look sometimes you do meet nice people out. It's not common, but occasionally it happens. What club was it?"

"*The Immortal,*" Gwen said.

"Really? I've heard about that place. It's supposed to be very exclusive. From what I've heard very few people get in. You almost have to know someone who works there to gain entrance. Even when large tips are offered to the bouncers, most people aren't admitted. How'd you get in?"

Gwen was quiet a moment, taking in what Bridget had said. Bridget and her husband, Raymond, were well known real estate developers in the Cove area of Panama City. The McIntyres knew anyone and everyone who had clout in the Panhandle region. If Bridget mentioned *The Immortal's* extreme secrecy and exclusivity, it was because she had credible sources. Images of the bouncer and his enthusiasm at her arrival to the club flashed through her mind. *Why did she get into the club so easily when others were denied, she wondered.*

"I don't know Bridget. I waited in line for a while when a bouncer came up to me asking for my license. He inspected my ID, stamped my hand, and directed me into the club. I noticed a lot of people around me were denied access, or ignored by him and the other bouncers. I haven't the foggiest idea why. But, once inside I can tell you that place is amazing! It's very mysterious and exotic. I've been to some cool clubs in my day, even in New York City, and this one beats them all, hands down! Anyway, it's where I met Connor."

"Well, have you two been out a lot?"

"We've only had one official date—but we've seen each other on a few different occasions. He's—interesting to say the least. I can't put my finger on it, but he's different from anyone I've ever met—anyway, I hope it continues," Gwen said. A smile broke out across her face.

"Well, I do too. You could use some happiness in your life, Gwen. It's been years since you were excited about anyone. Just enjoy it, no matter what the outcome. "

"I suppose you're right. I just have to watch myself that I don't get too excited, too early."

"Okay, I've got to go. I'll be home in a couple of weeks. Let's get together and have dinner when I get back."

"Sounds good. Give me a call when you get home. Enjoy the nice cool air, while you can."

"Oh, I definitely will. Bye."

"Bye," Gwen said before she hung up.

Gwen turned on the news while she changed into her nightgown. She wanted to hear if anything new had developed in the murder case before going to bed. The news reporter outlined a few more details of the case, stating that a homeless man, who had been sitting on one of the benches near the bay, had witnessed the murder victim running from two other men carrying knives or some other form of sharp weapon. He told the reporter that the men were running so rapidly he could barely see their feet touch the ground. The reporter visibly frowned as she listened to the man recount his version of events, doubt evident in her facial expression. The news team shot footage of the area where the man's body had been found, marked by blackened ash on the ground where the body once lay. Gwen winced recognizing the ash as remnants of the man's charred remains. The reporter also interviewed another witness who had been several blocks away from the Civic Center, where the murder took place. This witness told the reporter he had seen the men pursuing the victim on foot near Grace Avenue. Gwen's pulse quickened. *The Immortal* was located on Grace Avenue. Gwen got a sick feeling in the pit of her stomach that the murder and the club were somehow linked.

Monday was a fairly uneventful day. Gwen worked on another manuscript she wanted to submit for publication as well as a review for a journal that was due in a couple of weeks. She finished her revisions and the journal review shortly before four in the afternoon when her cell phone rang. It was the number Connor had called her from yesterday. She quickly answered it.

"Hello, Connor."

"Good afternoon, Gwenevere. How has your Monday been so far?"

"Good—yours?" Gwen answered, suppressing the urge to yell with excitement. She thought she heard Connor giggle on the other end of the line, but it was fleeting.

"Good. I met with my cousins yesterday to iron out some things related to the club. We've run into a few minor problems we need to address the next couple of days so we're shutting down until Friday night," Connor replied in a business-like tone.

"That sounds serious. Is everything okay?" Gwen asked, feeling anxious, sensing something was wrong. As long as the club was doing well, Gwen was certain Connor would stay, but if they went out of business she wasn't so sure he wouldn't head back to Massachusetts.

"It's fine. We just have a couple of issues to resolve. Anyway—I was wondering if you'd like to join me this Friday night. I'm going for a little drive to Pensacola and I'd like to take you with me. We could stop and have dinner along the way."

Gwen wanted to blurt out her answer, but refrained from displaying her exuberance. She composed herself before speaking. "Sure—that would great."

"Good. I'll pick you up at five,"

"Okay. See you Friday night," Gwen said, her voice steady and smooth.

Connor hung up seconds before Gwen did. When she was sure the phone was completely turned off, she screamed out in delight a resounding, "Yes!" in her office. A colleague who just happened to be walking by her office door frowned at her, sending Gwen a visual admonishment for her verbal outburst. But, Gwen didn't care. She was excited and had something to look forward, to now. She scanned her email one last time, making sure she had nothing of immediate concern to deal with before leaving for the day. She did notice a colleague had sent her another news link related to the murder near the bay, but Gwen didn't open it. She was in a great mood and knew reading the news story would deflate her spirits. As she left the university she thought excitedly about what Friday night would bring.

Friday morning, Gwen woke to the torrential rain of a thunderstorm. She was grateful she didn't have to teach as the roads near her flooded easily and the rain was coming down in heavy sheets. She opted to stay at home and work rather than venture out. Gwen tuned into the local news to get the weather report for the day and let out a sigh of relief that the forecast was favorable. The heavy rain would subside by the early afternoon followed by sunny skies. The roads would be bone-dry by this evening just in time for her road trip to Pensacola with Connor.

Gwen surfed the channels to view the other news stories of the day and was stunned to hear the reports of two additional murders. Like the first murder, both victims had had their heads severed from their bodies and were badly burned. However, this time the bodies were dumped near the water at St. Andrews State Park. A middle-aged couple camping at the park had found what was left of the bodies early in the morning before the rainstorms arrived. Gwen wondered if this was the work of a serial murderer or copycat killer. Whoever had killed these victims certainly wanted to keep their identities concealed. Although she had initially worried that there could be a link between the first murder and the club, it was highly unlikely that these two new murders would be associated with *The Immortal*. For one thing, the club wasn't open last night and second, the location of the bodies was in another part of town, far removed from Grace Avenue. In fact, she seriously doubted the first murder was related to *The Immortal* at this point, as well. Or at least she convinced herself there wasn't a link between the two. Gwen decided to put the news of the murders out of her mind. She went into her office to answer student emails and work on other university-related tasks until it was time to shower and get ready for her date.

The day had been a blur and before Gwen knew it, Connor had arrived at her doorstep. She could see the familiar outline of his strong, muscular build through the window. Gwen nearly stumbled over Panda as she ran to answer the door. Her kitten had a bad habit of lying in the middle of the wooden floor wherever he felt like plopping down. When Gwen opened the door, Connor stood before her in jeans, black racing sneakers, and a black t-shirt that hugged his well-defined physique. Gwen blushed as she caught herself staring at his arms. She hadn't noticed he was so developed before. Connor immediately pulled Gwen to him to lightly kiss her before speaking.

"You ready?" He asked his luminescent eyes squarely focused on hers.

"Yes."

Connor held Gwen's hand as they walked from her house towards his car. Gwen detected a subtle, but distinct change in her mood. Moments before Connor arrived at her house, she remembered being nervous and giddy, but now she felt calm and peaceful. It occurred to her that she frequently felt emotional and physiological changes around him that she had attributed to alcohol or some other cause, but that wasn't the case this time. In fact, Gwen couldn't think of another plausible explanation for the sensations she was experiencing at the moment. Another thought occurred to Gwen which disturbed her. She had noticed similar physiological sensations and clouded thinking when Derrick and Lucinda had touched her at the club. Although Gwen thought it silly, she decided to conduct her own little experiment to examine her hypothesis. She purposely dropped her hand from Connor's, noticing him glance in her direction with a slight look of curiosity. The pleasant sensations Gwen had experienced seconds earlier when Connor held her hand rapidly dissipated. The first phase of her experiment was complete, now she'd collect more data for replication to make sure she wasn't crazy.

"Something wrong?" he asked, looking into her face, his eyebrow cocked to one side.

Gwen smiled at him. "No—why?"

Connor appraised her expression carefully before smiling. "Oh, nothing."

Connor walked over to Gwen's side of the car and opened the door of the Porsche for her.

"Thanks," she muttered.

"You're welcome," he said, before Gwen got into the car. He waited for her to buckle the seatbelt around her body before he shut the car door. Gwen watched through the window as he gracefully moved to the driver's side and was soon seated next to her.

Connor started the ignition, and the Porsche's engine sprang to life. They backed out of Gwen's driveway and headed down the street of her development. Gwen thought she'd ask Connor a question to distract him so she could plan to touch him when he'd least expect it.

"So did you work things out with the cousins at the club this week?" Gwen asked.

Connor was quiet a moment before he turned to Gwen. "Yes."

Gwen stared into his eyes, noting the complexity of his facial expression. It appeared to be a combination of guilt and resolve, mixed with relief.

"Okay, care to share with me what happened?"

"We had to fire a couple of employees who were making life rather difficult for us," he stated, flatly looking straight ahead at the road.

"That's it? You had to shut down the entire club for a week to fire a couple of employees? I don't understand, that doesn't make any sense."

"It's complicated, Gwenevere, I really can't elaborate right now."

Gwen felt her face flush and her temper flare. "Why?" she asked indignantly, looking at his angelic face.

"Remember what I said on the beach about needing some time. I will tell you everything; I'm just not ready, yet. Besides the problem is solved—at least for the time being."

Gwen was quiet a moment as she processed Connor's last comment. She wondered if he was just toying with her. She decided now was the time to test out her hypothesis again and when she saw Connor move his hand for the gearshift she grabbed his forearm, holding onto him tightly. Connor stiffened, clearly caught off-guard by Gwen's response. He quickly glanced in her direction, seeing a look of recognition and triumph in her eyes. However, Gwen wasn't prepared for what happened next. The world started spinning and she thought she was going to vomit right there on the spot. She noticed her ability to control her musculature diminished and her grip on Connor slipped, as did the rest of her body. She slumped back in her seat with her head tilted in his direction staring at him, her body listless. Connor looked alarmed and pulled the car over on the side of the road. He turned to face Gwen, apprehension and distress noticeable in his facial expression.

"Gwenevere, are you okay?"

Gwen noticed some feeling coming back to her limbs and body. She also realized that she could speak, although it would be labored. "Yes, I think so—I don't know what happened," Gwen slurred, trying hard to be coherent. But, Gwen did know. Something about Connor wasn't normal. In fact, something about his whole family wasn't normal. She realized his touch could affect her mood and her bodily responses. When he stroked her face or touched her softly the sensations were pleasant, but seizing hold of his arm or direct touch with pressure resulted in her losing her ability to think clearly or move. Because she had experienced these sensations with two other members of his family, she realized this must be the *difference* Connor had told her about on the beach. Maybe it was a genetic mutation the cousins all shared, but whatever the cause, it would mean close physical contact had to be carefully approached with Connor or the consequences could be lethal.

Connor looked down, guilt apparent in his face. "You have to be careful with *how* you *touch* me, Gwenevere."

"I know. When Derrick and Lucinda touched me at the club, I remember feeling odd for lack of a better term. I had a hard time concentrating on what they were saying and was light-headed and nauseous. I thought the sensations were the result of the alcohol I had that night, but I've felt it with you too, even when I haven't had anything to drink," Gwen whispered, still slightly slurring, but starting to sound a bit more like herself. "Is this what you meant by being different the night at the beach in Destin?"

Connor looked at Gwen, his glowing eyes scanned the outline of her face before returning to look into her doe-shaped eyes. "Yes, it's part of it."

"Is this—ability related to a disease?" Gwen asked concerned for Connor now realizing how much this ability could come in handy in some situations, but could also lead to isolation in others.

"Sort of—" his eyes drifted down to the floor of the car.

"I've never heard of a disease that causes something like this. What's it called?"

"I—I don't know Gwenevere, I think it's a genetic anomaly. I'm not sure. It's not something I like to think about to be candid with you. It is one of the reasons I've avoided relationships. I have to be very careful or I could really hurt you."

Gwen looked at him a moment wanting to ask him a question she almost thought taboo, but she decided since he was opening up to her she'd ask.

"Can you be physically intimate?"

"Yes, but it's something I approach extremely cautiously. However, there's much more to intimacy than the physical aspects *humans* typically focus on."

"Humans?" Gwen asked.

Connor laughed for a moment. "You know what I meant. Are you feeling better?"

"Yes, starting to, anyway."

"Good. Just make sure you let me control how we touch okay?" he asked. "I promise I won't let you get hurt—"

She nodded.

"Well, let's get back on the road. I have to be somewhere by eight o'clock, " he said, as he smiled at her.

"Connor, I just need to clarify something before we move on."

"Sure."

"Do all your family members have this *anomaly*?"

"Yes, they do."

"Well—the man who grabbed me by my car—well—he had the ability too, but he isn't related to you, is he?"

Connor noticeably stiffened, a heavy sigh escaping his lips. "No."

"Then there are others like you? Like your cousins?" She asked, her voice soft like a child's.

He nodded.

Gwen suddenly and inexplicably felt a chill course through her body.

Chapter 7

By twilight Connor and Gwen were well on their way to Pensacola. Gwen felt like they were flying and realized why when she looked at the speedometer.

"Oh my God, Connor you're driving a hundred and twenty miles per hour. You're not worried about the police or an accident!" Gwen exclaimed, noticing how easily they navigated around other cars. *She thought it amazing how he seemed to have a knack for knowing what other drivers were thinking.* He never had any near misses and seemed completely in control of the road ahead of them.

"No, not a bit—" he said, with a mischievous smirk.

"Oh—I love driving fast too, but I'm not as fearless as you are. I once got a hefty speeding ticket that resulted in three points on my license. I guess I'm only willing to speed in small bursts," Gwen admitted.

Connor smiled at her, his gorgeous white teeth noticeable and prominent in the fading light of the sun. " I hate driving slow—makes me crazy. I have a terrible case of road rage. Fortunately, I don't have to do a lot of driving in town."

Connor briefly glanced in Gwen's direction, a sparkle in his eye. "So tell me more about what your life was like growing up.

"Well, what do you want to know?"

"You know—the usual—do you have siblings? What was your home life like as a kid? That kind of stuff."

"Well for starters I'm an only child. I grew up in a typical middle-class family in a rural area of Southern New Jersey—"

Connor interrupted Gwen, "Did you live on a farm?"

"No—just a basic bi-level house. Mom was an executive assistant or what they used to call a secretary and Dad was into the computer business."

"Are you close to your parents?" Connor asked.

"Very much so. I got lucky in the "parent lottery." My parents are wonderful people. I talk with them at least four or five times a week. What about you? Any siblings?"

"I had two older brothers, Cyrus and William, but they died years ago."

"Oh—I'm sorry to hear that."

"Thanks. It was a long time ago—but I often think of them—especially on their birthdays. Cyrus was quite the practical joker always pulling pranks on us. He could make you laugh when no one else could. William on the other hand, kept to himself, but he had a gentle nature that everyone liked. We fought like all siblings do, but I could always count on my brothers. As for my parents, Mom died when I was only five years old so I have practically no memories of her, but Dad lived well into his seventies before he passed away from a heart attack. I was never close to my Dad. Our views on things were radically different. Anyway, my existing family are my cousins and we've stayed close, even if we don't always see eye-to-eye on things."

"Did you grow up in the country or city? I can't remember what you said when we were on the beach."

"I spent the first five years of my life in the suburbs of Boston before Dad relocated the three of us to the city."

"Where did you go to school?" Gwen asked.

"Hey, I thought I was the one asking the questions today," Connor retorted, partially joking. "Harvard for both my Bachelor's and Master's degrees."

"Oh—wow, now *I* feel intimidated."

"*Hello*, you're the doctor in this car, so *who* should be intimidated here?"

Gwen laughed. "I went to a small state school in New Jersey for my bachelor's and the State University of New York for my doctorate."

"Which SUNY?"

"Stony Brook."

"Very nice. That's a hell of a school. Two Nobel laureates were among the faculty when you were there weren't they?"

"Yes—how you'd know that?" Gwen asked, surprised.

"Because I've donated money to Stony Brook before," Connor mentioned matter-of-factly. I always research prospective recipients of my money before investing—I want to guarantee they're going to make a significant contribution with the funds.

"Do you often donate money to universities?" Gwen asked.

"When I can. I love science. I excel in business, but science has always captured my interest and attention. I'm secretly a bit of a nerd. I love watching science shows and subscribe to several science journals. Derrick thinks I'm insane, but I feel sorry for him. He doesn't know what he's missing."

Gwen stared at Connor in utter fascination. If she weren't worried about causing an accident or self-inflicting bodily harm from Connor's touch, she'd take him right now in his car. Aroused and excited she had to take deep breaths to calm down. Connor laughed as he looked at Gwen.

"You okay there, you look a little— *flushed*," Connor grinned.

Gwen cleared her throat. "Hmm— it's a little warm in here. Do you mind if we turn down the air just a tad?"

Connor nodded and changed the setting on the air conditioning, turning the temperature down by a couple of degrees. He turned his head to look briefly at her before shifting his gaze back to the road. Gwen welcomed the cool air that filtered through vents in front of her face and torso. Connor wasn't the only one who would have to keep his arousal in check she thought.

"Is that better?" he asked.

"Much. Thanks."

"So what made you pursue a career in psychology? Was it a desire to help people," Connor tilted his head to the side as he stared at her a moment.

Gwen smiled as she spoke. "Believe it or not, I took a general psychology course in my junior year in high school and that did it for me. I loved everything we learned in the course and I had an epiphany that this was the field I was meant to pursue. It's funny, but I've never wavered in my passion for the field. I remember during my first college class, the instructor asked us to introduce ourselves and indicate our major. You know the basic kind of introductory information faculty use to break the ice. Anyway, when she called on me, I mentioned my major and that I wanted to be a psychologist and pursue my doctorate so we should get cracking with class because I didn't have a moment to waste. The instructor looked at me like I was crazy. But, true to my word, years later, here I am."

"I know you do research and teach, but you seem to prefer teaching. Why?" he asked.

"Well—I love both, but there is something special about the look on students' faces, the moment they grasp a difficult concept. It's very rewarding to be a part of that process for my students."

Although Connor was still observing the road, she saw the corners of his mouth twist into a big smile. "What about you? Why business since you love science so much?" Gwen asked.

"I don't know. I guess I just followed in my dad's footsteps. He ran a general store when I was a kid and he was quite successful at it. I learned most of what I know from helping Dad with the store afternoons following school. He wasn't wealthy, but he put food on the table for his three boys so he did okay for himself. For my part, I earned a scholarship to Harvard. Dad didn't have any formal education beyond the basics and always wanted us to go farther than he did. Had I to do it again, I would have gone into the biological sciences, but I'm good at what I do and I can do a lot for others with the money I've made on my investments."

"Why the biological sciences, if I may ask?"

"Life, the processes needed to sustain it, and how fragile it can be intrigue me."

A sign saying Pensacola was near appeared on the right of I-10. Gwen looked at the clock on the dashboard of the Porsche noting the time, seven o'clock.

"We're making good time," she said.

"*Yes we are*," Connor stated, as the winked at her.

Gwen smiled as she turned away from him, her face blushing again. Connor pulled off an exit for Pensacola. Gwen noticed he was quiet a few moments as he navigated through streets in the city, apparently looking for a specific location.

"So where are we going?" she asked.

Connor looked over at Gwen, his excitement betraying his facial expressions. "I just have a brief stop to make and then I'll take you to dinner."

"Okay—sounds good." Gwen's curiosity was piqued, but she didn't press him. A few minutes later, the Porsche pulled into a parking lot of an upscale jewelry store. The storefront had gorgeous landscaping, with several palm trees, a few gardenia bushes, and multiple hibiscus plants with flowers in bloom. The building itself was tan stucco with solid white columns on either side of the entrance. Connor parked in one of the empty spaces up front and turned off the ignition. He turned to face Gwen, his eyes playful as he spoke. "Gwenevere, I'm picking something up for Derrick, I'll just be a moment. Okay?"

Gwen wondered why he didn't want her to come inside, but she didn't want to force the issue. She simply nodded her head in agreement. With that, Connor quickly exited the car and went inside the store. Gwen sat watching the fronds of the palm trees sway back and forth in the breeze. The enormity of Connor's condition was starting to sink in and Gwen wondered how this relationship would work. At some point, she'd want to be physically intimate with him and she wondered how she'd do that without harming herself. Then she remembered what Bridget said about enjoying the moment. Gwen always overanalyzed things to death. It was one of her biggest problems. She wished she could just relax and not feel compelled to delve deeper into what people said or how they behaved. Her friends always warned her about her incessant worrying, but it was hard for Gwen. She had suffered from anxiety and depression for much of her life and it had become part of who she was. Sure, there were medications for anxiety, but many were habit forming and she didn't want to rely on medication to function. The positive tradeoff was that she could be wildly creative and fast paced in research and the classroom. It suddenly occurred to Gwen that Connor could be very good for her in this regard. When he lightly stroked her hand or face, she felt a calmness envelope her. Maybe his condition was a mixed blessing. She thought of how good it felt just to be near him and she decided that for now, that was what she was going to focus on.

Half an hour after they left the jewelry store, Connor took Gwen to Kearney's for dinner. Kearney's was an expensive and impressive Irish restaurant located on the water. The restaurant had a small microbrewery on the premises that offered a host of beers in addition to the typical domestic and imported beers people commonly drank. The male servers wore tuxedos while the female servers wore long full black skirts and crisp white button down blouses. Servers, regardless of gender, wore a carnation that was died green on their collar. The mood was festive and fun and Gwen was immediately comfortable the moment they entered the place. Connor asked that they be seated near a window overlooking the water. A young woman escorted them to their table, presenting them with menus, two glasses with a pitcher of ice water, a loaf of fresh-baked sourdough bread, and a small dish of homemade butter spread. Gwen surveyed the menu homing in on a corn beef and cabbage dish that looked particularly good. A tall male server with short blond hair and a ruddy complexion approached their table.

"Good evening, my name is Jared and I'll be your server tonight. Can I get you anything from the bar?" Jared asked, his expression plastic.

"Gwenevere?" Connor looked over at her.

"Yes, I'd like Baileys on the rocks. Thank you," Gwen said.

Gwen watched Connor's eyebrows raise and his lips form into a smirk. He then shifted his gaze from Gwen to Jared, motioning the young man to come towards him. Connor stood up and whispered something into the young man's ear. Jared looked at Connor, nodded, and swiftly walked away from their table towards the bar.

"What was that all about?"

"I just asked him for a glass of wine from the owner's private stash.

The owner of the restaurant and I are *good* friends.

"Hmm—so is the fellow here, I'd love to meet him."

"No, *she* is up in Boston running my company," Connor added.

Gwen sat back in her chair, her gray eyes fixed on his. "Oh—I see." There was a moment of uncomfortable silence between them.

"Cassandra Kearney and I are childhood friends. She built this restaurant a few years before I built my house in Destin. She spends most of her time in Boston, but comes down here once or twice a month to check on things. She's got an impeccable manager who runs the place like a well-oiled machine. Anyway, she has a private wine cellar that my cousins and I occasionally sample."

Gwen wondered if Connor and Cassandra had ever been involved. Something about the way he referred to her as being a good friend bothered her. Connor glanced around the restaurant appraising the situation. Gwen watched his furtive eyes dance from table to table. He snickered a moment while watching an older couple argue several tables in front of them before turning his attention back to Gwen.

"Enjoying yourself Mr. Blake?" Gwen asked.

Connor seemed to look right through her as he smiled. "You have no idea."

"Really? Enlighten me."

"Trust me—you don't want to know."

"Actually—I do. What's so amusing?"

Before Connor could open his mouth, the waiter had arrived placing Gwen's drink in front of her and a silver wine goblet with Connor's red wine in front of him. Gwen took a sip of the Baileys; it was excellent.

"Ma'am may I take your order?" Jared asked, his body turned towards hers.

"Yes, I'd like the corn beef and cabbage entrée with the boiled potatoes please."

"Yes, ma'am and for you, sir?"

"Nothing, I'm good. Thanks," Connor replied. The waiter looked at Connor strangely for a moment and then left.

"Connor, you're not eating dinner?"

"I had something at four before I drove to your place."

"I feel kind of uncomfortable eating in front of you. You sure you don't want anything?"

"Yes, I have to eat multiple small meals throughout the day or I get sick. I'm very, as they say, hypoglycemic. Anyway, don't worry, I'm fine."

Gwen stared at him. She realized she had never seen him eat before. *She thought that really strange.* "So back to what we were talking about before. What was so amusing a few moments ago?"

"Well, Dr. Ryan—if you must know, I thought that conversation the older couple was having was quite—humorous."

"You could hear their conversation? They are several tables in front of us. How is that possible?" she asked.

"I read lips," Connor announced.

"You do?"

"Yep. Done it for years now."

"Really—where did you learn that?"

Connor shrugged his shoulders. "I don't know, just picked it up somehow. It pays to be observant. Anyway, the older gentleman was arguing with his wife about her cooking. I didn't catch all of it, but suffice it to say—he compared her meatloaf to a piece of desiccated leather. She wasn't too cheerful about it, I'll tell you."

Gwen and Connor both chuckled a moment. "Guess he's going to be hungry for awhile," Gwen muttered.

"No, he apologized to her a few minutes later and they walked out holding hands. Guess the old guy figured dried-out meatloaf is better than nothing."

Gwen and Connor spoke for several minutes before Gwen's food arrived. The corn beef and cabbage looked great and Gwen dove in right away. She hadn't eaten since lunchtime and was famished. She almost felt sorry for Connor since she barely heard a word he said while she ate. He was talking about how beautiful Salem and Boston could be in the fall or something to that effect. When Gwen had eaten more than half her entrée, the hunger pangs ceased and she started to feel relaxed.

"How was everything?" Connor asked as he took a big gulp of his red wine. He seemed to be thoroughly enjoying it.

"Excellent."

"Good. I was thinking of stopping at my place before taking you home if that's okay. There's something I want to show you."

Gwen smiled. "Sure, do you mean the house in Destin?"

"No—my little place in Panama City Beach," he clarified.

"Okay, I'd love to see it."

"I'll get the check and we'll be off." Gwen watched as Connor finished the last of his wine. He seemed to be savoring every drop.

"Could I try some of that wine next time?" she asked, smiling at him.

"Perhaps." Connor grinned at her, the impish smile she loved facing her.

They left the restaurant and drove to Panama City Beach talking about fun, superficial topics like favorite music and movies. They both loved horror movies, action flicks, and romantic comedies. Gwen was surprised to hear that Connor was cool with chick flicks as long as they had enough action to balance things out. They also appeared to have the same eclectic musical tastes. Connor did appear to be a bigger fan of classical music than Gwen, but he too liked classic rock and alternative music. The topics eventually shifted to more meaningful discussions about politics and the state of the country. Gwen learned that Connor was socially liberal like herself, but conservative when it came to how the country's money should be spent. It was becoming clear that they had a tremendous amount in common and Gwen felt herself becoming increasingly more comfortable with him.

Connor lived in Bay Point, an exclusive gated community in Panama City Beach. His so-called modest home was a twenty-four hundred square foot house located on a lagoon. The house had every amenity you could think of including a temperature-controlled room just for Connor's massive red wine supply off the side of the pantry. The house was largely decorated in upscale style with plush sofas and loveseats, large ornate dining and living room furniture, stainless steel appliances in the kitchen, and impressionist artwork adorning the walls. The Impressionists were Gwen's favorite type of artwork and she salivated looking at the paintings hanging on Connor's walls. One of the paintings looked to be a genuine Monet, but Gwen was too bashful to confirm this with Connor.

"Wow, your house is so beautiful," Gwen, said in awe looking at

Connor as he approached her.

"You really like it? I think it's kind of stuffy."

"Connor? Are you crazy? Look at this place. It's a dream home," she retorted, visibly rolling her eyes in front of him.

Connor laughed as he gently pulled Gwen to him. "I'm joking my Dear. I'm very lucky to live here. Just wish I wasn't in this large house by myself. Anyway—glad you like my humble little home."

Gwen felt relaxed in his arms, letting her head lean against his chest.

"Come with me, Gwenevere," he said, gently holding her hand and leading her outside towards the patio. He motioned for them to sit in two lounge chairs overlooking the water.

"I have a little surprise for you," he whispered. "Close your eyes."

"Okay," Gwen said, her voice wavering with excitement. She felt something cool and metallic placed around her neck.

"Okay, you can open your eyes now," Connor ordered, in a soft voice.

Gwen looked down to see a beautiful pave diamond pendant hung around her neck.

"Connor—it's—it's beautiful. I don't know what to say—"

"Do you like it?"

"*Yes*!" she exclaimed, a tear forming in the corner of her eye. You didn't have to do this you know."

"I know, but I wanted to." He pulled her close to him. Gwen buried her face in the small of his neck, while his arms gently held her near him. He turned for one brief moment to look into her eyes before he kissed her. Coolness gave way to warmth and feelings of peacefulness. He held her like that for hours, before taking her home.

Chapter 8

It was five in the morning when Connor finally drove Gwen home. Gwen gently rubbed the diamond pendant back and forth between her index finger and thumb while she stared absently out the window. Connor glanced over at Gwen, noticing her playing with the necklace and smiled.

"Gwenevere, I'd like to ask you something?" Connor asked, breaking the silence between them.

Gwen tilted her head in his direction, "Yes?"

"I don't know what your plans are for the next two weeks, but I'd really like it—if you'd join me in Destin."

Gwen's heart fluttered. She knew the answer to the question before he'd finished asking. "Yes, I have a lot of time saved, I could take off from work and stay with you."

Connor smiled, his beautiful features seeming to glow from within. "Well—I have some business at the club later this afternoon. I'll just swing by and pick you up afterwards. I'll come by around six, if that's good for you?"

"Yeah, that's great," Gwen, said, a bit too enthusiastically! She had meant to sound more subdued, but her excitement got the best of her. She heard Connor laugh for a moment. She wished she were better at hiding her emotions, especially around him.

Connor dropped Gwen off at her home, giving her a light kiss and hug before he quickly hopped back into his car. As Gwen entered the house she realized how exhausted she was. Afraid she'd forget something before leaving later that afternoon, she wrote a list of things she'd need to do before Connor picked her up. Afterwards, she changed into her nightgown and climbed into bed, just in time for sunrise.

Gwen opened her eyes around one in the afternoon. She had a lot to do before leaving. She needed to pack her suitcase, line up friends to take care of the cats, and contact work about taking leave. Since Pam lived the closest to her, she called her first to ask if she could watch her cats and much, to her relief, Pam agreed. She also told Pam about her plans with Connor. Pam was excited for her, and said she'd stop by within the hour to get the spare key and alarm system code. Next, Gwen emailed the university, as well, as left a voice mail that she'd be out for the next two weeks on vacation leave. Finally, Gwen grabbed her suitcase out of the garage and packed. She wasn't sure what she'd need, so she over packed. She included a few dresses, some jeans, shirts, shorts, nightgowns, bras, panties, toiletries, and a couple of pairs of shoes. She had to sit on the suitcase so that she could zip it closed. Gwen was relieved the suitcase had wheels and a handle since it would be hell to pull by itself. Gwen heard a knock at the door, which interrupted her train of thought. She realized it must be Pam coming to get the key.

Gwen opened the door to see Pam holding a newspaper in one hand and her large bottle of water in another. Pam never went anywhere without a huge bottle of ice water. She smiled at Gwen as she walked inside the house.

"How are you, Miss?" Pam asked, in her sweet melodious voice.

"Great—you?" Gwen asked, her eyes twinkling with excitement.

"I'm doing better than the two dead men found near St. Andrews State Park. Did you read the story in yesterday's news?"

"No, I must admit I haven't. I heard about it on the local news, but

I haven't kept up with the story. Any developments?"

"No. The police don't have any viable leads. They're hoping more witnesses will come forward. They're starting to think we've got a serial killer in town. I don't know about you, but I'm worried," Pam said, apprehension evident in her facial expression.

"I guess I should be concerned, but I've been so caught up with—Connor—I haven't been able to think about much else," Gwen confessed.

"Oh boy, I can see it all over your face. You're into him in a big way, aren't you?" Pam asked, impatiently tapped her foot back and forth.

Gwen sighed a moment. "Yes," she said, with a look of defeat.

"You haven't told him how you feel about him, have you?" Pam folded her arms across her chest.

"No, I've been careful not to divulge the fact that I'm crazy about him yet, if that's what you mean. You know, Pam—this is ridiculous. I feel like I've known him for years, but it's only been weeks."

"Well, it's a relief you haven't said anything. Remember, feelings are subjective, Gwen. They aren't logical and often lead to us make snap decisions we regret later on. Just be careful."

"Yeah, I'll try." Gwen smiled at Pam. They both knew she was already in over her head. Gwen would have advised any one of her friends that going away with someone to their home for an extended stay this early in the relationship was ill advised, but Gwen had lost all her objectivity and she felt compelled to be near Connor.

"Well, Miss—I've got to go. I'll take the spare key and your alarm code and be on my way."

"Thanks Pam, I really appreciate your looking after the fur balls."

"Yeah, yeah—I know. Give me a hug," Pam joked as she hugged Gwen goodbye and took the key and a piece of paper with the alarm code. Gwen heard Pam humming a gentle tune as she shut the door behind her.

Around *five-thirty* Gwen called Andy to check in with him. There was no answer at Dan's house. Gwen then dialed Dan's cell and to her relief, he answered. Dan was taking Andy home after spending the day at a local park. Gwen briefly spoke with Andy who was distracted by a hand held video game Dan had bought him. Andy mentioned that he missed her, but Gwen could tell he was also enjoying his vacation with

Dan. She let Dan know she was leaving town for the next two weeks and staying in Destin in a hotel. She urged him to call her cell phone if he needed her. Gwen didn't fill him in on Connor or the details of her stay and Dan didn't question her story. He just seemed eager to get off the phone with her. This was fine with Gwen. She didn't want Dan prying into her personal life, anyway.

After she hung up with Dan, Connor arrived to pick her up. He grabbed Gwen's suitcase like it was filled with air and easily hoisted it into the trunk of the Porsche. Gwen watched him, amazed. Connor showed up in jeans, a faded white t-shirt, a thick black leather jacket, and black leather boots. He didn't so much as have a bead of sweat on his skin despite the fact that it was ninety-seven degrees with seventy percent humidity outside. Gwen was already starting to sweat just from the one-minute walk outside her house to the car. Although Connor cranked up the air conditioning in the car as soon as they left the driveway, Gwen noticed several beads of sweat clung to the skin of her arms and legs. She looked over at Connor in his jeans and leather jacket again and shook her head back and forth in disbelief.

"Connor, how can you stand wearing those jeans or that jacket in this heat?" Gwen asked.

Connor shrugged. "Just cold natured, I guess."

"You must love the sun's warmth and heat?"

"No, not really."

"Even though you run cold? I would have thought the sun's rays would feel good on your skin?"

"Actually—it just makes me feel weak," he said.

"Weak?"

"Yes, it's why I prefer going outside in the late afternoon and evenings."

"Oh—," Gwen said, glancing at him as he drove on the interstate. She noticed Connor looked uncomfortable, his lips drawn forming a tight line. "What's wrong?" she asked.

"Nothing." Connor said, before sighing.

Gwen frowned as she looked over at him. "No, there's something bothering you."

Connor pursed his lips, like he was debating whether he should divulge his concerns. He seemed to be mentally deliberating what he should say before he finally turned to her to speak. "I probably shouldn't have told you about the sun's effect on me."

"Why? What's the big deal?"

"I don't know," he said, shaking his head.

"Is it another symptom related to your *ability*?" Gwen asked, her eyebrows rose in response to her question.

Connor laughed nervously. "Yes."

"Okay, so you have extreme photosensitivity. That explains the heavy tint on your car windows. Is this something your cousins also share?"

Connor didn't say anything; he simply nodded.

"Will you tell me more over this vacation?"

"Perhaps," he whispered, as he leaned over towards her, his right index finger lightly stroking her hand. Gwen relaxed in her seat and turned to face him.

"That's not fair, Connor," she whispered to him, aware of his intensions to manipulate her mood.

"I never said I played fair. Do you want me to stop?" His sensual voice sliced through her defenses like acid through metal.

"No—" she said, feeling the patterns his cold white finger traced along her wrist and hand. A deluge of pleasurable sensations overpowered her and weakened her resolve. She looked over at his beautifully sculpted face in pure fascination and awe. "It's scary the kind of power you have over me, right now."

Connor turned to look at Gwen, his radiant eyes staring intently into hers. "I could say the same about you." His expression was serious and he held her gaze for a long period of time, before he turned his attention back to the road.

"I don't understand—it's not like I have your ability," she said.

"No, but you have others you aren't even aware of."

Gwen smiled and closed her eyes. She knew he was using his ability to influence her and she thought about fighting it. She knew she could push his hand away or simply ask him to stop. He wouldn't have fought her. But, she didn't want to. They drove the rest of the way to Destin without speaking. Normally, Gwen would have hated the prolonged silence between them, but sitting in the car holding Connor's hand in hers, she was at peace. She wondered how Connor felt, and noticed he had a serene smile on his face. She leaned her head back and sighed as she stared out the window watching the tree canopies fly by.

It was dusk when they reached Connor's house in Destin. The Porsche stopped in front of the gate that enclosed the entrance to the house. He rolled the window down and promptly punched in his code on the keypad located adjacent to the entrance of the gate. The large iron gates swung open allowing them access to the driveway. Connor quickly pulled the Porsche through the gates and parked. He turned to look at Gwen and gave her a playful smile.

"Home sweet home," he said a little too eagerly; Connor clearly had a cheeky side to his personality.

Gwen laughed a bit. She noticed the front door and stone walkway leading up to the house were dark and wondered how she'd navigate the steps without killing herself. Always in tune with her thoughts Connor noticed the poor lighting situation.

"Guess I'll have to remind the maid to keep the outdoor lights on. Sorry Gwen, I didn't realize it would be this dark. You stay here and relax while I run up to the house and turn on the lights to the door and grounds. There is a bit of a slope on your way up to the door and I don't want you to trip. I'll be quick, okay?"

"Okay." Gwen watched him hop out of the car and race up the steps to the door. She couldn't make out his form very well, but it looked like he was practically floating up the stairs. Gwen closed her eyes and rubbed them, lamenting her poor night vision. When she opened her eyes a few seconds later she was startled to see Connor standing right beside her with the front yard brightly illuminated.

"Wow, that was *fast*! How did you do that?" Gwen asked.

"I told you I can run quickly," he stated flatly.

Gwen shook her head in disbelief. "Let me guess. Your ability to run is part of your condition, too, isn't it?"

Connor simply smiled at Gwen.

"Well?" Gwen pressed. She wasn't going to let this one go that easily.

"Well, what?" Connor had a look of amusement on his face.

"Well—either you're Superman—or you can fly."

"No—I can't *fly*."

"But, you can run like the wind can't you?" Gwen asked.

"No. Not *quite* like the wind." His lips curled into an impish smirk.

"Are you going to tell me what's going on?"

Connor sighed as he looked at her. "*Soon*, now let's get inside before the mosquitoes devour us whole."

Connor walked past Gwen and grabbed her suitcase out of the trunk. He carried her luggage up the stairs with what seemed like minimal effort while Gwen followed him. Connor waited patiently holding the door open for Gwen when she reached the top of the steps leading to the door's entrance. Gwen loved that Connor was the consummate gentleman.

The house was just as beautiful as she remembered it, although she didn't get a full tour of the place on her last visit. Gwen noticed that Connor managed to quickly turn on several lights in the house as he made his way to the bedroom where she would sleep during her stay. Gwen followed Connor towards the bedroom, noticing several impressionistic paintings that hung on the walls. Gwen also took in the surroundings of the massive living room and hallway. It didn't take a trained eye to detect the high quality craftsmanship of the home's painting, molding and woodwork. The furnishings were expensive and tasteful, not ostentatious and garish like many homes of the wealthy. Gwen loved the causal elegance of the place and felt relaxed.

Connor placed Gwen's luggage on a king-sized mattress in the bedroom before turning on the antique lamp beside the bed. Soft white light filled the room and Gwen noticed the beauty of the ornate furniture that surrounded her. The headboard, bureau, and end tables were all made of sturdy solid oak wood with an ornate scalloped design. The bed itself was covered in linens made of silk and brocade material that looked delicate in contrast to the heavy oak wood furniture. Gwen noticed the draperies that hung from a stylish curtain rod above the French doors overlooking the Gulf were made of the same silk and brocade material. A large ivory and gold Lennox vase that held a dozen fresh-cut white long-stem roses stood on the bureau. Gwen loved white roses and their fragrance filled the room.

"I hope you'll be comfortable here. There's a bathroom that adjoins the bedroom over there," Connor said, pointing out the entrance to the bathroom that was larger than Gwen's kitchen and housed a porcelain whirlpool bathtub.

"It's beautiful! Thank you, I'll be *extremely* comfortable here," Gwen whispered as she smiled at him.

"Good. Are you hungry? I can make you something, if you'd like."

"Yeah, that would be great. Can I help?" Gwen offered.

"No. But, you can keep me company while I cook," Connor said.

"Sure. Lead the way."

Gwen followed Connor into his mammoth-sized kitchen. He opened the stainless steel refrigerator and pulled out a large bag of shrimp, a few garlic cloves, scallions, and a chilled bottle of Chardonnay. He quickly uncorked the Chardonnay and filled a large wine goblet with the rich elixir; handing it to Gwen. Gwen lifted the glass close to her nose, smelling the wine's buttery aroma before taking a sip. This glass of wine was slightly sweeter and more pleasant than the wine she'd had on their first date. She raised the glass to him in a gesture of thanks and smiled. Connor grinned in response as he placed the rest of the food contents onto the island in the middle of the kitchen and pulled out a large cutting board from one of the many drawers that lined the bottom cabinets. Grabbing a large chef's knife from another drawer, Connor quickly diced the garlic cloves and scallions into fine pieces. A few moments later, he opened the door of the massive pantry and selected a box of angel hair pasta from the top shelf. He placed a large saucepan on the burner of the stove and started boiling water in preparation for making pasta.

Gwen watched Connor move about the kitchen with ease. He snatched a large frying pan from beneath a cabinet near the stove and retrieved olive oil from the pantry. Shortly after sprinkling the frying pan with olive oil, Connor scooped up the garlic cloves and pan-fried them until they were tender, before he added the scallions. The aroma of the garlic infiltrated the kitchen and Gwen's nostrils flared in delight. Connor added the shrimp and other seasonings to the pan, before he tossed the angel hair pasta into the saucepan. After stirring the shrimp and garlic sauce, he removed the pan from the burner. Connor drained the pasta-filled water into the sink before placing several strands of it onto an ivory and gold china plate. He then ladled the shrimp and garlic sauce onto the pasta before handing the dish to Gwen.

Gwen noticed a twinkle in Connor's eyes as she eagerly accepted the plate from his hand. She couldn't suppress a smile after taking her first bite of the shrimp dish.

"Oh my God, this is wonderful! Where did you learn how to cook so well? I have to work hard not to burn toast."

Connor laughed for a moment. "I've picked up a few tricks here and there. So, I'm guessing cooking isn't one of your strong suits."

"I'm what some might call culinary-challenged. I can make some basic staples, but I don't have the talent you do—God, this is *so* good," Gwen commented, as she dipped a large shrimp into the garlic sauce mixture before gingerly taking a bite.

"I'm glad you like it. I haven't cooked for anyone in awhile."

"What about you? You don't want any?" Gwen asked; a small bit of scallion dangling from her fork.

"Nah. I'm not very hungry at the moment."

Gwen stared at him befuddled. She realized she had never seen him eat.

"I'm kind of on a restricted diet, Gwenevere. I eat by myself most of the time since I can't eat the kinds of food most people eat."

"What does your diet consist of?"

"It's a liquid protein diet of sorts. Anyway, I'm happy to see you enjoy my cooking."

"You can cook for me anytime. It's too bad you can't enjoy these shrimp, they're amazing," she stated, before chomping down on another one. Gwen didn't say anything more regarding Connor's diet to him, but it clearly bothered her that he didn't eat in her presence. She wondered if his diet was another factor related to his medical condition.

"Want to walk the beach after dinner?" Connor asked, his lips forming into a beautiful smile; his shiny white teeth prominent in the soft light of the kitchen.

"Absolutely."

Following dinner Connor removed Gwen's plate along with the cutting board that he placed in the stainless steel dishwasher. Gwen offered to clean the stove and island, but Connor wouldn't hear of it. Although it was quite a mess Connor reassured her it wasn't a big deal. Gwen excused herself to use the restroom and, when she returned to the kitchen, was amazed to find that it was spotless.

"Ready to go?" Connor asked, his hand held out to her.

"You're finished cleaning the kitchen already?"

"Told you it was no big deal."

"I don't understand, it would have taken me at least twenty minutes to clean up in here," Gwen said, her expression one of disbelief.

"I can move very fast when I want to."

"I see that," Gwen looked puzzled. She expected him to elaborate, but he simply stared at her with those beautiful luminescent eyes holding his hand out to reach hers. Still shaking her head, she gently grabbed his hand and they walked out of the house to the beach. Although she had a number of thoughts racing through her mind associated with Connor's amazing speed and other talents, her concerns were soon mollified by the hypnotic power of his touch. Within a few minutes she no longer cared about the superhuman abilities he seemed to possess.

Connor and Gwen walked along the beach for a couple of hours talking about their favorite movies, books, artwork, and various other topics related to culture and education. The sheer volume of books Connor rattled off his reading list astounded Gwen. She wondered where Connor found the time. He'd clearly read all the classics as well as a plethora of scientific journals in a variety of disciplines. With all the daily hassles and responsibilities of life it was surprising that someone as young as Connor would be so well read. It was also obvious that Connor acted significantly older than his age. Gwen was beginning to feel like the *younger* person in the relationship. Nevertheless, Gwen was enthralled with Connor. She was quiet much of the time as he spoke this evening, because she didn't want to divulge what she was really thinking. *Although Gwen had only known Connor for a short time, she knew she was falling for him.* He was clearly everything she wanted in a person, and more. Yet, there was something he was hiding from her and this worried her. She wondered what this big secret might be and would it impact their relationship. "When were the pieces of the puzzle finally going to come together?" she thought.

Sometime close to midnight, Gwen began yawning. It had been a busy day in her preparations for coming to Connor's and she was starting to feel weary. Connor wrapped his arm around Gwen's shoulder and they slowly walked toward the house.

"Wearing out on me, huh?" Connor joked, stroking Gwen's shoulder with his right hand.

"Yes, guess all the excitement of the day is catching up with me."

"That's good. You'll sleep really well tonight."

"I think I will," Gwen said turning to look into his shining blue eyes. "Will you stay with me?"

"I'll tuck you in, if that's what you mean."

"Okay."

Gwen was disappointed, but she didn't complain. When the two of them reached the house, Gwen quickly went into the bathroom to change into her nightgown. Connor was waiting patiently by the bed for her. She walked over to him and he wrapped his arms around her. He held her close for a few minutes before he lightly kissed her lips. Then he pulled the covers of the bed back so that Gwen could slide under them. Connor sat down on the bed looking into her beautiful face.

"I'll see you in the morning. Sweet dreams," he whispered.

"You, too. Goodnight."

Gwen stared up at Connor for a few moments, feeling him stroke her forehead with his ice-cold fingers before her eyelids became heavy and she succumbed to fatigue.

Chapter 9

Connor and Gwen were inseparable the next two weeks. Every morning Connor made Gwen a large gourmet breakfast before they would venture out for the day. The first two days she spent with him they went fishing on a small yacht he chartered. Although Connor didn't like the sun, this craft had a large awning to protect him from the sun's direct rays while they fished in the deep waters of the Gulf for marlin and sharks. Connor seemed to be quite the fisherman, with a keen instinct for even the subtlest changes in the fishing line or movements of the water near the boat. He caught a marlin and a Mako shark, both of which he released back into the water. It appeared that Connor clearly enjoyed the thrill of the hunt more than the kill. Gwen, on the other hand, would have loved catching a marlin to bring home as a trophy, but she only caught an eel, which she tossed back into the Gulf. She never did have much luck with fishing, but had to admit that sport fishing was really quite exciting.

The next five days Connor and Gwen spent lounging at his house, watching some of their favorite old movies, spending time walking along the beach, and talking for hours it seemed, about art, science, culture, and politics. Gwen marveled that the conversation never lagged and she had much to learn from Connor. Gwen also spoke with Connor frequently about Andy gauging his reaction. If she were to have a future with Connor, he'd have to be there for her and Andy. To Gwen's delight, Connor showed great interest in learning about her son and would sit with her when she made her daily call to check in with Andy.

On the seventh day of her stay, Connor surprised Gwen with a quick flight to Miami, where they spent the next six days enjoying the shops, the local artists, and the food. In actuality, Gwen was the only one enjoying the food; Connor simply watched her gorge herself on seafood and rich chocolate desserts. They stayed in a five-star hotel with a breathtaking view overlooking the Atlantic Ocean. Each night Connor would take Gwen to a play or some other interesting venue that displayed the city's artisans and entertainment. Afterwards, they'd return to their suite to sit on their balcony and watch the white caps that swept onto the sand from the surf. Although they were staying in the same room, Connor slept on the couch leaving Gwen to sleep alone in the king-sized bed. When Gwen asked him to stay with her, even just to sleep, he refused. Evidently, his sense of chivalry was stronger than his desire, much to her annoyance. The following Friday they flew back to the Florida Panhandle. On the drive back to Connor's house from the airport, they stopped to gaze at an aquarium loaded with exotic fish and dolphins.

It was late afternoon when they arrived at Connor's house in Destin. Gwen was tired from their trip and Connor suggested she take a nap. She slept for several hours and was surprised it was dark when Connor woke her.

"Hey sleepyhead, how are you feeling?" Connor asked, sitting on the bed beside Gwen examining the outline of her face.

"Hi—what time is it?" Gwen asked, rubbing the sleep out of her eyes.

"It's close to eight. You've been asleep for several hours. How are you feeling?"

Gwen's eyes opened wide in shock. "Connor, why didn't you wake me earlier?"

"Well, you looked quite peaceful and I didn't want to disrupt your sleep. Are you hungry?" Connor stroked her hair.

"Actually, I am kind of hungry. Did you eat yet?" Gwen fought the desire to yawn.

"Yes, about an hour ago. I took the liberty of grilling some salmon for you knowing that you'd probably be starving when you woke up."

"Connor, you're so damn thoughtful, how did I get so lucky to meet you?"

"I think you've got it the other way around, Love," he whispered.

Gwen sat up and quickly kissed him before he could protest or keep her at arms length. The familiar feeling of peacefulness infiltrated her consciousness, making her feel a little dizzy and slightly disoriented.

"Gwenevere," Connor protested, gently pushing her away from his lips, but still holding her close to him. "Remember, we have to be careful."

"I know—but I couldn't help myself."

They both laughed for a moment.

"Well, I'll be strong for the both of us. I just worry that I'll cave one day and overpower you. I really must be careful, you know."

"I know," she said, smiling at him.

Connor changed the topic, with the slightest hint of irritation evident in his tone. "I got a call from Derrick that he really needs to speak with me. I'm going to have to go to the club tonight. I'm sorry, I didn't anticipate this disruption in our time together this week. I can go and be back by midnight."

"It's okay, I understand, but I want to go with you. Besides I haven't seen your family in awhile. Maybe *this* time they'll like me."

"Of course, they like you. What are you talking about?" Connor asked annoyed, his brows furrowed.

"They really didn't seem to like me that first night I met them at the club and neither did you for that matter. *Remember?*"

"I told you, you reminded me of Elizabeth and it was a bit disconcerting, at the time. Anyway, they know how I feel about you, so don't worry about them."

"How do you feel about me?" Gwen's doe-shaped eyes were wide open, eager for his response.

"I would think it's obvious by now," Connor whispered, his luminous eyes searching hers.

"Humor me," she said.

"I've been looking for someone like you most of my life. You have the ability to make me smile and laugh, something I haven't done much of for many years, and simultaneously, you can irritate the hell out of me with your stubbornness and inquisitive nature. You think yourself weak, but you are stronger than most and I can't imagine life without you now."

Gwen was speechless for a few minutes. She stroked the side of his cold perfect face pulling him closer to her. She felt his breath near her face and neck before he kissed her with an intensity that surprised her. He pulled away from her a moment to look into her eyes. "Your turn, Love."

Gwen stammered as she tried to speak. What could she possibly say to top him? She realized at that moment that she was hopelessly in love with him. She remembered Pam's warning about disclosing her feelings too soon, but it took everything in her not to say the words. Still she wanted him to know she felt just as strongly for him as he did for her.

"Connor, I feel the same. All I know is that my life has completely changed since you came into it. I, too, can't imagine life without you," she stroked his face wanting desperately to say more, but didn't feel it was quite the right time. At least for now, she knew they felt the same about each other and that was enough for her. She sensed he knew what she was thinking for some reason, based on the gentle and loving look in his facial expression.

Connor held her close to him, his hands stroking her back. "Well, I should let you shower and change so you can eat something and we can leave for the club."

"I wish we didn't have to leave."

"Me too," he whispered before exiting the room.

Gwen quickly showered and changed. The salmon, cooked to perfection as usual, was waiting for her with some asparagus spears and a nice glass of white wine when she entered the kitchen. Gwen consumed the dish in minutes and they left for Panama City. They spent the hour-and-a-half drive talking and joking about a number of things on their way to the club. Gwen was happy and she could see a giddy side to Connor that was new. He was relaxing around her letting her know more about him and who he was. The time seemed to fly when Gwen realized they were pulling into the parking lot next to the club.

Connor parked the car in a spot in the back reserved for one of the owners and he escorted Gwen through a back entrance into the building. She could hear the driving beat of the band as they played a techno song she didn't recognize. Holding her hand, they walked up a dimly lit staircase to the second floor. Connor moved a pair of plush red curtains out of the way, so that he and Gwen could enter the band arena where the cousins were sitting. It was extremely dark in the room and Gwen was glad Connor was holding her hand to guide her through the maze of people and tables scattered throughout the room. Gwen briefly examined the patrons of the club noticing many of them were wearing black and Goth-like attire. It was then that she spied them. The cousins were all seated at a table near the back; they appeared to be closely scanning the crowd. She felt a strange, nervous sensation in the pit of her stomach. She didn't know why, but something about them made her tense. Gwen thought it odd that Connor seemed so different from his family and yet she reminded herself that he had come across as cold to her on their first meeting as well. She wondered if she wasn't being a bit too harsh in her judgment of them. Gwen noticed that the three relatives seemed preoccupied by her presence when she and Connor reached the table. She sensed a difference in their demeanor; they seemed less threatening than before.

"Hey, Gwen. How are you this evening?" Derrick asked, his devilish grin spreading across his entire face.

"I'm great, actually," Gwen said as she quickly glanced from Derrick to Connor before speaking. "It's nice to see you all, again."

Lucinda and Aidan nodded in her direction. She noticed Lucinda's expression was actually pleasant as she smiled at Gwen.

"Gwenevere, Derrick, Aidan, and I are going to speak for a few moments in the back. Do you mind sitting with Lucinda for a few minutes?" Connor asked

"No, that would be fine," Gwen said, a little apprehensively, but she smiled anyway to put Connor's mind at ease.

"Okay, we'll be back shortly." The three cousins quickly fled towards the back room, disappearing behind the red curtains, leaving Gwen with Lucinda, who appeared to be staring at a young man across the room. The young man was likely in his early twenties and his attention was singularly focused on Lucinda, as well. Lucinda smiled at the man who tacitly took that as an invitation; he quickly approached their table and sat down beside Lucinda slipping his hand into hers. Gwen noticed he had a blood drop stamp on the back of his hand and she watched in fascination as his demeanor changed around Lucinda. He seemed almost giddy as Lucinda spoke to him in a voice too low for Gwen to hear. Gwen hated to interrupt, but she needed to use the restroom.

"Lucinda, I'm just going to the little girl's room, I'll be back shortly in case Connor comes back looking for me."

Lucinda simply nodded and went back to speaking with the young man who was clearly captivated by her. Gwen got up and found one of the red doors leading to the women's restroom. She used the facilities and combed her hair before leaving the bathroom. Near the bar, she noticed a man staring at her with a sneer on his face. He was tall like Connor, but a few years older, with long thick snow-white hair and a pair of luminous blue eyes. Gwen was caught off guard by his eyes, which matched those of Connor and his family. Gwen started to walk towards Lucinda's table, but there was no sign of her. She sat down on one of the stools waiting for Lucinda to come back when she felt a cold hand grab her wrist. Startled she looked up to see the man with the dark sneer firmly holding her wrist in his hand. Gwen sensed the man was very dangerous and she tried to pull away, but his grip was like iron and her will rapidly weakened. She felt her body collapse as he pulled her close to him. His mouth was near the nape of her neck and he was speaking to her in a language she didn't understand. Gwen felt herself continue to weaken and she no longer had the ability to fight. She didn't feel content or peaceful, as with Connor, but paralyzed and terrified. The man started pulling her away from the table towards the curtains, which led to the exit of the club. Gwen tried to scream, but nothing came out. She realized the man was going to rape her or worse and she would be powerless to stop it or even call out for help. Then, she heard a snarl and deep-throated scream that came from behind her.

Gwen couldn't see anything in the dark, but heard what sounded like a small group of animals growling. In the commotion, the stranger released Gwen from his grip and she fell to the floor with a thud. She heard Connor yelling at the man who had tried to abduct her.

"Stay away from her, she's mine," he growled in a voice so low and guttural that she barely recognized it.

"I didn't catch your scent on her, nor have you changed her. She's open to anyone who wants her," the man snarled back.

"She's mine! Get the hell out of here, before I rip your throat out myself," Connor screamed as he stood over Gwen protectively.

"You'd better change her if you value her," the man warned as he stormed out of the club's exit.

Gwen had no idea what was going on, she didn't understand what they were talking about.

"Lucinda, I left you in charge for two minutes and you couldn't keep an eye on Gwen. What the hell is wrong with you? You know what she means to me!"

"Oh my God, Connor! I didn't mean to—I'm so sorry, please forgive me," Lucinda cried.

"Connor, you'd better take Gwen home. She's conscious and she's frightened," Derrick ordered.

"You're right. We'll talk tomorrow."

"Yes. We will," Aidan agreed staring at Connor before he walked off in a huff.

Gwen felt Connor pick her up off the floor. Although she was frightened, she instantly felt better in his arms. He carried her out to the car and placed her in the passenger's seat before they left the club breaking multiple speeding laws on the drive back to Destin.

"Gwenevere, are you okay?"

"No—what did that man mean about changing me?" she asked frightened, her heart thumping loudly.

"He was just some lunatic. I'm so sorry he grabbed you—and so help me God, Lucinda's going to pay for her neglect," he said through clenched teeth.

"It's not her fault. I simply went to the bathroom and the man followed me to our table. He came out of nowhere."

"Gwenevere, I told you there are some dangerous characters at the club. Lucinda should have followed you to the bathroom just to make sure," Connor huffed.

"So, what he said was nonsense?" Gwen asked.

"It was rubbish. Clearly the man is mental."

"He seemed quite emphatic to me!"

"Well, pay no attention to him. He won't ever come near you again."

Gwen was confused and fearful; she knew Connor wasn't being completely honest with her. She felt Connor touch her hand and her discomfort eased a bit.

"Connor, you're going to tell me everything right?"

He looked over at her briefly, with a sober expression on his face. "Yes."

Gwen examined Connor's expression as he stared out the window of the Porsche. His lips pursed.

"When are you going to tell me what's going on?" she asked.

"Later this weekend. For now you've had a rough night. You should rest and get some sleep."

"But I'm not tired.

Connor looked over at Gwen and said softly, but firmly, "You will be," as he stroked her hand. She felt a wave of fatigue envelope her, but she forced her eyelids open.

"Stop it, Connor! You're reminding me of *him*," Gwen cried as she pulled her hand from his with tears streaming down her face.

Connor nervously moved his hand through his hair forcing strands away from his eyes and face. He looked distressed and worried.

"Gwenevere, if you want I can make it go away."

Gwen abruptly turned to look at him. "What do you mean?"

"I can erase the memory if you want. It will be like it never happened."

Gwen stared at him in shock. She was pretty sure she didn't hear him correctly. She stammered as she spoke. "What did you just say?"

"You heard me."

"Are you saying you can manipulate my memory?"

He looked over at her, clearly regretting this line of conversation. "Forget I said anything."

"No! Answer me, damn it!" she screamed.

"Yes," he said, in a soft voice that was barely audible.

Gwen suddenly felt nauseous. She remembered a conversation in the car during their first date where she couldn't remember a question she had asked him. She wondered in horror if he had erased one of her memories that night.

"Gwenevere, I just thought—you wouldn't want to remember what happened tonight. I just wanted to erase *that animal* from your mind. Forgive me, I didn't mean any harm," he pleaded.

This time it was Gwen's turn to speak through clenched teeth. "Connor, the one thing I need from you more than anything else is your honesty and trust. If we don't have that we don't have anything."

He sighed as he lowered his head a bit. "I'm sorry. Maybe I shouldn't have started this."

"Now, what are you talking about?" she asked, alarmed.

"Maybe I'm not the right man for you."

"Oh, so now you're having second thoughts, when earlier this evening you said you couldn't live without me!" Gwen yelled, crying.

Connor abruptly pulled the car over to the side of the road. He looked over at Gwen his eyes wild with fury. "I meant every word of what I said tonight! But, you'll have to make sacrifices to be with me and I don't know if I'm willing to put you through that. I don't want to let you go, but I sure as hell don't want to be the person who damns you either!"

"What do you mean?" she said frustrated.

"I mean that I'm not the best person for you, Gwenevere."

"What if I don't agree with that assessment?"

"You don't understand. Being with me will come at a steep price. Maybe a price that's too high for you to pay."

"Why don't you let me make that decision for myself, Connor?"

He stared at her, his lips drawn tight. His eyes glanced down to the floor before coming back up to rest on her eyes. He sighed heavily, in defeat. "Okay."

"You are going to tell me everything this weekend right?"

"Yes, I will, like I said."

"Oh—and one last thing. I need to know. Have you ever erased my memory before? Don't lie to me to "protect" me. I want the truth."

He looked at her, guilt covering his face. "Yes, once."

"When?"

"You asked me a question regarding my past on our drive to Destin during our first date. I answered you honestly, but I didn't want you to remember my answer."

"Why?"

"Because you asked me if I had ever killed anyone."

"And?"

"I have," he whispered, remorse in his tone.

"Oh," she said. "Is that part of the secret you've been hiding from me?"

"Yes. Are you frightened of me now?"

Gwen hesitated only for a moment as she pondered his question. "No. If you wanted to hurt me, you would have done it by now—and it's pretty clear that you want to protect me."

Connor looked over at Gwen relieved; he whispered softly to her. "I would rather burn alive than harm you."

"Well, please don't do *that*. I may be angry with you for the moment, but I want you sticking around for the long term," she whispered, a smile crossing her face as a tear rolled down her right cheek.

"Gwenevere, I'm so sorry for the secrecy. I will tell you everything; I just wanted to do it when I was ready. It's not an easy topic to broach and I know I risk losing you once I do. But, I respect you and I owe you as much. Please forgive me."

"I do, but from now on I need your honesty no matter how painful the information might be."

"Agreed," he whispered.

"Good."

"Can we drop the topic for tonight and go home?" Connor asked.

"Yeah, we can do that," Gwen mumbled.

Connor pulled the car back on the road and they were both silent for the rest of the drive. Gwen was worried about the cryptic things Connor had mentioned, but she felt emotionally drained and didn't want to talk with him about it now anymore. When they arrived at the house, Connor walked Gwen to her room and hugged her close to him.

"I really want you stay with me tonight. Please—" she implored.

Connor smiled and stroked her back with his cool fingers. "Okay."

Gwen changed into her nightgown and slipped under the covers. She waited patiently for Connor who quickly disrobed down to a pair of boxer shorts. He slid in the bed beside her, holding her close to him. The coldness of his smooth skin momentarily sending chills down Gwen's body, before being replaced by familiar sensations of peacefulness and comfort. She sighed a few moments before falling asleep in his arms.

The sound of a door opening and muffled noises woke Gwen in the middle of the night. She reached for Connor, but found the sheets were empty. She was going to yell out his name, but refrained when she heard voices coming from the kitchen. She quietly got out of bed and walked towards the door to listen. That's when she heard the four of them speaking.

"How is she?" a female voice asked. Gwen could tell from the beautiful quality of the soft velvety voice that it was Lucinda speaking.

"She was pretty upset tonight. I wish I had insisted she stay here while I came into town. Then nothing would have happened," Connor said.

"It was only a matter of time, Connor. You have to tell her everything. You risk putting her life in danger if you don't."

"I know—I just wanted to have some normalcy in my life for a change. And—how do I tell this lovely woman I'm in love with what I really am?"

"You have to; you have no choice. You've gone public with her, but she's still mortal. Several of our kind, are beginning to question your motives. Remember Connor; she's an AB positive—one of the most coveted types. If you want a life together, you'll have to change her," Lucinda stated, a hint of sadness detectable in her voice.

"I've never changed anyone before. What if I fail to stop in time?" he asked.

"Don't be ridiculous, you've had many human *familiars* in your time. You'll know when to stop in the process." Derrick retorted, almost jovially.

"It's been over eighty years since I took a human *familiar* and I don't like being reminded of my roguish past. After Elizabeth died I was mad at the world and believed it owed me something. Besides, there is a big difference between taking a human *familiar* and changing a mortal. Anyway, I'm a different man from those barbaric days, you all know that from my hunting preferences."

"How you choose animals over humans is beyond me! I can't stand the stench they produce," Aidan said, in disgust.

"Easily Aidan, no one gets hurt," Connor remarked.

"Our human *familiars* get something out of it too, Lad. Have you forgotten so quickly? It's why we never have difficulty getting new recruits," Derrick said.

"Oh, yeah that's right. So we can take advantage of their feelings for us. What about poor Jasmine? The girl wants nothing more than to be changed and your companion, yet you parade numerous *familiars* in front of her. I pity the girl, she deserves better," Connor retorted, his voice inflections rising sharply.

"Well, at least I've been honest with Jasmine about what I am. You've kept poor Gwenevere in the dark for your own selfish motives," Derrick scoffed.

"Boys, lets not fight. We don't to want to wake the human in the other room," Lucinda said.

Gwen shuddered as she listened to the conversation. She realized that something was very wrong with Connor and his family. They didn't have a genetic disease. They weren't human. What did they mean by changing mortals? She remembered the man who attacked her by her car the first night she went to the club. He had said something to Connor about being unaware that she was his *familiar*. What did that mean? And—Connor's comments about hunting preferences concerned her. She continued to listen as they spoke.

"All we're saying is that you've got to tell Gwen what's going on and let her decide what she wants to do. If she decides she wants out, you've got to let her go. But, you will have to erase her memory to protect her and us. We can't risk having her telling others what we are," Aidan said.

"I'm going to tell her tomorrow night."

"Why don't you tell in the morning?" Lucinda asked.

"Because my stash has run low and I have to hunt tomorrow."

"You should have been more careful about that having her in the house with you," Lucinda snapped.

"I would never hurt her. But, you *are* right. It was careless of me to let my supply run low. If I can't find decent game, I'll head to Pensacola and raid Cassandra's cellar."

"Connor, I think it will be okay. If it's meant to be, it will happen. At least you're going to give Gwen the choice. You refused to change Elizabeth and she died as a result. It doesn't have to be that way," Lucinda said.

"Please don't remind me. It may have happened over three hundred years ago, but the wounds still run deep."

"Good, than you won't let it happen again this time," Lucinda admonished.

"What about our other problem?" Aidan asked.

"We've taken care of it, I see no reason to be concerned," Derrick said.

"Really? You think the elder clan will be so forgiving of what we've done? I'm not so optimistic," Connor said.

"We'll be fine. We just have to keep the number of predators in the club down," Derrick said.

"Our cover's blown, the elders aren't happy with us," Lucinda quipped.

"Well, let's just see if any more come to town. We'll have our answer then," Aidan said.

"Yeah, but at the price of losing another one of our own. Let's hope the two we dealt with were the last of the lot," Connor said.

Gwen sat mesmerized listening to the cousins. She didn't know what to make of their conversation, but she felt a mixture of fear and curiosity. Who were they, or more appropriately, *what* were they? She went to move closer to the door, when she heard a commotion in the kitchen.

"She's up. Let's go," Lucinda said.

Gwen heard the door open and voices trail off as the cousins rapidly fled the house. She quickly jumped into bed and pretended to be asleep when she felt Connor slide back in the bed next to her. She hoped he wouldn't notice her heart racing; practically exploding in her chest.

She felt his cold hand pull her close to him and her anxiety diminished. She wondered if he knew she had heard the entire conversation, but she didn't want to give away that she was awake. However, Gwen's concerns were short-lived as Connor's ability to subdue her worked, and she fell into a deep and dreamless sleep.

Chapter 10

At ten the following morning, Gwen woke to an empty house. Connor had left a note indicating he was shopping and running other errands, but Gwen knew otherwise. He was out hunting; she just didn't know what *type* of game. She replayed the cousins' conversation she'd overheard the night before in her mind, searching for any missing details that might explain the situation. Gwen also thought about the stranger's comments during the scuffle; something about his remarks registered a deep-seated fear within her that she actively tried to suppress. She raided Connor's pantry, nibbling on some bread and crackers while she made herself a cup of tea. Gwen wondered what she should do next. She was tired of Connor's evasiveness and would insist on answers when he arrived home. However, the thought of sitting around and waiting for him was unappealing. Gwen decided to start searching Connor's house. Under normal circumstances she would rather cut off a limb than go through someone's personal things in their home without their knowledge or consent, but nothing about this situation was normal. She couldn't ignore what she'd heard or experienced and she wanted answers.

Gwen searched the kitchen first, noting nothing unusual except that there wasn't much food. She was lucky to find the bread and crackers she had eaten. Connor didn't even have canned goods, which was odd for any home in Florida. After all, tropical storms and hurricanes were frequent unwelcome visitors to the state and having an ample supply of canned goods was necessary in emergency situations. Of course, Gwen realized that Connor didn't stay in Destin that often, but still to have no canned goods whatsoever was odd to her. She continued searching through the bedrooms, living room, bathrooms, and the porch out back, but came up empty. Gwen was about to give up her search when she noticed a door that seemed out of place. It was located inside of Connor's bedroom closet; partially hidden beneath some of Connor's suits and trousers.

Gwen tried to open the door, but it was locked. She tugged vigorously on the door handle for several minutes in frustration hoping the lock would release under pressure, but it wouldn't budge. She sighed to herself in disappointment as she started to walk away when something shiny and metallic on the wooden floor caught her eye. Her attempts to yank the door open had inadvertently dislodged a key that was lying on top of the molding above the door. Gwen grabbed the key and eagerly inserted it into the lock allowing access to the secret room hidden within the closet. When she opened the door she found the room was sparsely furnished with a small desk, a chair, and a filing cabinet that was jammed with papers. She also observed a wooden bookcase filled with old books that looked worn from years of wear. Gwen walked over to inspect the books, noting they consisted of several classics Connor had mentioned he loved. She picked up one of the books, and began leafing threw it, detecting the musty smell of the paper. Gwen was about to place the book back onto the shelf when she saw *it*.

On the wall, hung an oil painting of a petite young woman with dark red hair, warm brown eyes, and pale skin standing on the beach with hundreds of small round rocks scattered along the sand. The woman had a lovely smile and gentle features, but what struck Gwen the most was the young woman's attire. She wore a plain long black dress that covered most of her body with a starched white apron that hung over her shoulders and extended down the length of the dress. In her hand, the young woman held what appeared to be a white linen headdress or bonnet that normally would have covered her beautiful red hair. Gwen stood with her mouth agape in wonder at the painting. She moved closer to the portrait to inspect the script at the bottom right hand corner. It read, "Elizabeth in Salem," signed with Connor's signature and the year 1693 below it.

Gwen stood frozen in place, the book dropping from her hands to the floor with a loud thump. Suddenly, she was inundated with an onslaught of thoughts and imagery. If the portrait was genuine, and there didn't seem to be any rational reason why it wouldn't be, then it proved Elizabeth Blake *had* lived in the late 1600s. The computer search Gwen had conducted weeks ago had been accurate after all. Gwen began to shake; the grim realization that Connor himself must have been alive in the 17th century registered in her mind. He told her he was older than he looked their first date on the beach. Could he actually be over three hundred years old she wondered? If so, how was it physically possible? Gwen thought about Connor's other unusual characteristics. His ice-cold perfect pale skin that never seemed to sweat, his ability to run at speeds that were beyond the range of human capabilities, and his amazing strength. With nothing more than his touch, Connor could manipulate her mood, her physiological activity, and even erase her memories. And—most importantly, Connor didn't eat. Gwen had never seen Connor eat nor any evidence of the so-called diet he said he was on. She started the mental process of tying the concept of *hunting* with the idea of a *liquid protein diet* and the pieces of the puzzle finally clicked into place.

Beads of sweat broke out all over Gwen's body and she experienced a sickening feeling in the pit of her stomach. Gwen was a rational data-driven scientist and what she was contemplating was beyond the scope of what she thought physically possible. Yet, as much as she racked her brain, she couldn't think of a more parsimonious explanation to fit the facts than the one she was thinking now. She thought to herself in exasperation, *it can't be true, it just can't be.*

"Why not?" he asked.

Gwen abruptly turned to see Connor standing behind her. Her pupils widened. Although she sensed he wasn't surprised to see her in his private room going through his things, he didn't seem angry.

"Connor?"

"Gwenevere, I see you found the portrait of my late wife."

Gwen nodded, visibly shaken.

"She died a month after that portrait was painted."

Gwen looked directly into his stunning blue luminous eyes. In a voice that was barely above a whisper she spoke. "Connor, how old are you?"

"I'm 346 years old," he said with a grave expression.

Gwen gasped, placing her hand over her mouth. She didn't know what to say. She couldn't believe this was happening.

"What are you?" she whispered.

"I think you already know the answer to that question."

"I need to hear you say it—I need to know for sure that I'm not imagining this whole thing, because in my logical, rational world someone like you doesn't exist."

"Give me your hand, Gwenevere," Connor ordered.

"I don't want you manipulating my mind. I need to know the truth."

"I'm not going to manipulate you or your memories. I want you to—feel something. You're going to have to trust me," he said, his eyes looking intently into hers.

"Okay."

Gwen allowed Connor to place her hand over the left side of his chest beneath his shirt. She felt the icy coolness of his skin, but nothing more. Her eyes widened further in panic. There was no heartbeat. How was this possible? She started palpating the wrist of his hand frantically searching for a pulse in an effort to prove he was mortal.

"Gwenevere, you won't find anything. My heart stopped beating in 1692."

"You *can't* be dead! You can't be! How are you standing in front of me right now? How?" she yelled at him, as tears began to flow freely down her face.

"There are many names to describe what I am. The most common term is vampire, but my cousins and I like to call ourselves immortals," Connor said flatly.

"You can't be a vampire, vampires don't exist!" Gwen screamed at him, hitting him with her fists as hard as she could. She didn't want to accept the truth; Gwen felt like she was going insane. She collapsed in his arms crying.

Connor picked Gwen up off her feet, cradling her in his arms as he left the small room and walked into the master bedroom. He set her down on the bed beside him and held her hand in his. She felt her anguish ease.

"Gwenevere, I can't change what I am. I do have a conscience and unlike my family, I predominantly hunt animals instead of humans. But, I live each day with deep regret over the innocent lives I've taken," he said with a look of anguish.

Gwen sat transfixed on the bed. "You said you predominantly hunt animals instead of humans. Does that mean you still hunt humans on occasion?"

Connor looked over at Gwen, reaching with his finger to wipe dry a tear that had slid down her cheek. "Yes, once in a great while. However, I never hunt an innocent. If I choose to hunt a human now, it's because I hear the evil deeds he or she has committed or is planning to commit and I decide to protect others from their violent acts. I'm not saying its right or even condoning it. The thirst for human blood is powerful and occasionally I lose control."

Gwen stared at Connor still processing something he had said a few sentences earlier. She realized why he was always in step with her thought processes. She asked the question to confirm her suspicion. "Can you hear my thoughts?"

"Yes," he said, looking away from her, guilt apparent in his facial expression.

"So you've known what I've been thinking the whole time I've been with you?"

"Well, I don't listen to everything you think, only when I want to. I wasn't listening the day you grabbed my arm in the car, which is why you caught me so off guard. Lately, I've tried to avoid prying into your mind because I feel it's rude and intrusive. But, sometimes I just can't help myself. I'm sorry about that."

Gwen was visibly uncomfortable, but she pressed on with her

questions now that he was revealing himself to her.

"Do all vampires have the ability to read minds?"

"The ones I know do. Some of us are better at it than others. Of the four of us, Derrick is the most expert at it, while Lucinda has the strongest influence with touch."

Gwen's brow furrowed. "Which ability or talent are you superior at compared to your cousins?"

Connor grinned from ear to ear. "That's easy. I can move faster than any of them. That's one of the so-called talents of this curse I actually like."

"You think of it as a curse?"

"Don't you Gwenevere? I've been alive for so long, nothing is new anymore. I never had children and everyone I've ever loved with the exception of my cousins has died. And—there is the little matter of what I eat to survive. Every moment I'm near a human, the potential is always there to attack."

"But, you've never tried to attack me."

"Oh, yes I have. I nearly bit you when we danced the first night I met you. It took every ounce of my willpower to pull away from you."

"Then why did you pull away?"

"Because I didn't want to feed on you." Connor sighed as he got up from the bed and walked over to the opposite side of the room. He dropped his head in his hands rubbing his temples.

"Why did you cut in on the dance when I was with Derrick?"

"Because, I didn't want him feeding on you either."

"Is that the only reason?"

"No—I was moved by your spirit and strength. You are so much like Elizabeth, but a strong and vibrant person in your own right."

"I don't feel that strong," she admitted.

"Gwenevere, you approached a table full of hungry vampires and asked to sit with us. That would practically be a death sentence for most. And—you had the strength to resist Lucinda, which I've never seen any human successfully do before. We were all quite impressed."

"It's not like I knew you were vampires. If I had, trust me I wouldn't have come anywhere near you."

"That fact became obvious to us, as well, from your responses."

"Were the strange men who tried to abduct me also vampires?" she asked.

"Yes."

"Why would they want me? I mean—they could have had their pick of anyone in the club." Gwen studied Connor's expression, her head cocked to the side.

"Humans are always in danger of being attacked simply because they are humans. But—the reason why you've been targeted more than once has more to do with your blood type."

"I don't understand. What's so special about my blood type?"

"You possess a very rare blood type in the US that is desirable to our kind. Only a small percentage of the population here has AB positive blood, so your scent is very inviting to immortals."

"How did you know I have AB positive blood?"

"I could smell it when you walked into the room at the club. We all could, which was why we were so amused when you approached our table. It was like a filet mignon parading itself in front of a pack of hungry wolves. You also wore a rosebud stamp identifying your type as rare so we weren't the only ones to recognize it in the club. You see—rosebud stamps are reserved for the rarest of the blood types, which are AB positive, O negative, and AB negative. A blood drop is used to identify rare, but slightly more frequent types like B positive, B negative, and so forth. The most common types such as O positive and A positive get the script stamp," Connor said, his shimmering azure eyes focused on Gwen.

Gwen quivered as she processed this information. She now understood the bouncer's eagerness to usher her into the club the night she met Connor. Gwen thought of the cousins' conversation and started to understand a bit more of their concerns. "What's so special about rare blood types to vampires?"

Connor sat down next to Gwen keeping a small distance between them, so she'd feel comfortable.

"Extremely rare blood types like the kind you possess give off a unique aroma and flavor. The B allele, which isn't very common in North America, has a distinctively sweet taste that is coveted like fine liquor that has been aged. It's why some of these other immortals have followed you."

"So I could be attacked and killed by one of these vampires, because of my blood type?"

Connor nodded.

Gwen's heart began to race with the gravity of Connor's words. She suddenly felt frightened and vulnerable.

"Gwenevere, I'll make sure nothing happens to you."

"How can you be so sure? You left me alone with Lucinda and look what happened?"

Connor visibly cringed at her words. "That will never happen again, you can trust me on that. But, in the long run, there are two ways in which I can protect you. The first involves you moving on with your life and simply severing your ties with me—"

Gwen looked alarmed and cut Connor off mid-sentence. "What's my other option?"

Connor sighed heavily, like he had an invisible weight on his shoulders. "I can *change* you."

"Change me?"

"I can make you an immortal," he whispered, his eyes a bit downcast in a loathsome expression.

Gwen gasped a moment before she regained her composure. The thought of becoming an immortal was both terrifying and exhilarating.

"Let's say I was to consider that option—and I'm not saying I am yet, but for the sake of argument—how does it work? How would you change me—into a vampire?"

"You'd have to drink my blood co-mingled with yours to become an immortal. The vampire blood would attack your human body replacing your human cells with vampire cells. The process takes several hours and you'd experience human death before being reborn as an immortal," Connor replied.

"Then what?"

"Then you'd be like me."

"Could I still live a fairly normal existence?" Gwen asked, surprised to hear those words uttered from her own lips. She couldn't believe she was considering this.

"You'd have to learn how to hunt, how to act *human*, how to protect the people you love who are mortal from knowing your secret. And— you'd have to move every ten to fifteen years because you won't age and people will become suspicious."

"Oh—"

"You would also have to change your identity each time you move. It's best to move to big cities since you get lost in the crowd that way. Small towns like this posses greater *complications*."

"What about my son and my parents? Would they be safe around me?"

"Actually yes, a vampire cannot change a mortal with whom they share a bloodline. In fact, you would be repelled by the scent of their blood."

"That's a relief," she said with a sigh.

"Oh, but it's a dual-edged sword, Gwenevere. Your loved ones are safe from you harming them, but you can't change them to prolong their lives either."

"What if I asked a vampire who doesn't share genetics with them?" she asked eyeing Connor.

"Oh no, not so fast. I'm not thrilled about the idea of ending your human life, let alone that of your family."

"Connor, if I were to become immortal how would it affect Andy? I mean he'll figure out pretty quickly that I'm not human right?"

"He'll definitely figure out that you aren't human. There is the real possibility that you'll frighten him, but there is also the strong possibility that he'll accept you as his mother regardless of *the change*. You'd still be you, Gwenevere, but your strength, speed, ability to read thoughts, as well as the hunger will be a part of your life for eternity. Unfortunately, you don't know how Andy will respond. Seeing his mother remain the same, frozen in time may bother him as he ages over the years. But, it will also give you the ability to be physically strong for him, as he matures and grows into manhood. You should speak with Aidan about this. He has a lot of experience mentoring children and he could provide you with more information than I could. As for your other concern about us moving in a decade, Andy will be twenty by then and likely on his own working or in college. That part of the change will likely have little influence on his life and he could always choose to move with us. Again, this is assuming you become immortal."

"Why does Aidan have so much experience with children?"

"He loves children and has worked with various boys clubs providing them with a male mentor."

"Don't the children figure it out? You know, that he's not mortal."

"Sometimes, but to a kid without any male role model, someone who wants to spend time with them and protect them is all that matters."

"Really?"

"Think about it Gwen. Kids are very perceptive and often pick up on cues when someone has negative intentions towards them. Aidan genuinely loves spending time with kids, and they sense that about him. He'll have insight into your concerns about Andy."

"Well, what about my parents?" Gwen asked, concerned.

"Your parents will notice the changes too at some point so you'll have to decide whether they can handle the news of their daughter's new identity as a vampire or whether they'd be better off believing you dead."

"Are you saying I'd have to stage my own death for my parents benefit if I think they can't handle the news?" she asked.

"I'm not saying you should, but I've known other vampires that have staged their deaths to spare their loved ones knowing what they'd become. It will depend on how accepting your parents will be of your rather *unusual condition*," Connor said.

Gwen was becoming uncomfortable with this aspect of their conversation and abruptly changed the topic, knowing she'd have to consider everything Connor had just said about her family as she thought over her decision. For the moment, she was overwhelmed. "What's a human familiar?" she asked. Gwen had heard the cousins talking about this last night.

"It's a human who allows a vampire to drink a small amount of their blood. I've heard several humans say the sensation associated with being bitten by a vampire is greater than any human sexual or pharmacological experience, which is why there is never a shortage of humans who want to be familiars. Being a *familiar* doesn't offer protection from other vampires. It's more or less a symbiotic relationship between a vampire and a human. The vampire feeds off the *familiar* and the *familiar* experiences the high of the experience. In fact, many familiars will actively seek out several vampires to bite them because the experience is so reinforcing. And—the problem with taking a *familiar* is the longing it will create in that human for the change."

"So you can drink a small amount of a human's blood and not kill them?"

"Yes, but it can be challenging. The vampire has to will himself or herself to stop, which is difficult when the blood tastes as exquisite, *as yours would.*"

Gwen cringed at Connor's last few words momentarily experiencing revulsion.

Connor chuckled a minute to himself. It wasn't laughter associated with amusement; it was the kind of nervous laughter one produces in moments of extreme awkwardness and discomfort.

"If I chose to walk away then what?" Gwen asked.

"Then we would have to part ways. But, I could as you know, erase your memories of me to make it an easy transition. I'd live with the memories, but you'd be free to start over without any baggage."

"That hardly seems fair to you."

"I know, but I'd do it for you if it meant maintaining your safety. It would be your choice, but I'd do it in a second if that's what you wanted." Gwen looked into his beautiful eyes for a moment seeing the depth of his emotion. He really meant what he was saying.

"Is that what you want?" she asked.

"What I want isn't important here. It's what's best for you."

"No—you don't get off the hook that easily, Connor. If you are telling me you don't want me then my answer is easy. But, you have to be honest with me. Do you want me in your life?"

Connor's glance at Gwen was filled with agony and frustration. He hesitated a moment, but then acquiesced to her question. "Yes, more than anything, but I don't want that to sway your decision."

"Well, like it or not Connor it does matter."

He nodded in defeat knowing she was right.

"Did Elizabeth die because you refused to change her?" Gwen asked.

Connor winced at her question. "Yes, I refused to feed off of my wife, and she was killed one night when I left to hunt." Gwen got the impression this was the root of the self-loathing that she'd seen Connor occasionally express. "I'm giving you the choice I never gave Elizabeth. She pleaded with me to change her, but I refused. I couldn't stomach drinking her blood. But, my stupidity cost me everything including her life and it's why I haven't become seriously involved with another human since. You're the first in over three hundred years."

"So you weren't a vampire when you met Elizabeth?"

"No, I was bitten long after we were married. In fact, the same vampire, who sired me, also sired my cousins. He wanted us to be part of his new coven in America, but we rejected him once we were strong enough to break free of his hold on us. None of us asked for this."

"And—so that's why you refused to change Elizabeth?"

"Yes."

"What happened after Elizabeth died?"

"What do you mean?" he asked.

"I overheard you speaking with your cousins last night. You mentioned to Derrick you didn't want to be reminded of your roguish past. I'm sorry I eavesdropped, but I have to ask what he meant."

Connor's eyes lowered to the floor as his shoulders slumped. His voice wavered a bit when he spoke. "After I found Elizabeth dead, I went into a deep depression for a time barely feeding. Months later, near skeletal proportions, I was foraging for rodents near a popular tavern when I happened to overhear the thoughts of a man who was planning to kill another man for the money in his billfold. I became so enraged at the man's utter lack of humanity, that I killed him on the spot, draining him bone-dry. I noticed that for a short period of time I felt better, but the pain soon returned. So, for years, I actively searched for and hunted murderers or rapists. Unfortunately, in my bloodlust an innocent would occasionally get in the way and I would drain them too. It wasn't intentional. *I was in a frenzy of rage and pure hatred.* I was suffering and wanted others to suffer as well. I also took many familiars like Derrick, just for sport. Finally, after about seventy years, I grew to detest everything about my existence. I contemplated suicide for a time, but one day it occurred to me that I could use the talents I'd been given to actually do something positive for the world, instead of taking innocent lives. That's when I started carefully listening to the thoughts of others around me in the business world to make good decisions for my fund company. That way I could heavily invest in charities and scientific foundations, contributing something other than death to society. I also decided I'd hunt animals instead of humans. As I said, once in a while I will hunt a human, but only one who is more dangerous to the world than I am."

"What about the bottles of wine that I've seen you drink? I'm guessing they contain human blood?" Gwen asked, taking Connor's hand in hers. She noticed he smiled at her in gratitude for her gesture of faith and trust in him.

"Yes, they contain human blood, which should explain why I was quick to snap at you when you asked for some our first date during dinner."

Gwen was going to ask Connor where they blood came from, but he finished her thought for her.

"Don't worry, Love; the blood I'm drinking is tainted and comes from a blood donor bank that would simply dispose of it anyway."

"What do you mean by tainted?" She looked at him in horror.

Connor laughed a minute before he spoke. "I've arranged a contact who works within the local blood bank to sell me infected blood. When the blood bank receives donor blood that tests positive for an infectious disease like HIV or hepatitis C, they are required to dispose of it. However, the infected blood won't harm me and the contact has made a nice little side income out of our arrangement. This way I get to drink a steady supply of human blood without having to harm anyone."

"Why don't more vampires simply have similar arrangements?"

"Because most vampires love the hunt—and the kill. My cousins actively hunt humans as well as feed off of *familiars*. They think me insane for my hunting preferences, but I'd like to think I'm a bit more in touch with my humanity than they are."

"What about the stories of crosses, garlic, and stakes through the heart? Is there any truth to the folklore and vampirism?" Gwen asked.

"You mean do those things repel us?" Connor asked with his head titled in her direction; subtly revealing a few of his obscenely white sharp teeth.

"Yes—do crucifixes cause you pain, and that sort of thing?"

Connor broke out into full body laughter. Gwen looked at him at bit irritated that he was trivializing her line of questioning.

"I'm sorry, Gwenevere—but that was too funny for me to hold back— In all seriousness, crosses, garlic, and stakes through the heart won't hurt me. If you'll remember I made you garlic shrimp one night. I didn't die or burst into flames when I touched it, so a lot of the folklore is really just mythology."

"Do you sleep?"

"Yes, for about two to three hours a night. I can go for days without sleep, but then I'll need a six-hour nap to catch up. And—no I don't sleep in a coffin as Hollywood might have you believe."

"What about sunlight, obviously we went out on the boat so that doesn't bother you much right?"

"I just can't be in direct sunlight for hours at a time or I get violently ill. But, I won't burst into flames in the sun either."

"It's probably impossible, but can you die?"

"Actually, yes we can—there are two ways you can kill a vampire. One is to burn the vampire alive, which makes me shudder to think about. The other is to decapitate the vampire."

Gwen looked at Connor a bit alarmed. Something about the manner of death, besides the obvious gruesome nature of it, bothered her. Why did that sound so familiar to her?

"Are there any specific rules of being a vampire? Like a code of ethics?" Gwen asked, very curious to hear his answer.

"One big one—we are to remain secret about our existence. We're not supposed to flaunt it to the mortal world."

Gwen's jaw dropped. She looked stunned. She stammered as she spoke. "But—your club actively advertises what you are. I mean—it may just seem like a cool themed club to humans, but in actuality *The Immortal* isn't hiding the fact that you and your family members are vampires. And—with the different stamps used to identify the particular blood types—well there isn't that much secrecy regarding your motives or nature at all."

"I know. We are breaking the sacred rule of the Immortals."

"What are the consequences for your actions?"

"If the Elder clan in Romania found out about what we were doing here, they'd send their vampire hunters here to kill us."

"Oh my God—then why are you doing it?"

"Because, when I came to Florida to start the club with my cousins I no longer cared whether I lived or died. In fact, I came here knowing I was likely signing my death sentence. Then—you walked into the club and changed everything. Now, I have a reason to stay alive, but it may be too late—"

Gwen was troubled. "What do you mean? Does this Elder clan know what you've all been doing?"

"Yes, they've already sent two of their best vampire hunters here to kill us. They killed one of our kind a few weeks ago. Remember the body they found near the Marina Civic Center. That was one of our employees."

"What about the two bodies found near St. Andrews State Park?"

"Those were the bodies of the vampire hunters. Aidan, Derrick, and I hunted them after they killed Marcus. We cut off their heads and then burned the bodies to destroy the evidence. Just like they did to poor Marcus."

Gwen sat processing what Connor had to say. His words confirmed her initial intuition that the club and murders were linked.

"Do you think this Elder clan will send more hunters?"

"I don't know—we'll see."

Gwen saw the obvious concern on Connor's face and couldn't help but feel a deep sense of dread.

Chapter 11

Connor and Gwen talked through the night. She still had many questions for him, but she noticed for the first time that he seemed weary. It might have been more mental fatigue than physical exhaustion, but Gwen sensed Connor was struggling with the choice he had given her. He was clearly conflicted and she could tell it weighed heavily on his mind. They had left the confines of his bedroom hours earlier for some fresh air and were now walking on the secluded beach behind his home. The wind gusts were stronger than usual, and they huddled closely together as they walked so that they could hear each other over the breeze coming off the Gulf.

"How much time do I have to make my decision?" she asked.

Connor smiled as he draped his arm around her body while they walked.

"Take as much time as you need, this isn't a decision you'll make lightly."

"What about safety issues in the meantime?" Gwen asked.

"Don't be afraid. I'll stay with you the nights I can and have one of my cousins watch your house on the nights I can't."

"What about what happened with Lucinda?"

"Don't worry, I've laid into her about that, trust me you won't be able to breath without her knowing about it."

Gwen sighed, somewhat relieved and yet slightly unsettled by that thought. She was quiet for several moments before Connor interrupted her thoughts.

"What are you thinking?" he asked, eyeing her carefully.

"You tell me. You're the mind reader here."

"I told you, I've been avoiding that, lately. I'm trying to respect your *privacy*."

Gwen laughed nervously for a few moments. "You really want to know? You may not like it."

"Yes, Gwenevere I really want to know."

"Well—I've been wondering what it feels like to—be bitten."

Connor glanced at Gwen looking less than enthusiastic. "I don't think that would be such a great idea."

"Why?"

"As I mentioned before, it will create a longing for the change, and I'd rather not bias your decision, before you've thought things through."

Gwen frowned as she looked into his perfectly chiseled face. In the moonlight, he looked positively stunning, like a moving statue from a forgotten era. "What if it's what *I want*?" she asked.

Connor laughed a moment. "That's not very fair to *me*."

"Fair to *you*? You've had the upper hand since the day I met you. I hardly think *that's* fair, at all."

Gwen immediately regretted her comment as she could see the obvious pain in Connor's eyes. She had struck a nerve. "I'm sorry that was mean of me. I shouldn't have said that."

"No, you're right. I've definitely had the advantage the whole time we've been together. What can I do to make things right between us?"

"You say you are going to give me the choice to pursue the relationship, or not, right?"

"Yes," he muttered, looking at her cautiously.

"Well, then I need to know you'll make me your human *familiar* if I want to know what it's like."

"Is it really that important to you?" he inquired.

124

"Yes."

"I'd rather not," Connor pleaded, stopping to face her while he lifted her chin with his fingers so that her eyes were staring directly into his. "Just hours ago you learned the complete truth of my identity and you were horrified. How can you go from that, to wanting me to feed off of you so quickly?"

"I'm not saying for certain that I want to be bitten; I'm saying I want to know that you'll do it if I ask you to," Gwen said.

"I will if that's truly what you want—but I really don't want to. It would be very difficult for me."

"I know, but this is not about you. It's about me and my decision making process."

"It sounds like you've already made up your mind that you want to be my familiar."

"Don't put words into my mouth. I didn't say that. But, I'd be lying if I didn't say I wasn't leaning in that direction. In the very least, my curiosity is piqued."

"Gwenevere, I haven't taken a *familiar* in over eight decades. There is the very real concern that I might not be able to stop myself. There is a large risk involved."

"Have you ever accidentally killed a familiar?"

"Yes, once, my first time."

"And how many *familiars* have you had in your lifetime?"

Connor looked embarrassed when he spoke. "Regrettably, I cannot recall. I took many *familiars* in the early days."

"You can't give me a ball park figure?"

Connor laughed at Gwen's remark. "Maybe a few *hundred* or so."

Gwen glared at him. Her gaze reflected a combination of shock and disgust. "A few hundred or so?"

"I'm not proud of it."

Gwen shook her head back and forth. "Well, the point is that in a few hundred *familiars*, you only managed to kill one of them. So the odds are in my favor."

"You're right, I can't debate the statistics. Nonetheless, I worry about the longing it will create for the change."

"Well, that's my choice isn't it?" she affirmed.

"Okay, your point is well taken."

"Have you ever changed a mortal?"

"No. There is a much bigger risk in that process than in my taking you as a familiar."

"Then if the day comes that I want to be changed, we'll face it together."

Connor simply nodded in response. "It's nearly dawn and I'm tired. I'd like to rest," he said changing the topic.

"Yeah, I guess we're both exhausted," she replied.

"I do feel like a giant burden has been lifted, at least for now. It's a relief that I won't have to hide what I am from you anymore."

"Good. I want to know the real you anyway," she whispered.

Gwen noted the obvious relief in Connor's expression as they walked towards the house. She also felt somewhat relieved by the epiphany of Connor's immortality. At least she knew she wasn't crazy and all the odd behaviors had a logical, albeit supernatural explanation. It wasn't that she was completely comfortable with the information. Indeed, a part of her was frightened by it. However, she also realized that Connor could have killed her the first night they met and he had gone out of his way to protect her multiple times. Gwen thought of the duality that lies within all humans; we each have an inherent dark side that lurks within us. It just so happened that in Connor's case, the dark part of his persona wasn't metaphorical. Gwen had much to think about in the days that lay ahead and her future with Connor was uncertain. She also had to think about how her decision would affect Andy and her family and friends. For the moment, she decided to live in the present taking each moment as it came.

Connor and Gwen slept until late Sunday afternoon. He made Gwen dinner shortly before he loaded her suitcase into his car and drove her home to Panama City. By the time they reached her house it was nearly dusk. Misty and Panda, Gwen's cats, were excited to see her arrive home and eagerly rubbed against her leg when she and Connor walked through the door. However, within a few seconds, both cats began hissing at Connor. Gwen had never seen them do that before, and was surprised by their behavior.

"Do they know, Connor?"

"They know I'm a predator like them and they are being territorial and protective of you."

Connor reached down to pick up Misty in his hands. She hissed and lunged for him trying to bite him, but he calmly stroked her little head and held her so that he could look into her eyes. Her hissing behavior ceased and she started to purr, rubbing her head against his fingers, licking the fingertips. Gwen watched in awe at the transformation of her cat's behavior.

"What did you do to her?" Gwen asked.

"Just used touch to assuage her fears."

"Similar to how you can manipulate human emotions with touch?"

"Yes."

"So, now what?" Gwen asked.

"I'm going to spend the night at my house in Panama City Beach. Don't worry, Aidan's coming to camp outside your door tonight. He drives a Nissan Xterra truck so don't be shocked when you see it in your driveway. He'll likely hang outside on your porch, occasionally walking around to make sure he doesn't detect any unusual activity or the scent of another vampire. If he thinks anything is awry, he'll contact me immediately."

"When will I see you again?"

"In a few days, or sooner, if you need me."

"I'm not going to see you for a few days?" she asked, disappointed.

"It's up to you Love, I'm just a phone call away. Just figured you'd need some time by yourself to think."

"Okay," she replied, nodding her head.

Connor pulled Gwen towards him, wrapping his arms tightly around her waist. She felt herself relax in the comfort of his solid, strong arms wishing she could sleep next to him tonight. He lightly kissed her lips goodbye before he left. Gwen listened as Connor's Porsche revved it's engine exiting her development. Although she knew it was ridiculous, she suddenly felt very alone in her empty house.

Gwen hadn't spoken with Andy in a couple of days and realized she'd better call him. She had managed to call him nearly every day of her trip, but the last two days were a blur and he was probably worried about her. She picked up the phone and dialed Dan's cell number. She soon heard his familiar annoying voice answer.

"Hello Gwen, what's new?" Dan asked, with obvious conceit in his tone.

"Not much, just got back from my trip. I haven't spoken with Andy in a couple of days and wanted to touch base with him."

"Sure, let me get him. He's playing a video game in the living room," Dan added as he put the phone down. Gwen heard him calling Andy's name. A few moments later Andy came to the phone.

"Hi, Mom," Andy shouted loudly into the receiver. Gwen instinctively pulled the phone slightly away from her ear; she was temporarily deafened by his shrillness.

"Hi, Baby, how is your vacation with Daddy going?" Gwen asked.

"It's great Mom. We've gone to the zoo and aquarium twice and Dad says we can go to a Braves ballgame next week," Andy said.

"That's great, Honey. Are you getting enough food and sleep?" she inquired, making sure Dan was keeping his end of the bargain.

"Yes, Mom. Can I go now? I want to play my game?" Andy asked his attention unmistakably focused elsewhere.

"Oh—sure, Sweetie, I just wanted to hear your voice. Mommy misses you," Gwen admitted.

"I miss you too, Mom."

"Well, we'll talk later this week. Have fun with your game and I'll talk with you, soon."

"Okay, bye Mom."

Before Gwen could reply, Andy had already hung up the phone. She'd have to talk with him about that when he got home. That was a behavior pattern typical of her ex-husband that she didn't want her son modeling. Gwen thought about what Connor had said about Andy possibly being frightened of her if she were to become a vampire. The thought of Andy recoiling from her in fear deeply distressed her and Gwen's knee-jerk response was that she'd have to remain human. Yet, she wasn't ready to say, "no," just yet. She had much to consider and it overwhelmed her.

Gwen unpacked her suitcase putting most of her soiled clothing in the hamper near the laundry room. She started her first of several loads, laundering the clothes she had worn in Miami before doing some minor house cleaning and checking her email. She had several email messages from students and colleagues to address, which kept her busy most of the night. Finally, around eleven, she got dressed for bed.

Gwen pulled on a robe and briefly walked outside the front of her house. Right away she saw Aidan's truck in her driveway, with no sign of him inside. She was going to call his name, when she heard a swoosh sound behind her. Startled, Gwen jumped as he felt Aidan lightly touch her shoulder.

"Hi, sorry to scare you, I was just patrolling your backyard," Aidan said.

"Oh, that's okay. I'm just still getting used to the idea of—well, you know," she said, a little nervously as she spoke to Connor's cousin.

"I know, it must be a lot to take in. For our part, none of us can remember being human, it was so long ago."

"Does that bother you?" she asked.

"It did for awhile, but with time you get used to it. Are you thinking of becoming one of us?"

"I don't know. I have a lot to consider."

"I understand. None of us were given the choice."

"What would you do if you were me?" she asked.

Aidan smiled at Gwen. "I honestly don't know. I guess if I were you, I'd determine what would be best for my family. Sorry, I can't offer more than that." With that Aidan waved goodbye to Gwen as he walked towards the back of her house where he'd stay the night keeping watch. Gwen watched Aidan disappear behind the palm trees that led to the back of her yard before going into the house for the night.

Gwen woke shortly before dawn. The first rays of sunlight were threatening to break through the clouds overhead. She groaned when she looked at the alarm clock and managed to capture another hour of sleep before waking for the day. When she got out of bed that morning to make her morning coffee, the reality of the weekend's revelations hit her. Gwen had met the man of her dreams, and he was a vampire. She would have to decide whether to continue living her life as a mortal, which meant losing Connor, or join him by becoming immortal herself. She could stay human for a short period of time, but inevitably she'd have to make a choice. The enormity of the decision and its ramifications for her life and those of her loved ones loomed in her mind.

Gwen ambled around the house looking for Aidan, but found no evidence of him anywhere and his truck was missing from her driveway. She assumed the cousins would be watching her house at night when she was most vulnerable and gone by the mornings when she went to work. Gwen wondered which cousin would be sitting watch on her porch this evening. She felt a mixture of gratitude and annoyance that Connor's family would become a permanent fixture in her home until she had made her decision. She appreciated the safety they were providing, but the utter lack of privacy and reminder of her human frailty bothered her. Gwen's independent streak was one of her sources of strength and her new vulnerability threatened the self-reliance she was so accustomed to. She'd have to get over it though. Soon, Andy would be coming home and she couldn't let her pride get in the way of safety. Gwen shuddered a bit when she thought of Andy's homecoming. How would she explain the strange aloof people hanging outside the porch at night? For that matter, would Andy like Connor? Gwen's head began to hurt as she processed this information. She walked over to the refrigerator in the kitchen and leafed through the calendar. Gwen realized Andy would be coming home in three weeks. That didn't give her much time to think things through. Even though Connor wanted Gwen to take her time making her decision, she got the distinct feeling that time wasn't on her side. The Elder clan had sent two of their best vampire hunters to kill Connor's family; she doubted they would sit idly by while *The Immortal* remained fully operational. Fearful thoughts began coursing through her mind and Gwen chose to actively suppress them. She knew from past experience that once her anxieties took over, her ability to function would shut down. She couldn't risk that happening now; too much was at stake.

Later that morning, Gwen drove to the university to work. She hoped she'd have lots of email to answer to keep her mind preoccupied and distracted from the scary thoughts she'd been experiencing earlier. Gwen wasn't disappointed as her inbox was loaded with messages. She spent several hours catching up on email from students and colleagues. Gwen also received the good news that one of her papers had been accepted by a prestigious journal. It occurred to Gwen that among other reasons, scientists published their work to gain a small sense of immortality. Of course, the predominant reason to publish one's work centered on making contributions to the scientific literature and field. But, the idea that someone could read a paper you wrote over a hundred years ago meant that your ideas would survive long after your physical demise. She surmised that artists, musicians, and writers, like scientists, in their quest to create and contribute, were aiming for a semblance of immortality.

When whole civilizations of people disappeared like the Incas in Peru, all that had been left of these people was their architecture, art, and scientific work. That's why relics and art were so important to a society; they provided evidence that people had existed and made a difference in the world. However, what if immortality was granted and you didn't have to worry about physical death? How much research could Gwen conduct if her life were to be extended indefinitely? She would witness technological changes that would dramatically alter her perception of the world and humanity. Connor had lived in a time before the invention of indoor lighting, cars and planes, amazing medical advances that significantly prolonged life, even indoor plumbing. She wondered what that must have been like for him to observe each of these events knowing how primitive life had been during the time of his mortal life. Would it be like that for Gwen if she chose to become immortal? The thought of being around to witness change appealed to her in a way she had never considered. Of course, immortality also brought with it salvation from physical death, one of Gwen's biggest fears. Yet, if she chose to become a vampire there was the strong possibility she'd outlive her parents and Andy, a thought that filled her with dread and sadness.

The phone in Gwen's office rang interrupting Gwen's train of thought. Reflexively, she grabbed the phone and answered it.

"Hello, Dr. Ryan speaking."

"Hello, Miss—how was your vacation?" Gwen recognized the voice on the line immediately.

"Pam, how *are* you?"

"Good—how about you?"

"I'm great! Just catching up on email and I found out I got a paper accepted. I'm so excited," Gwen said, hoping she could mask any concern in her voice.

"That's great. How'd your trip go with Mr. Blake?" Pam asked.

Gwen paused for a moment. What should she say? It's not like she could tell the complete truth. She sighed before she spoke knowing she'd have to alter her story.

"I had a wonderful time. We spent most of our vacation in Miami sightseeing."

"*Wow*—that sounds fantastic. I want details. When can we meet? I want to hear everything. Plus, I've got your house key for you."

"I don't know. Maybe I could get Cindy and Bridget to join us somewhere for dinner this evening. Then we could all catch up and I can give you the juicy details. What do you think?" Gwen asked, buying herself some time to figure out what she'd say.

"Yeah—that sounds great. I have tonight free. Have you spoken to Cindy or Bridget yet to clear it with them?"

"No—but, I can call them and then get back to you. Will you be free in a few moments to answer your phone?" Gwen inquired.

"Yeah, but call my cell since I'm out running errands, right now."

"Okay, call you back in five minutes."

"Okay, talk with you then." Pam hung up on the other line.

Gwen called Bridget and Cindy. To her amazement, both were available to join her and Pam for dinner that evening. Gwen called Pam back to confirm the evening's plans and then hung up to finish answering emails. A couple of hours later, she left the university to run errands of her own before heading home to change. When she pulled onto her street, she saw Connor's black Porsche in her driveway. Gwen hadn't expected to see Connor this soon and was concerned something had happened at the club. When she pulled into her driveway she didn't see any sign of him in his car. She figured he was waiting for her on the back porch, but when she opened her front door, she was surprised to see him sitting on her couch watching network news.

"Hi, wasn't expecting to see you for a few days. Everything okay?" she asked with trepidation bracing herself for bad news.

Connor flashed Gwen one of his million-dollar smiles. "Yes, Love, everything is fine. I just couldn't stay away from you for longer than a day." He stood up and pulled her close to him lightly kissing her lips; the frigid coolness of his skin sending chills down her spine.

"Guess absence *does* make the heart grow fonder, after all," she replied, smiling back at him. "Oh, and how did you get in my house without a house key?"

"Well, there is one little talent left that I haven't told you about. If I concentrate hard enough, I can move small objects such as deadbolts and locks with my thoughts."

Gwen sighed as another question she had had about the night he drove her home was finally answered. "I should have known you'd have telekinesis too. Is there anything else you can do that I don't know about?"

"That's it. No more hidden abilities— I promise," he replied as he took Gwen's hand in his and sat down with her on her couch. "Regrettably, I can't stay long. I've got to oversee things at the club tonight. I just wanted to spend a little time with you before rushing off. How was your day?" he asked, his radiant blue eyes studying the contours of her face.

"Well, it was a nice day. I found out I got a paper accepted to a journal and I'm having dinner with my girlfriends tonight."

Connor's eyes lit up at her news. "Congratulations on the paper acceptance. Well done! Also glad that you're spending time with your friends this evening. You definitely need to go out and celebrate. I only wish I could be there to join you."

"I do too. I want them to meet you."

"I wonder how your friends will feel about me," he added, failing to suppress nervous laughter.

"Well, obviously I can't give them all the details of our vacation."
"Yes, somehow I don't think they'd be too keen on the idea of their good friend being romantically involved with an immortal."

They both laughed for a few moments at the thought. Connor stroked Gwen's hand in his for a few moments before he spoke. "Have you given any thought to what we talked about the other night?"

"Like I can think about anything else, Connor?"

"I feel awful about putting you in this position," he commented, with guilt in his eyes.

"Don't. The situation is what it is."

"There are moments when I look back with regret on my decision to follow you to the beach the night you came looking for me at the club. If I had just let you go and never contacted you, you would have forgotten about me by now and be living your life as usual. Instead, I put my own selfish motives first and now I've given you an ultimatum. It's so unfair Gwenevere, and I'm truly sorry."

"Are you saying you are having second thoughts about me?" she asked.

"No, not at all. I just feel if I were a better man I would have left well enough alone. As it turns out, I'm somewhat human after all," he said, shrugging his shoulders.

Gwen sighed feeling a sense of relief. "Connor, what if we had met while you were human and something terrible happened to you. Say for example, you were diagnosed with a degenerative disease that left you debilitated, weak, or worse. What kind of woman would I be if I just abandoned you like that?" Gwen asked, her eyes looking intently into his perfectly sculpted face.

"Well, it's not quite like that with us, now is it? In the scenario you described, I wouldn't have prior knowledge of my condition. But, in our case, I knew from the moment I met you that I was a vampire and kept it from you as long as I could. I should have revealed myself to you earlier before you became so heavily involved with me. The truth is—for the first time in centuries, I felt a sense of normalcy in my life and I didn't want to lose you. It wasn't right to put you in this situation and I loath my selfishness and weakness."

"Well, counterfactual thinking won't change anything. We can't go back in time and change what has happened and I wouldn't want to. I've been hurt more times than I can count by men who claimed they loved me. I don't regret meeting you or the fact that I'll have to make a choice. I know that must sound really strange to you, and I'm not really sure I understand it myself, but it's how I feel."

Gwen watched as a single red tear ran down one of Connor's pale perfect cheeks. She had never seen him cry before and was amazed to see his tears consisted of blood. Connor turned to look away, but Gwen pulled his face towards hers, gently using her finger to dry the blood tear, which partially smudged red across his cheek. "I guess I never told you that we cry blood," he mentioned, looking uncomfortable and embarrassed.

"No, you didn't," she whispered.

Connor pulled Gwen close to him and stroked her back. He spoke softly into her ear. "I never thought I'd meet someone like you. I had given up that anyone would ever see anything good in a wretched soul like me."

Gwen pulled away for a moment to look into his eyes. "Please don't say things like that."

"I'm sorry, but it's how I've felt for a long time."

"Well, I certainly don't feel that way about you."

"How'd I get so lucky to find you, Gwenevere?"

"I was actually thinking the same thing about you."

"You know this is crazy, right? This whole situation is completely insane," Connor, said, his expression sincere and calm.

"I know. But, here we are."

"Yeah—here we are," he said, looking into her gray doe-shaped eyes.

Connor held Gwen close to him for several minutes lightly humming a beautiful tune in her hair. She felt the peacefulness she always did when he touched her and could have stayed on the couch close to him like that for an eternity. But, soon it was time for him to leave and she had to change for her dinner with her friends.

"Well, I'll see you in a day or two."

"Okay," she replied.

"You know it will likely be tomorrow right?"

Gwen giggled, "I figured as much—you're a glutton for punishment."

Connor laughed as he hugged her one last time. "Have a good night."

He lightly kissed Gwen's lips before opening her front door. Gwen interrupted him just before he exited the house. "Connor, who's keeping watch tonight?"

"Lucinda will be here when you get home. And don't worry; she'll be keeping a very close eye on things. She knows I'll have her head if she doesn't," Connor said, only partially kidding right before he shut her door.

Gwen shuddered a moment, before walking into her bedroom to

change. This time it wasn't her safety she worried about. She hoped for Lucinda's sake that everything did go well, because if it didn't; she was pretty sure that Connor would kill Lucinda in an instant, blood relative or not.

Chapter 12

Pam, Bridget, and Cindy were all waiting for Gwen when she walked into K's Shrimp and Steakhouse on Panama City Beach. The three women were sharing a pitcher of margaritas and looked like they were having quite the party when Gwen joined them at their table in a secluded back section of the restaurant. Bridget poured a margarita in Gwen's empty glass as she sat down in her chair.

"Hi ladies, nice to see you. Looks like you got the party started early," Gwen said, smiling at her friends.

"Hey, it's so nice to be home. I can't get shrimp like this in the mountains of North Carolina, you know what I'm saying," Bridget remarked, her russet colored hair gently swaying back and forth near the nape of her neck as she spoke. Gwen noticed how beautiful she looked; the fresh mountain air agreed with her friend.

"Well, I don't need any excuse to eat shrimp, I'm just happy to get a break from the kids. I feel bad for my husband, but I really needed a night out with the girls," Cindy said, taking a big sip of her margarita.

"Tell me about it, my teenage daughter is driving me nuts lately. I love her to death, but sometimes I wonder whether that child is an alien, because she sure has some bizarre ideas about life. She didn't get those cockamamie ideas from me that's for darn sure," Pam commented in her eating a cracker with cheese on it.

Gwen laughed a bit under her breath about Pam's alien comment. If she only knew about Connor—

" fill us in on Connor Blake. Don't spare any of the details. We want all the dirt," Cindy asked, with an impish grin on her face.

Gwen felt her face flush. She didn't want to panic, but beneath the table her legs began to shake. She couldn't tell them the full truth; she'd have to be careful with some of the details. "Well, what would you like to know?"

"Well, what did you do with this mystery man for two weeks?" Pam asked, her attention squarely on Gwen.

"Okay, okay—I'll spill. We spent most of our trip in Miami."

"My, my I'm starting to like Mr. Blake already. Does he have an available brother?" Bridget joked.

"Bridget! You're married," Gwen blurted out.

"Yeah, but it's good to keep your options open if things don't pan out—I'm kidding you know that," Bridget said, smiling from ear to ear.

"I know, I'm just busting your chops," Gwen said, her face flushing from the alcohol.

"So what'd ya'll do in Miami?" Cindy asked, her eyes sparkling with delight.

"Everything, but what you're thinking," Gwen said, with obvious disappointment in her voice.

"You're—kidding—us—right?" Bridget asked, a look of shock on her face. "He didn't put any moves on you at all?"

"Well, he kissed me, but that was it," Gwen said.

"Wow, a real gentleman. I like this guy, " Pam stated.

"Pam, we love you, but you are so old-fashioned," Cindy joked.

"I know, I know. I should have been born a hundred years ago—you know I love the simpler things in life," Pam said.

"Personally, I wouldn't buy a car I didn't take out for a test drive, so if things get more serious I'd pounce on him," Bridget said, raising her glass in a gesture of triumph.

Laughter broke out around the table.

"Yeah, I have to say I'm in agreement with Bridget, I'd definitely want to take that sucker out for a long test ride. And—for that matter, maybe you'll need multiple test drives on different terrains—to make sure things are—you know—working properly." Cindy winked at Gwen.

"You two are incorrigible!" Pam said.

Bridget and Cindy replied simultaneously almost like a chorus, "We know."

Gwen was red-faced with embarrassment. She felt like climbing underneath the table. "Okay, then—moving right along. In Miami, we went to plays, museums, sampled lots of different restaurants, and enjoyed watching the drunken locals meander from bar to bar," Gwen said. She edited out the part where Connor didn't eat anything.

"Wow! He does sound great. So how do you feel about him?" Cindy asked, now being serious.

Gwen thought about Cindy's comment. She wondered if she should be open with her thoughts. She figured there was no harm done in answering this question completely honestly. "You know Cindy, I'm falling in love with him."

All three of Gwen's friends were suddenly silent as their eyes scanned each other's faces. It was Bridget who broke the awkward silence. "Really—so soon Gwen? Does he know how you feel?"

Pam looked concerned and Gwen knew what she was thinking. "Well, I haven't come right out and told him if that's what you mean. He knows I'm extremely fond of him, but the feeling is mutual."

"That's a relief. I thought you were going to tell us you spilled your guts to him. I'm glad my warning kept you from divulging your real feelings. Keep him guessing, Sweetie," Pam said.

Gwen wanted to take Pam by the hand and tell her everything, but she couldn't. How could she really tell any of them? This was the part of tonight's conversation she had dreaded. She felt guilty, holding back pertinent information regarding Connor, but it couldn't be helped.

Gwen looked at Pam and simply nodded that she had heeded Pam's warning, to which everyone smiled at her.

"Where is he tonight?" Bridget asked.

"He's helping his cousins with the club."

"Oh, that's right. He's their financial wizard isn't he?" Cindy asked.

"Yeah, you could say that. The man is a genius when it comes to money; he runs a very lucrative fund company, but he also gives a lot of it away to charities," Gwen said.

"You think he would mind sending some money our way?" Cindy asked, slightly joking. Cindy was the director of a school for developmentally disabled children. She was passionate about helping children with autism and related disabilities, but the behavior therapy was expensive and the center was always in need of funds. State funding to assist the school had dwindled over the past few years, which was a constant source of stress for Cindy.

"I'll ask him."

"Oh, he doesn't have to Gwen, I was just kidding."

"No, it's okay. It never hurts to ask right?" Gwen smiled at Cindy.

"So when do we all get to meet Connor?" Pam asked.

"Oh I'm sure it will be soon," Gwen said.

"Gwen is everything all right, you don't quite seem like yourself today," Cindy asked, concern in her voice.

"Yeah—I'm fine, why?"

"Well, to be candid, you don't seem fine," Bridget said, her brows raised like a question mark.

Gwen scanned the eyes of all her friends at the table. She could tell they were worried about her. "I'm fine. I just haven't eaten in hours and our server seems to be ignoring our table. I just need some food and I'll be great."

"Okay, just making sure. You know we all love you. We're just looking out for you" Bridget said.

"I know—but really you don't have to worry about me. I'm happy," Gwen said. And—the truth was she really was happy. She just wished she knew what she'd decide, but for now she tabled her anxieties to spend the night with her friends. If she did choose to be immortal, this might be one of the last times she would spend out with them drinking alcohol and eating food. That thought briefly saddened her, but she suppressed it. The four women spent the next three hours eating dinner, dessert, and having a couple of pitchers of margaritas. Everything tasted great and Gwen wanted to enjoy herself as much as possible. Gwen told them a lot of details about Connor, but nothing that would compromise his secret or identity. After eleven, when she knew she was sober enough to drive, she hugged all her friends' goodbye and drove home.

A brand new red Corvette was parked in Gwen's driveway when she got home. Evidently, Lucinda, like Connor, enjoyed the perks of a fast car. Gwen entered the house and turned on the lights of the back porch looking for Lucinda, but noticed it was empty.

"Looking for me?"

Gwen jumped when she heard the beautiful feminine voice come from behind her.

"You scared me. I didn't see you standing there," Gwen cried slightly out of breath and three shades paler. Lucinda really unnerved her.

"Sorry, I was sitting in the end of the hallway. I figured that would be the best place to launch an attack should a vampire break into your house," Lucinda replied in a business-like tone.

"Oh—okay. Can I get you something from the kitchen to make you comfortable?" Gwen asked reflexively before remembering Lucinda wasn't human. "Oh, sorry, that was stupid of me. I was just out with friends and I guess the alcohol hasn't completely worn off yet."

Lucinda smiled briefly at Gwen. "I make you anxious don't I?"

Gwen failed to suppress nervous laughter before speaking. "Yeah, you do."

"Guess it's my fault. I came on strong the first time I met you. I thought you wanted to be a *familiar* when I saw you approaching our table with the rosebud stamp. I'm not as good at reading thoughts like the boys."

"The boys?" Gwen asked, looking puzzled.

"You know—Derrick, Aidan, and Connor."

"Oh—yeah—the boys."

"Look Gwen, I'm really sorry about last week. Connor asked me to keep an eye out for you and I underestimated the chances of your being attacked. I should have known better and I'm really sorry about that. If it's any consolation, I feel terrible about the whole thing and from now on, I'll guard you like a hawk."

Gwen nodded her head to acknowledge she understood.

"Gwen, Connor is special to us. He suffered a great deal when Elizabeth died and went off the deep end for years. Now, for the first time in well over two hundred years he actually seems *happy*. We know how precious you are to him and we want you to feel welcome in our family," Lucinda whispered.

Gwen was a bit taken aback. "Thank you, Lucinda. That means a great deal to me."

"Well, it's the least I can do, considering I nearly got you killed last week."

"Would that vampire really have killed me?"

"He wanted you, Gwen—and not as a *familiar*. When I got close enough to him, his thoughts became clear to me. He was going to drain you dry."

"So I really am in danger remaining mortal around Connor—"

"As long as we're watching you, you should be okay. But, I wouldn't wait too long to make your decision."

"What would you do if you were me?"

Lucinda frowned as she looked at Gwen. "I don't know what I'd do if I were given the choice. But, I do know that if I found someone who loved me the way Connor loves you, I'd consider it seriously. You will never find someone more devoted to you or your child than Connor. I don't know if he ever told you, but Elizabeth was pregnant when he and the rest of our family were attacked and subsequently changed. Not long afterwards, Elizabeth lost the baby. Connor was beside himself. After the change, he couldn't father any more children and the miscarriage devastated him. When Elizabeth was killed a year later, his whole world collapsed. Now, with you and your son, he has a second chance for happiness."

"He never told me about that."

"Well, he hasn't spoken of the situation in years. Anyway, I don't want to sway your decision one way or another. But, you've managed to make Connor happy and none of us have seen this side of him in years. I would gladly welcome you into our family if you should choose to become one of us. We all would. However, we want it to be your decision on your terms."

"I appreciate that Lucinda. I wish Connor had told me about Elizabeth and the miscarriage. I would be very sympathetic."

"He knows that, Gwen. It's just that some things are just too painful to discuss."

"Lucinda, after Elizabeth died, what happened to Connor?" Gwen asked.

Lucinda's perfect features morphed into an uncomfortable expression. "Gwen, you really don't want to discuss that with me."

"Why?"

"Connor's changed and is a very good man. But, for a period of time, he let his rage and anger control him. You really don't want to know what he was like back then."

"Was he really that bad?" Gwen pressed.

"You sure you want to know?" Lucinda asked.

"Yes."

"When he found Elizabeth's dead and blood-drained body, he became despondent. He starved himself to death and withdrew from the world. None of us could say anything to reach him. He was suicidal for a time, but then one day he snapped and started seeking out any criminal he could find. Soon innocents would get in his way and they, too, would succumb to his blood lust. You see, Gwen, of the four of us, Connor is the most expert in killing. Back then; he was the most bloodthirsty immortal I had ever seen. No one got in his way, even Derrick. He was like that for years, before he radically changed his ways. Sometimes, I think Derrick forgets what Connor is capable of, but when *the boys* had to kill the two vampire hunters recently, Derrick had a reminder. It was Connor who literally ripped their heads off with his own bare hands. You see Marcus, the vampire they killed, was like a little brother to Connor. So when he says he would rather burn to death than hurt you—*he really means it*. He's been the way you've known him for well over two hundred years. He is constantly haunted by the faces of the innocents he killed and has atoned for it since."

Gwen wasn't sure what to say. Hearing Lucinda's words corroborated Connor's story, but it gave her more insight into why he thought of himself as wretched.

"Lucinda, may I ask why you and your cousins still hunt humans while

Connor prefers to hunt animals now? I—just want to understand—because it's hard for me to think of you as a killer, right now," Gwen asked. She hoped she wasn't offending Lucinda.

"I think that's a fair question, given what you know of Connor and his preferred prey these days. The truth is, as a vampire the thirst for human blood dominates your thoughts everyday of your existence. No other blood quenches our thirst like human blood and we need it for survival. In fact, Connor cannot exist solely on animal blood. He must supplement his food supply with human blood or he'll become ill. This is why he has his little arrangement with someone in the local blood bank. As for me I can't stomach animal blood. It has a stench that is vile and incredibly repulsive. So I try to avoid harming humans while simultaneously satisfying my hunger by drinking the blood of multiple *familiars*. That way no one person gets hurt or killed. But, occasionally the hunger can get out of control and on a few rare occasions I've unintentionally killed innocents. I will also admit that like Connor, I have had my moments where I've sought out a criminal or thug that won't be missed if he or she were to permanently disappear."

Gwen didn't know what to say. She realized that she'd be plagued with the same thoughts and needs if she were to undergo the change. The thought of killing an innocent person horrified her. However, Gwen hated to admit it to herself—but the thought of taking out a murderer or child molester didn't bother her nearly as much. She could almost rationalize choosing such human monsters as victims.

"Thank you for explaining this to me. I'm worried about you and your family with the club being fully operational. Are you worried about the Elder clan sending more vampire hunters for you?" Gwen asked.

"Yes, I am. I think we've really ticked them off, especially, the leader of the Elder Clan, Josef. But, Derrick refuses to shut it down and we're hoping that they just forget about us, for now, and deal with other renegade vampires instead. I don't know. We'll have to see what happens."

"What will you do if more hunters come?"

"We'll kill them like we did the first ones. That is, unless they kill us first."

"What if they just keep coming for you?" Gwen asked, worried.

"If it becomes clear that Josef has it in for us, then we'll torch the club and leave the area."

"What about Connor?"

"He won't leave you, Gwen. *Ever.*"

"What if I decide to remain mortal? Won't he leave once my memory has been erased?"

"No, he will never leave you. He'll stay here and keep watch over you and Andy from afar to protect your safety. You would be blissfully unaware of his presence, but he would always be aware of yours and your son's until the day you died. He loves you that much."

Gwen stood silent for a moment stunned by Lucinda's words. "Lucinda, how do you know this?"

"Connor and I are very close and I know him better than he knows himself. He told me of his plans to protect you regardless of your decision. He will *never* leave you. But, please don't ever tell him I told you this. He doesn't want you to know his plans. He's afraid it will sway your decision. His choosing to stay in town is his decision and has nothing to do with yours."

"But, he could die staying here for me."

"He knows that, but you're the only thing that matters to him anymore and it's a risk he's willing to take. "

Gwen was overwhelmed by the magnitude of Connor's devotion to her and her son, a child he would die to protect who wasn't his own, and whom he hadn't even met. Lucinda must have read Gwen's mind as she mumbled something about giving Gwen her privacy and walked out onto the back porch to keep watch. Gwen barely heard her as she walked by. She was too busy reeling from the enormity of Connor's decision. Unable to control her emotions she went into her bedroom and wept. They weren't tears of pain or sadness, but of joy. Connor really loved her and the enormity of his willingness to sacrifice for her and her child moved her beyond words.

Chapter 13

The following morning rainstorms drenched the Panhandle, flooding most of the streets near Gwen's house. Unable to leave her house, Gwen worked in her home office on syllabi for the fall semester, as well as last minute edits to a paper she was revising for resubmission. Like Aidan, Lucinda was gone when Gwen woke up in the morning. Her conversation with Lucinda occupied her thoughts for a good chunk of the day. Gwen's opinion of Lucinda had dramatically changed for the better and she felt more comfortable knowing Lucinda would be keeping watch in the days that lay ahead. Of course, Gwen also knew that Lucinda had a motive for mentioning Connor's intention to remain near her and Andy. Nevertheless, Gwen didn't hold it against her. After all, Lucinda and Connor were very close and Lucinda liked seeing him happy. Connor's utter devotion to Gwen and her son weighed heavily on her mind and would definitely factor in her decision. How could it not? Nevertheless, Gwen wanted to make sure that whatever decision she made, it was for the right reasons.

Gwen was deep in thought when she suddenly heard footsteps in her hallway coming towards her office. She wasn't expecting anyone and immediately jumped out of her office chair and hid behind the door. She scanned the room for anything that could be used as a weapon and noticed one of Andy's baseball bats leaning in the corner. Gwen grabbed the baseball bat and held it upright against her body bracing herself for a fight. Although she tried to remain calm, her respiration increased and she could feel her heart pounding in her chest. She heard Misty hissing and screeching in the living room, which only heightened her fear. She knew the cats wouldn't be hissing if Connor were present.

"Gwen, don't be alarmed. It's me, Aidan. You can put down the bat."

Gwen slammed the office door open to face Aidan, the baseball bat still tightly clenched in her hands. "Holy crap, Aidan, you scared the living hell out of me!"

Aidan produced a loud sigh as his shoulders slumped. His eyes, which had been squarely focused on Gwen, shifted to the wood flooring near her feet. "Sorry, guess I should have knocked."

"Yeah, that would have helped. I thought I was going to have a heart attack."

"I promise I'll knock next time. I just wanted to check on you," he said, his lips pursed.

"Is there something wrong?" Gwen asked alarmed.

"No—we're just being extra cautious."

"You'd tell me if there was something wrong wouldn't you?" she pressed.

"Of course, I'm not one to keep someone I care about in the dark."

Gwen didn't know how to respond instead she ignored Aidan's dig against Connor.

"I brought something for you. I hope you don't mind. I just thought they might brighten your spirits on such a bleak day," Aidan replied as he pulled a small bouquet of wildflowers from behind his back.

Gwen smiled as she dropped the baseball bat to the floor and reached for the flowers. "Oh—thank you, Aidan. They're lovely. That was so sweet of you."

Aidan smiled wide, clearly pleased with Gwen's reaction. "You're welcome. So is all forgiven?"

Gwen giggled a moment. "Yes, all is forgiven. Let's put these in a nice vase with water. I don't want them to wilt," she said, taking the flowers from Aidan's cold hand and walking down the hallway towards the kitchen.

"So, how was your day?" she asked.

"Okay. Nothing really exciting—just cleaning things up at the club and that sort of thing."

"You?" Aidan asked, sitting down on Gwen's loveseat.

"Just catching up on work—getting ready for the fall semester, which will start in less than two months. You know—the usual. Have you heard from Connor?"

"We spoke this morning. He'll be over tonight to stay with you, but he asked me to swing by and make sure everything is okay here."

Gwen opened the cabinet above her sink and removed a large square shaped vase, which she promptly filled with fresh water. She grabbed a pair of scissors and cut away the clear cellophane wrapping that surrounded the flowers before placing them into the vase. "Did Connor ask you to bring me the flowers?" Gwen asked.

"No, that was all my idea." Aidan grinned at Gwen.

Gwen really liked Aidan. He seemed like a pretty easy-going and pleasant person. It was hard for her to accept the idea that he was a vampire, but his physical features and stealth reminded her wasn't human.

"Thank you, Aidan. So, does some other lucky lady receive flowers from you?" Gwen asked.

Aidan seemed to flush a moment, which for a vampire meant being slightly less pallid for a few seconds. "No—not really. I have a few *familiars* who would like to be my partner in life, but I don't feel the same way they do."

"That's a shame," she whispered.

"Well, it's hard to find a woman of your caliber who would be willing to die to be with me for eternity," Aidan replied, with a slight chuckle.

"I can imagine," Gwen, said, a bit uncomfortable with the gritty reality of Aidan's remark.

"You have no idea. I mean, I've met some great women in my time. In fact, many that I knew I could easily live with, but not a single one I knew I couldn't live without. I hope that makes sense."

"It makes perfect sense. Settling is worse than being alone, because you have this expectation that you should feel happy and connected to the person you're with, but something's missing. Meanwhile you're biding your time either hoping things will change or the right one will come along. Honestly, I'd rather be alone the rest of my life than settle. In fact, I had all but given up when I met Connor. I'm still waiting for the moment when I wake up and find out this is all an elaborate dream."

Aidan stared intently into Gwen's eyes. "Sounds like you've had your fair share of heartache."

"Yes, unfortunately I have."

"So do you think you could give up your human life to be with Connor?"

"I don't know," she said, clearly uncomfortable. Aidan's remark had caught her off guard and she felt cornered.

"Sorry, I have difficulty with subtlety."

"*Really*, I hadn't noticed."

"Okay, I guess I deserve that—I'm just curious to know what you're thinking."

"Guess your not reading my thoughts, huh?" she asked.

Aidan laughed a moment. "No, Connor's asked us to refrain as much as possible from intruding into your mind. I'm trying to be polite, but I'm obviously missing the mark."

Gwen smiled to herself in response to Connor's request. "Well, Aidan, to more fully answer your question, I find myself thinking about it constantly. Part of me really wants to become immortal while the other part wonders what I'll be giving up. I don't want to lose Connor, but I have Andy to think about as well. There are so many things to consider. I really don't know what I'll decide, yet and it frustrates me to no end."

"Well, you're being honest with me and yourself. I respect that. You know I did have someone special once and I gave her the choice, but she turned me down."

"Really?" Gwen asked, her brows rose.

"Yes, her name was Lilly. I met her the year before I was changed. She was lovely, with long dark brown hair and eyes a mixture of dark green and brown. I guess you'd call them hazel. In any event, I met her at church and spent every free moment I could with her, which wasn't easy because Puritans weren't big on contact between the sexes. We spent most of our time together studying Scripture, but it wouldn't have mattered what we did as long as I could be near her. I knew fairly soon after we met that I wanted to marry her. I planned to propose to her the day after meeting with my cousins for a brief family reunion at an inn near my home, but fate had other plans. That evening, along with the others, I was attacked and changed—" Aidan said, before briefly becoming silent. He looked deep in thought, like he was reliving the event.

"What happened the next day?" Gwen asked, as she sat down on the edge of her couch.

"I couldn't see her for a long time after that night. I was still struggling with controlling my thirst. We all were. But, after a couple of months, I learned how to keep myself in check. I decided that I had to see her, if for no other reason than to say goodbye. But, I foolishly hoped that by some miracle she'd be willing to overlook what I had become and spend her life with me. I would have taken any condition she had to offer to be with her, even if she were to stay mortal."

"So what'd she say?"

"When she saw me, she knew something was wrong. She noticed my dark green eyes were now brilliant bright blue and that my ruddy complexion had turned pale white and frigid to the touch. It was like Lilly could see right through me. I explained to her what had happened and that we could still be together, whether she stayed mortal or not. But, she was terrified of me and pleaded with me to leave." Aidan choked up a minute before continuing. "She said that I was an abomination on this earth and that if I ever loved her, I'd never see her again. The pain was unbearable and I immediately fled from her home. Anyway, my heart, which no longer worked, turned to stone. Since that day, I *have* come to love other women, but no one like Lilly and in my nightmares, I can still see the look of fear in her eyes when she saw me that morning."

Gwen felt an overwhelming sense of compassion for Aidan. She wished she could hug him and tell him how sorry she was for his loss, but she wasn't sure how he'd react. She also worried that Andy might have the same reaction if she were to change. "Aidan, I'm so sorry for your—"

Aidan interrupted Gwen mid-sentence. "It's okay, Gwen. I've had a long time to process it. But, now maybe you'll see why I'm so curious about what you're thinking and planning to do. I mean I was amazed you didn't tell Connor it was over immediately. Obviously, you and Lilly are different people living in a different time. Still, it fascinates me that you are considering it. So, I hope my line of questioning makes more sense to you now. It's not out of guile, but of sheer astonishment," he whispered.

"I think I understand more about you, now. But Aidan, Lilly was terribly wrong to treat you the way she did. Even if she couldn't bring herself to continue the relationship, she couldn't blame you for what you'd become. For heaven's sake, it wasn't your fault."

"I know, but the memory is brutal and has haunted me for years. I guess I never quite got over what happened. I suppose on some level, I feel a moral responsibility to avoid changing a mortal. It's like—I would be creating another monster for my own selfish reasons."

"Is that what you think Connor is doing with me?"

"Sort of—but then again—I can't blame him anymore than he could have blamed me for trying with Lilly. I guess I'm a bit jealous that your reaction wasn't one of disgust."

"Aidan, I do have mixed emotions. I don't want you to get the wrong impression that I was overjoyed at the news. Trust me—I wasn't. It's just that Connor is such an amazing person that I feel compelled to at least consider becoming like him. I hope you can understand my predicament." Although Gwen wanted to speak with Aidan about her concerns about Andy and how he'd take it if she decided to become immortal, she didn't feel this was the time to broach the subject with him. She'd talk about it with him in the future when the time felt right.

Aidan nodded. "I wish Lilly had given me the chance that you are giving Connor. You're a remarkable woman, Gwen. Regardless of your decision, Connor's lucky to have met you."

"Thanks, Aidan."

Aidan and Gwen were both silent for several moments. Gwen wasn't really sure what to say. She hadn't planned on having such a deep conversation with Aidan, or Lucinda, for that matter. She realized that Connor's family members were as conflicted as he was regarding the status of her mortality. Although, she respected their opinions, she couldn't let their views influence her decision.

Aidan suddenly spoke, breaking the silence of the room. "Gwen, I've got to get back to the club. Thank you for talking with me. It's been a real pleasure."

"Sure, anytime—thanks again for the flowers."

Aidan's face lit up when he smiled. "You are very welcome. See you later this week."

"Okay—see you later."

Aidan swiftly walked to the door carefully avoiding Misty who swiped at him with her paw. For hours after Aidan's visit, Gwen thought about what had happened with him and Lilly. She imagined the look on his face when Lilly recoiled from him in horror. Gwen could tell by Aidan's expression that he still loved Lilly even after all these years. Yet, Lilly's actions had left a permanent scar on his soul, leaving him bitter and resentful. Gwen promised herself that if she chose to stay mortal and leave Connor behind, she would be kind in her words and actions. She wouldn't damn Connor to a life of misery, like Lilly had done to Aidan. It would be the least she could do.

Connor arrived at Gwen's shortly after nightfall. He came to her door carrying a DVD in one hand and a bag of buttered popcorn in the other. Gwen greeted him with a soft kiss before briefly surveying the box in Connor's hand.

"I thought we could watch a movie tonight like a normal couple," he said, with a wink.

"Okay—sounds great. So what are we watching?" Gwen asked.

Connor didn't answer, he simply handed Gwen the DVD, before putting the popcorn down on the coffee table.

"Dracula?" she asked, with one eyebrow cocked.

"Yeah, it's the version with Frank Langella. It's my favorite," Connor said, smiling.

"*You* like vampire movies?"

"Love them. Most of us do. Unfortunately, the movies usually don't get the details right, but they are entertaining."

"Vampires watch movies about vampires? Who knew?" Gwen shrugged her shoulders. "So why is the Frank Langella version of Dracula your favorite? It happens to be mine, too, by the way."

"Langella is suave, sophisticated, and makes vampires look good. What about you?" he asked, eyeing Gwen.

Gwen smiled and turned her head briefly away from Connor in a weak attempt to conceal that she was blushing. "Do I have to answer that?"

"Ahh—let me see—yes!"

Gwen giggled. "Okay, you win. It's because he's the most gorgeous *on-screen* vampire I've ever seen. And his voice is *so sensual*. I think he could melt steel with that voice."

Connor rolled his eyes at Gwen.

"What? You asked and I told you."

"Well, you didn't have to lay it on so thick about his voice."

"Are you jealous?" she asked, laughing.

"Absolutely not."

"Oh my God—you *are* jealous," she replied, giggling.

"Please—" Connor said with little enthusiasm, as he walked past Gwen over to the DVD player and inserted the disc. Gwen watched Connor's movements with fascination. He made even the most mundane of activities look graceful and polished.

"What?" he asked, when he saw her staring at him.

"Oh, nothing."

"Gwenevere?"

"I was just noticing how graceful you are. It seems like each movement you make is orchestrated with purpose."

"I hadn't noticed," he said, with a cheeky grin.

Gwen stared into Connor's sparkling ice-blue eyes wishing she could read *his mind* for a change.

"No, you don't—it's not that interesting," he said, interrupting her train of thought.

Gwen's eyes opened wide. "Excuse me?"

"Oh—sorry. Forgot for a moment. Didn't mean to pry."

Gwen frowned at him. "Well?"

"Well, what?"

"What was so amusing about my comment?"

"Which one?"

"How quickly they forget?" she muttered aloud to herself. This time it was Gwen's turn to roll her eyes.

"Oh, you mean about each movement being made with purpose?"

"Yes—that one—care to elaborate?"

"Well, you're right. Each movement does have a purpose. Or more specifically, I have to think carefully about producing each movement I make in front of you," he said, with a genuine smile.

"I don't understand," she asked, puzzled.

"If I were to move at the speed that is comfortable for me, instead of the speed at which most humans move, my individual actions would no longer be perceptible. It would look like you were watching me in "fast forward" mode."

"Really? I want to see," she asked, excited.

"I don't think that would be such a good idea. You'd probably just be freaked out by it."

"It's okay. I really want to see it."

"Are you sure, I'd hate for your evening to be ruined."

"I'm a empiricist, remember? Please, show me. I'd like to see the way you move when you're by yourself or more aptly, when you're being yourself."

"Okay, but you asked for it," he warned. "Any requests of what you'd like to see me do?"

"Well, I had wanted to straighten up my kitchen before you got here, but I got sidetracked by Aidan's visit. I could use some help," Gwen asked as she glanced into the kitchen. The white tile floor clearly needed to be swept and mopped. There was also a fairly large pile of dishes in the sink, the result of breakfast and lunch, as well as some crumbs that were scattered along one of the countertops near the sink.

"Your wish is my command," Connor said, his classic roguish grin in place.

Gwen saw what looked like a blur of dark hair and pallid skin move to the pantry of her kitchen. Connor's movements were so quick and distorted she couldn't tell whether or not he had opened the pantry door until she saw him sweeping the floor with the broom. *He seemed to flit across the floor like a humming bird.* Gwen couldn't see any individual movement that Connor produced. Rather, he seemed to generate a flow of movements that were seamless from their start to end with no breaks in bodily position in between. Of course, logically Gwen knew that Connor must be taking breaks in between each movement, but the sequencing of the movements, as well as the abrupt onset and completion of each action, were imperceptible to her. It was just like Connor had said; he appeared to be in fast-forward motion. Gwen didn't see Connor exchange the broom for the mop and only realized he was mopping the floor when she detected the smell of bleach. A couple of minutes later, Connor stood at the sink, his hands moving at an insanely rapid pace cleaning dishes. It took him seconds to clean off the countertops leaving them spotless. When Connor had finished, he stopped moving to smile at Gwen without as so much as a hair out of place. Gwen stared at him in amazement. She would have been huffing and puffing, out of breathe with sweat across her brow by now. Of course, she reminded herself that Connor didn't sweat or need to breathe. His breathing was likely for her benefit.

"Wow! I don't know what to say. I feel so incredibly slow by comparison. It must be difficult for you having to wait for me to keep up?"

"No, I'm used to it. Remember, I have to concentrate on looking human to function in the world. So I take it you are feeling okay, right? No dizziness or anxiety?"

"No, I'm great. Frankly, I'm in awe that you can do that."

Connor shrugged his shoulders. "It's no big deal."

"You just cleaned my whole kitchen in less than five minutes. That's a pretty big deal to me."

Connor laughed a bit. "Well, if I made your life easier then it was worth it."

Gwen smiled at him. "Thanks!"

"You do realize how that level of speed makes us the deadliest predators on the planet, right?"

"Yeah, of course," Gwen said in a matter-of-fact tone.

"I don't think you quite appreciate what I mean," he said.

Before Gwen could even respond to Connor's statement, she noticed he was standing a couple of inches in front of her face. She instantly jumped back startled by his actions, her hand clutching the left side of her chest. Connor had moved over ten feet in a fraction of a second and Gwen hadn't heard or seen him coming.

"Okay—you proved your point," she said, gasping for breath.

"Sorry, I didn't mean to frighten you. I just wanted you to know what you're dealing with when it comes to other vampires."

"I get it!" she huffed.

Gwen felt Connor's cold hand envelope hers and the anxiety immediately vanished. He pulled her to him and wrapped his arms around her; coolness radiated down her body enshrouding her with feelings of peacefulness and tranquility.

"I'm sorry, Love, my behavior was uncalled for."

"It's okay—just don't do that again. We were having such a good time and you purposely frightened me for no good reason. I'm well aware of how deadly you and others of your kind can be. I don't need constant reminders of my human frailty."

Connor pulled away from Gwen a moment to look down into her gray-blue eyes. He was going to apologize again, but Gwen interrupted him. "It's alright, Connor. Just lighten up a bit. Can we just watch the movie and relax?"

Connor nodded and pulled Gwen towards the sofa, where they sat side by side with his arm wrapped around her shoulder. He grabbed the remote control for the television and DVD player and set up the movie. Connor's actions were forgotten a few minutes into the film. Gwen unexpectedly noticed a flash of something brown quickly darting back and forth in her peripheral vision. Distracted, she turned to observe the flurry of activity to find to her amusement that it was her kitten, Panda, leaping onto the coffee table. The scent of warm buttered popcorn must have attracted him. Panda managed to stick his snout into the bag biting into a few kernels before Connor swiftly grabbed the sack out of the kitten's reach. Connor and Gwen both laughed before Connor gingerly picked the kitten up and placed him on the floor next to his mother.

Gwen snuggled close to Connor lying with her head only inches away from his, while they watched the movie. Although Connor was cold, the sensations his touch produced generated warmth and closeness.

They laughed at the comical scenes in the movie as well as the cheesy special effects. When it came time for the love scene, when Dracula took Lucy as his *familiar*, Gwen's heart began to race, but Connor only laughed.

"What's so funny?" she asked, miffed he was killing the mood for her.

"The lame bat flying through the red mist. Where do they dream this stuff up anyway? They have no idea what it's like for a human *familiar* or for the vampire. It's really a bit insulting if you think about it."

"Connor, you forget that most of the world has no idea vampires are real. Until you and your family—I thought it was all folklore and fodder for the entertainment industry."

"I know, but seriously, they can do better than that."

"Well, what's it really like?"

"You know—we talked about it before."

"You mentioned it was very pleasurable for the *familiar*, but you didn't elaborate. You also didn't tell me that it was pleasurable for the vampire."

"I didn't?" he asked, looking uncomfortable like he'd let something slip he wasn't supposed to divulge.

"No, you didn't."

"Well, what do you want to know?"

"Tell me what its like," she said, as she stroked his hand feeling the coldness of his smooth hard skin.

He spoke no louder than a whisper with his lips close to hers. "Imagine being so intimate with another person that you can hear every thought, feel every sensation of the body, and experience total and complete joy in their presence. For the *familiar* there is an overwhelming sense of contentment, heightened senses, and pleasure beyond all measure. For the vampire, it is even better—"

Gwen sighed as she thought about it. She wanted to know that level of intimacy with him, even if just once. Gwen was fairly certain that Connor would protest, but he had made a promise to make her his *familiar* if she asked. Connor was silent for a moment and Gwen was fairly certain she knew why. He was hoping she wouldn't ask.

"Connor—" Gwen said, turning to look at him, his lips only

millimeters away from hers.

Connor sighed heavily. "I know Gwenevere—you don't have to say it."

"You read my mind again?"

He shook his head back and forth. "Didn't have to. Your actions are easy enough to decipher."

"When?" she asked.

"I'll leave that up to you," he whispered, before lightly kissing her lips.

Chapter 14

The next few days passed uneventfully. During the day, Gwen spent her time preparing for the fall term, editing papers, and meeting with students in her lab to discuss progress on her research program. At night, she stayed with Connor watching movies, having dinner out, and talking, their favorite pastime. It amazed Gwen how easy it was to speak with Connor. Connor and Gwen were very similar in their interests and passions, for the most part, and he got her weird, offbeat sense of humor.

Gwen suggested that she and Connor spend the weekend at his place on Panama City Beach for a change of pace. Before leaving for Connor's, Gwen packed a small suitcase with some overnight clothes and toiletries. She also called Andy to check in with him to make sure things were going well with his visit with his Dad. Andy seemed to be excited he'd be home in a couple of weeks, which came as a relief to Gwen. She wondered how he would receive Connor and hoped it would go well. The impact of her decision on Andy was constantly in her thoughts. Gwen finished with her packing and locked up the house. When she joined Connor by his car in her driveway she noticed he had a peculiar expression on his face that Gwen hadn't seen before.

"Something wrong?" she asked.

"I don't know," he said, looking troubled.

"Want to tell me what's going on?"

"I smelled something outside your bedroom window that concerns me a bit."

"What did it smell like?"

"Vampire," he said.

Gwen felt all the air leave her lungs. She couldn't breath for a moment and sensed a dark void in the pit of her stomach. For a moment she thought she was going to wretch, but was thankful the feeling quickly dissipated. "Couldn't that be Aidan or Lucinda you're smelling?"

"No. I know their scents very well. It's a foreign scent."

"What do we do?" she asked, frightened.

"Well, for one thing we're leaving tonight. I'm going to have to make sure you are watched at all times from now on until—well—you know."

"Until I make my decision, right?"

"Yes," he said, with a pensive look.

"How do you know they won't still come for me if I choose to stay mortal?" Gwen asked, her lips drawn tight.

"I don't. But, usually vampires respect boundaries and I'd make it known that you had your memory erased and there would be no need to harm you since you couldn't divulge our secret."

Now, Gwen understood why Connor would never leave her alone here. Even if she stayed mortal, there was no guarantee she'd be safe from harm. But, Connor would see to it that she was safe by guarding her every night of her mortal life, even though she'd never know it. This thought both comforted and saddened Gwen. "Is that the reason why I'm being stalked, now?" she asked.

"It's likely the most important reason why an immortal is coming by your home, now. You see because you are still a mortal and I'm spending so much time with you, my motives are in question. Most vampires think I would have changed you by now, if I had good intentions. They don't understand that I'm giving you the choice. Leaving you a mortal makes them wonder what I'm up to."

"Why don't they just confront you, instead of stalking my house? I'm no threat to them."

"But, you are a huge threat to them. In their minds, you could expose them. They don't understand that you'd never do that."

"Connor, I'm scared."

"Don't be. I'll make sure you're watched wherever you are."

"What about Andy? He comes home in two weeks."

"I'll have Andy watched at all times as well. I've already spoken with Aidan about it and he's happily agreed to protect Andy."

"That's right, Aidan loves kids."

"He sure does. Like I told you before he's volunteered with several organizations, like the Big Brothers for decades. Andy will be well protected with Aidan by his side."

Gwen was encouraged by Connor's comments and would speak with Aidan about it in more detail, but she was also worried about the news of a foreign vampire's scent outside her bedroom window. She was frightened, but didn't want Connor to know just how much. What if he or one of his cousins was momentarily distracted? Would they be able to get to her in time?

"Gwen? Gwen!" Connor asked.

"Huh?" She looked up dazed; she'd been deep in thought and hadn't heard Connor saying her name.

"It's going to be fine. Stop worrying. I won't let anything happen to you. Please trust me on that."

"Reading my thoughts?"

"Well, you were broadcasting a large signal I couldn't filter out. When you worry, I can hear it for miles. Sorry, not trying to pry, but you have to believe that I will do everything possible to protect you."

"Okay," she said, softly.

"Good. Now, let's get out of here!"

Gwen nodded and they both got into Connor's car. A short drive later they were at his house on the beach. Connor went to great lengths to keep Gwen's attention occupied from thoughts about the vampire's scent near her home. Fortunately, for Gwen, Connor was quite good at distracting her. He'd made her a gourmet dinner of grilled grouper with a special hollandaise sauce and steamed vegetables followed by kiwi-lime pie for dessert. After dinner, they went swimming in his pool, before sitting outside his patio stargazing. Connor surprised Gwen with a massive telescope he had purchased, so they could view the night's sky in Florida with the same power as the telescope he had in his home in Massachusetts. Connor was adept at programming the telescope to find various constellations, star clusters, and planets. The telescope was so powerful, that one could even see the faint image of other galaxies. It was one of the best nights they had spent together.

Later, cuddled up with Connor in his bed, Gwen lightly stroked the hard cool skin of his chest. It was still strange to hear the sound of his breathing without an accompanying heartbeat.

"Connor, why do you breathe when you really don't have to?"

"I want to sound human to those around me."

Connor shifted his position so that his face was next to Gwen's. His beautiful luminescent blue eyes peered into hers as he gingerly stroked Gwen's cheek, pausing to feel the bones beneath her skin.

"You're so beautiful," he whispered.

"So are you," she whispered.

Gwen pulled Connor towards her. Her lips rested lightly on his. The coolness of his skin sent a cascade of sensations throughout her body. She instinctively pulled him closer, wrapping her arms around his hard cold torso while her legs entwined themselves around his. His kisses become stronger and Gwen noticed she felt a bit lightheaded. Rather than pull away, she clung to him more fervently, wanting to experience every aspect of his touch and taste of his lips. Gwen noticed her heart rate slowing, which surprised her because she was so aroused. She brushed it off, moving her lips down the side of his perfect face towards his neck. Connor abruptly, pulled away and sat a good distance from her, his body no longer touching hers.

"I'm sorry—but that's too dangerous for us," he said, looking flustered.

"Why?" she said.

"My touch—it was having too strong an effect on you. Your heart was slowing to a dangerously slow pace and I had to stop."

"Would my heart have stopped beating altogether?" she asked, half jokingly.

"Eventually—yes."

"Oh—I didn't know that."

"My touch—it's designed to subdue prey. At least, if I'm not careful, it can."

"Connor, I want to be intimate with you. Can't we—figure this out?" she asked.

"In theory, yes. But in practice, your heart would likely stop before we finished. And there is the little matter of your bones."

"What about them?"

"Well, I'd probably break most of them in the process. Unintentionally, of course, but I doubt that would matter much to you if you ended up in a full body cast."

"So we can never be intimate?" she asked, bitterly disappointed.

"Not safely while you're still human."

"And if I were immortal?"

Connor looked a bit embarrassed as he laughed. "Oh yes, then anything would be possible."

Gwen blushed a minute at the thought. "Well, that doesn't help us now does it?"

"No, afraid not," he said, pulling the covers over his torso as he lay closer to her again.

Gwen was quiet a moment. She looked over at Connor who was staring at her, a beautiful expression on his face. He looked serene. It occurred to Gwen that there was a way she could be very close to him without sexual intimacy. The time felt right and she knew what she wanted.

"Connor, I'm ready."

"For what?" he asked, alarmed. "The change?"

"No, to be bitten."

"Are you sure I can't talk you out of it?" he whispered.

It occurred to Gwen that she'd heard him say something like this to her once before. Then it dawned on her, she had dreamt of this moment long ago. Of course, it had taken place on the beach somewhere, but the sentiment he uttered was the same.

"Yes."

"You know this will change things between us, right? You'll have a longing you didn't have before."

"I know, but I'm ready and I *want* this."

He smiled in resolution and pulled her to him. His lips found hers and he kissed her softly, holding her close to him. The kisses became a bit more urgent before she felt him moving his lips in soft caresses down her face to the nape of her neck. Gwen's heart was beating wildly in anticipation and excitement. She tried to relax, but was struggling with the adrenaline coursing through her body. Connor must have sensed her thoughts, because he stroked her neck with his fingers, calming her down by degrees. Familiar feelings of comfort and peacefulness engulfed her and she was no longer anxious. He kissed her lips again, likely to distract her from what was coming, but Gwen no longer thought about it. Instead, she concentrated on experiencing each kiss and stroke of his hand. Before Gwen realized what was happening, she felt something sharp pierce the skin at the base of her neck. She instinctively gasped for breath, surprised at the amount of pain the bite had caused. She moaned a bit in discomfort, before the pain receded and was replaced with ecstasy.

The feelings of peace and tranquility that Connor's touch typically produced, were minor compared to the feelings she experienced while being held in his arms as he drank her blood. Waves of euphoria enveloped her, body and soul. She could hear the movement of ants and flying insects outside the sliding glass door of Connor's bedroom, the hum of the refrigerator in the kitchen, friction of the sheets sliding around the bed, and even the faint sounds of surf coming from the Gulf. Connor's scent, which had always been sweet and pleasant, was now overwhelmingly so. Gwen could even feel the sensation of her blood being siphoned from her carotid artery, but was strangely unconcerned. Rather, Gwen felt a thinning of boundaries as her life flowed into Connor's.

Although her eyes were closed, a stream of images of her with Connor flitted through her mind in amazing clarity and detail. She saw herself with Connor lying on a blanket on the beach under the dim light of the moon. They were kissing and he was gently moving inside of her body. She saw her arms stroking his back while her long legs were wrapped tightly around his. Gwen was enraptured, but something soon distracted her from the image of intimacy with Connor. She heard a rhythmic beat that had a familiar ebb and flow. It was faint at first, but soon grew intense. Gwen found herself drawn to the hypnotic sound that had considerably slowed its pace. She saw herself on the beach alone; searching for the sound that captivated her, but the more she looked for it, the farther away it appeared. Feelings of euphoria were replaced with lethargy and Gwen felt her limbs become heavy and numb. She was more aware than ever of the beautiful rhythmic hum, until she was distracted by an even more appealing sound. It was a smooth and silky voice whispering in her ear that she needed to rest. Her eyelids becoming heavier with each second, Gwen fought hard to hold onto one last moment of consciousness, before she slipped into darkness.

An unfamiliar sensation roused Gwen from her deep, dreamless sleep. Despite her exhaustion, she couldn't ignore the need that was gnawing at her insides. Her lips and mouth were dry and her throat felt hoarse and raw. It wasn't until she opened her eyes that she recognized the sensation forcing her into awareness. *Thirst.* Gwen had an urgent need for water and lots of it. She called out to Connor, but didn't receive an answer and his side of the bed was empty. Gwen glanced at the clock on the nightstand noting the time, eleven-thirty. She had slept in late. Although Gwen routinely slept in during the weekends, this was later than normal for her. She must have really needed the rest.

Gwen sat up in bed for a moment thinking about the events of the previous evening. For a moment she wondered if Connor really had made her his *familiar*. Any doubt she might have had was instantly shattered when she touched the two small round scabs that had formed on the skin of her neck. Gwen played with them a few minutes, moving her fingers back and forth across the closed wounds noting their rough texture. However, her thoughts about her bite marks were interrupted by the relentless thirst that was growing in severity. Gwen sighed as the rolled out of bed and walked into the master bathroom. Flipping on the light switch, she was instantly blinded by intense light that overpowered her visual senses. She closed her eyes and managed to find the light switch with her hand, turning the lights off. Gwen had always been light sensitive, but now it appeared that sensitivity was temporarily enhanced. *She surmised it could be a side effect of last night.* Minutes later her eyes adjusted to the ambient light in the bathroom, enabling her to see her reflection fairly well. Gwen noticed that she was paler than normal and that there were dark circles beneath her eyes. She turned her head to the left side and saw the bite marks on her neck adjacent to the carotid artery. They were fairly sizeable and Gwen doubted anyone would believe they were mosquito bites. She'd have to use a scarf to cover them, rather than place it in her hair. Other than looking a bit tired, she felt wonderful.

A dry cough escaped Gwen's lips and she remembered why she had come to the bathroom in the first place. She scanned the vanity for a glass, but didn't see one. Frustrated she wandered out of the bedroom to the kitchen. The thirst was getting worse, and her mouth felt like it had wads of cotton in it. Gwen opened the refrigerator and was relieved to see a large bottle of spring water on the shelf in front of her. Grabbing a tumbler out of one of the cabinets, she poured herself a large glass of water, which she immediately drank. She poured herself a second glass, followed by a third until she couldn't drink anymore. Relief from the thirst came instantly as her body absorbed the fluids it desperately needed. Yet, the water did little to abate the feelings of dizziness and vertigo that she now experienced. Gwen worried that she might faint and sought refuge on the large sofa in the living room. She closed her eyes a moment, before she felt something cold and smooth slide across her forehead. Normally, this sensation would have resulted in Gwen being startled, but the scent that accompanied the cool sensation was pleasant and familiar.

"Connor," she whispered, with her eyes still closed.

Connor leaned over to kiss her lips briefly, before sitting down next to her. "Good morning. I ran out to the store to pick up some things for breakfast. Are you all right? You look frail."

Gwen opened her eyes to see him staring down at her, his brow furrowed. "I'm okay—just a little dizzy. It's no big deal." Gwen downplayed her nausea; she didn't want him to worry.

Connor frowned, sighing heavily. "I was afraid of this. I thought I was being really careful last night, but I guess I wasn't careful enough. I must have taken a little too much blood. You should relax today. I'll

166

make you a good breakfast."

"Connor, don't worry about me. I'm all right, just a little tired," she said, straightening up in the sofa trying to look normal.

"Gwen, you know I really wasn't keen on the idea of you being my *familiar*. Maybe we'd better not repeat the experience."

Gwen looked alarmed. "No, you promised me you'd respect my wishes if I wanted this."

"Gwenevere, you're as white as chalk and I can see you are dehydrated. The fatigue you're experiencing is likely the result of an iron deficiency from blood loss. This is my fault and I don't think it's safe for us to do it again."

"Connor, you told me it has been many years since you took a *familiar*. You are just out of practice that's all."

Connor looked irritated, his lips forming a tight line. "Gwenevere, I'm not going to argue with you about this, right now. I'm going to make you breakfast and then send your stubborn behind back to bed."

"Connor, please don't do this. Last night was one of the most amazing experiences of my life. I want to be close to you."

"Your safety is the most important thing to me. Everything else is secondary. Besides, you are close to me. Closer than anyone has been in a long time."

"I'm fine—really. Okay?" Gwen smiled at him, her eyes pleading.

"Okay, for now. But if you have this severe a reaction the next time, then all bets are off."

Gwen was relieved. She stared at Connor's beautiful angelic face that had a torn expression on it. She wanted to distract him from having second thoughts about her being his *familiar*. She tried to think of something interesting to discuss with him to divert his attention, but was coming up empty when she spied the plastic grocery bags on the dining room table.

"So what's for breakfast?" she asked.

Connor turned to face Gwen, a small smile replacing the frown. Her question seeming to work, Connor's attention now squarely focused on her nutritional needs instead of her human weaknesses. "Eggs, toast, and fruit. Oh—and some vitamins."

"Vitamins?"

"Yeah, you need iron and other vitamins to supplement your diet when you have blood loss."

"Oh, okay," Gwen, said, in a flat tone. She didn't want to draw his attention back to her frailties again. "Eggs sound great. Can I have two over easy, please?"

The corners of Conner's mouth erupted into a large grin that covered his face. "As you wish." He laughed a moment to himself as he got up from the sofa and walked into the kitchen. "How hungry are you by the way?"

"Ravenous. Why?"

"Well, I could make the eggs in human time, or I can make the eggs in immortal time. I'll leave it up to you."

"Immortal time, please. I'm really hungry," she replied watching him from the comfort of the sofa in the living room.

"Okay, will do. But, you may not want to watch this since you're feeling a bit dizzy."

"Actually, I'm feeling more normal now. But, since I'm tired, I'll close my eyes while you're cooking, if that's okay."

"Of course," he said, before turning his attention to his task.

Gwen lay her head on a pillow on the sofa, and shut her eyes. She heard a series of noises that occurred in rapid time. Some of the noises were clear such as the sound of cabinet doors opening and closing, eggs cracking, and a frying pan sizzling, while others were harder to define. Gwen smelled warm eggs within a few minutes, and her mouth reflexively salivated.

"Breakfast time, Love," Connor said, sitting down beside her.

"Wow—that was fast! Even for you," Gwen said, opening her eyes and sitting upright on the couch. She saw the plate of eggs, buttered toast, and freshly sliced strawberries on the coffee table in front of her. "This looks great. Thank you," as she kissed his cheek.

"Oh—I've got coffee ready, too. It's in the kitchen. Be right back," he said, before he got up from the sofa. Gwen saw a glimpse of Connor leave the living room followed by a quick glimpse of him returning with her coffee. It almost looked like he never left the room, his movements barely visible.

"I don't think I'll ever get used to that," she said, when he sat down next to her, with her coffee in his hand.

"Sorry."

"Don't be. It's just t shocking to see. So, if I were immortal like you, would I move that fast too?"

"It's possible. I'm unusually fast for an immortal. But, to answer your question, yes, compared to humans your movements would be rapidly accelerated."

"Unlike humans, would you be able to see my individual movements in immortal time?" Gwen asked, while biting into a piece of egg.

"Sure. To mortals our actions would barely be perceptible, but to each other, we'd see them perfectly."

"What else would I be able to do?" she asked, holding a piece of toast in her hand. She'd already wolfed down the eggs.

"Well, you'll be able to hear nearly everything around you, including people's thoughts, as well as, smell their scent. It can be very overwhelming at first, and you'll have to learn how to filter out what's unimportant from what's salient. Of course, you do that now as a human, but it's much more difficult as a vampire."

"Can you give me an example?"

"Sure. Imagine you are in a classroom of twenty students. You will be able to hear each of their hearts beating, their individual thoughts, the shuffling of feet under the desk, the sound of equipment projecting your lecture onto the screen, pens and pencils moving, mini-conversations students are having, and so forth. That level of detail can drive you insane unless you learn how to focus your attention to what's vital. It takes practice. Oh—and there is the minor issue of smelling the blood running through each of their bodies."

"My God, it does sound overwhelming. How do you learn to attend to what's important?"

"Your sire, which would be me, would train you how to focus properly. It's a skill you'll learn quickly. Vampires live in secret and so adaptability is key to survival. The more we blend with humans, the easier it is to live among them undetected."

"What else?" Gwen's eyes examined the outline of his face.

"You'll have to learn how to control your thirst. It's the most important skill you'll learn and comes before all else. Of course, it will be difficult at first. Luckily, Andy and your family will be perfectly safe around you as we talked about before, but other mortals won't be so lucky. You'll need to keep all your friends and coworkers at a distance until you gain control. Fortunately, it only takes a couple of weeks to master."

"Just a couple of weeks? I'd thought it would be longer! Aidan said he couldn't divulge his true identity to Lilly for a couple of months because he needed that time to get his thirst under control," Gwen said.

"Aidan wasn't being completely honest with you. He waited a while before confronting Lilly because he needed time to work up the courage to face her. Learning to control your thirst is the easiest of what you'll have to master as an immortal. It's ignoring people's thoughts that will take more time. Trust me; you'll not be thrilled at what you hear. People will disappoint you with what they really think."

"How would I explain the physiological changes? You know—the luminous eyes and cold skin?"

Connor laughed softly for a few moments. "Gwenevere, you'd be amazed at what people will believe. They want rational explanations to understand the people and situations around them. You can simply tell them you've come down with a rare disorder that affects the iris of your eyes and that you have a circulatory problem that leaves your skin cold; they'll likely believe you. As long as you act like yourself, most will accept your explanation because it sounds plausible. Even if they really doubt what you're saying, they'll go along with the idea because they don't want to be perceived as crazy. However, your explanations will only last so long. Within ten years or so when it becomes clear that you haven't aged, suspicions will be raised and you'll have to move."

"You know, even when the evidence was in front of my face that you were a vampire, I didn't want to believe it. I guess it just seemed too fantastic to be true."

"I know and that actually works in our favor. The fewer people know we are real, the better."

"But Connor, the club goes against the rules of your very existence."

"I know and we discussed why that was the case. If I had known I was going to meet you, I never would have agreed to help Derrick. It was foolish of me. But you know what they say about hindsight.

Anyway, the damage is done, so we'll have to see what happens."

"Why don't you just close down, now that the Elder clan is on to you?"

"We've been discussing it, but Derrick is stubborn. We're waiting it out a little longer. We haven't had any activity in over a month. Maybe Josef has bigger issues to deal and he's forgotten about us. Of course, he does hate us so we do have a reason to be vigilant."

"Why does he hate you?" she asked, concerned. Gwen put her fork down, no longer hungry.

"It's complicated."

Gwen glared at him. "I have a doctorate, I'm sure I can handle it."

"Okay, I'll tell you. At one time, Josef and his brother Matthias, ruled the Elder Clan, which is the oldest coven of vampires in the world. They each had radically different ideas as to the direction the coven should take. Josef was more sensible in his rule and wanted the vampires to remain hidden among mortals. But, Matthias had other plans. He felt vampires should live out in the open among mortals. One thing led to another and a bitter rift split the coven. Half of the members stayed with Josef in Romania, while the other half followed Matthias to America. Matthias came to Salem with plans of starting another coven that would, among other things, control the mortal world. He targeted the members of my family as well as another, the Kearneys. Matthias waited until we were all together for a family reunion, one night. One minute we were laughing and enjoying ourselves, the next we were brutally subdued and attacked."

"Why were you and your cousins targeted?" Gwen asked.

Connor took Gwen's hand in his while he spoke. "Matthias knew we'd all get along as vampires, since we were such a close-knit family. But, he never counted on the fact that we would join together to defy him. It took us time and planning, but when we were strong enough, we fought his coven, killing most of his followers. We couldn't kill Matthias himself. He was much too strong for us, but he fled from us, and we haven't heard from him since. Josef got the news of what we had done, and summoned us to Romania. We were sure we'd all be executed, but surprisingly he let us live. He was willing to overlook most of our actions because Matthias wasn't harmed and because he was relieved his brother's followers were taken care of."

"So if you killed Matthias' followers, who violated Josef's view, than why does Josef hate you so?"

"Because we're still the product of Matthias' bloodlust for power. He sees us as a symbol of his own brother's betrayal. For that reason alone he distrusts us."

"I'm worried Connor. I don't think he's forgotten about your family at all. I think he's biding his time."

"I know, but Derrick thinks he's bored with us by now since we haven't had any visitors."

"Who is the leader of your coven?"

"Isn't it obvious?"

"You right?" Gwen asked.

"Heavens no. Derrick is our leader."

"But only because you let him," she replied.

Connor smiled. "How did you know?"

"It wasn't hard to figure out you were the Alpha," she said as she smiled. "It was obvious the first night I met you at your table and when you cut in on my dance with Derrick. He may officially be your leader, but you run the show. At least that's my take on it."

"Much of what you said is true. For well over two centuries, I led our coven. But, I tired of all the infighting. You see Aidan and Derrick always stick close together. I don't hold it against Aidan. After all, he is Derrick's brother. Still, I got tired of butting heads with Derrick all the time. So one day when I had simply had enough, I told Derrick that if he wanted all the headaches that went along with the leadership position he could have it. Life has been so much more pleasant since I gave him the reins."

"Somehow I don't think Derrick realizes the danger he's putting you all in, now."

"Probably not. He's so damn stubborn it's ridiculous. But, he's our leader and unless I want to fight with him I'm staying out of it. I'm just hoping for the best and preparing for the worst. If they come, I'm ready. As long as you and Andy are safe that's all I care about. Now, enough questions you need to rest awhile. We can talk more later."

Gwen started to protest, but Connor insisted. He picked her up from the sofa and carried her into the bedroom where he tucked her in bed. Gwen decided not to argue. At least she knew he'd agreed to answer her questions later that evening. As soon as she'd closed her eyes, she was fast asleep.

Chapter 15

It was dark when Gwen finally awakened. She heard a melodious female voice coming from the living room, which she recognized immediately as Lucinda's. She got up and grabbed her robe out of the suitcase and tied it around her body. Gwen shivered ever so slightly from the air conditioning that Connor had lowered for her benefit. She strolled out of the bedroom down the hallway to the living room. She overheard Connor and Lucinda speaking as she approached the living room.

"We found traces of the vampire's scent near the back porch as well as outside Gwen's bedroom window," Lucinda said.

"I didn't detect anything near the porch, just Gwen's bedroom window. This immortal is definitely keeping tabs on us."

"I'm in agreement. There's something else. The scent smells old, possibly predating us," Lucinda remarked.

"You think it's one of Josef's followers?" Connor asked.

"Could be. Hard to say—but, this does mean we'll have to be more vigilant than ever. When does the boy come back?"

"In a couple of weeks. Aidan's going to cover Andy, and the rest of us will keep an eye on Gwen. I'll stay with her as much as possible, but I'll need you and Derrick as back up. We can't afford to make a mistake. This immortal is up to something."

"Does Gwen know about the vampire's scent?"

"Yes. I'm not keeping anything from her anymore. She wants complete honesty and I'm respecting her wishes."

"Has she said anything regarding her decision yet?"

"No, but I think she's leaning in the direction of joining us. I just don't want her to do it for me. I don't want to be a factor in the equation."

"Well that's not very realistic, Connor. Of course, you factor in her decision. Nevertheless, Gwen is a smart woman. I know she'll make the decision that is best for her and her child."

"Sounds like you've warmed up to her. Are you telling me your chilly exterior is melting?" Connor chided.

"Don't make me hurt you, Connor. I like Gwen, but I will always be the ice queen," Lucinda said, smiling.

"I don't doubt it, Lucinda," Connor said.

Gwen walked into the living room, where Connor and Lucinda were sitting. She didn't mean to interrupt them, but she felt uncomfortable standing in the hallway eavesdropping. Gwen smiled when she saw Connor with his cousin. It almost looked like they could be siblings rather than cousins, with how comfortable they seemed around each other. Connor stood up when Gwen entered the room; his smile large and inviting. Lucinda, on the other hand, surprised Gwen by walking over to her and giving her a kiss on the check. Up close, Gwen was reminded of Lucinda's elegance and remarkable beauty.

"I didn't mean to interrupt you. It's great to see you, Lucinda," Gwen said, grinning.

"It's nice to see you too Gwen. How are you feeling today?" Lucinda asked, as she glanced at Gwen closely. No doubt Lucinda knew that Gwen had become Connor's *familiar*.

"I'm great, just a little tired. Of course, I don't know why, it's not like I haven't slept today," Gwen muttered, a little nervously. She liked Lucinda, but still found being around her a little intimidating.

"It's okay. Your first time being a *familiar* can be somewhat draining. You'll be less tired the next time."

Connor glared at Lucinda. Gwen wasn't sure whether he was annoyed at Lucinda's tacky pun, her reference to a *next time*, or both.

"I'm not so sure that would be the brightest idea. Gwen looked very worn out today," Connor said.

Lucinda moved closer to Gwen, pointing to the bite marks on Gwen's neck. "May I have a look?"

"Ah—sure," Gwen stammered.

Lucinda lightly held Gwen's face in her hands examining her coloring and the purple circles beneath her eyes. She gently moved Gwen's face to the side so that she could examine the bite marks more closely. "You're a shade paler than normal, but you'll be okay," Lucinda said, winking at Gwen, when Connor wasn't looking.

"Lucinda, Gwen was nauseous and dehydrated this morning."

"Connor, you're making a mountain out of a molehill. Gwen's fine; you're just rusty from lack of practice."

"You're not going to budge are you, Lucinda?" Connor said, annoyed.

"Nope."

"Gee thanks, cousin."

"Anytime," Lucinda said, with a smirk. "Well, I should be going. I'm going to head over to Gwen's house to feed her cats and keep an eye on things."

"Thanks, Lucinda, I appreciate that. I was going to ask Connor about swinging over there tonight to do that myself, but I'm still kind of beat. That's really nice of you," Gwen said.

"It's no problem. Glad to help. Besides, I don't want your cats hissing at me every time I enter your house. I'll let you all know if I detect anything new. It was nice seeing you Gwen. Connor, I'll be in touch," Lucinda said, as she hugged Gwen before walking towards the front door of Connor's house.

"Bye, Lucinda," Gwen said, waving.

"Talk with you later," Connor replied, looking in Lucinda's direction as she marched out of the room.

Connor smiled as he came to Gwen, placing his arms around her, lightly resting his lips against the top of her head. She was momentarily amused by how short she felt standing next to him. They stood together there quietly taking in the moment, before Connor produced a heavy sigh. That usually signaled his concern, or worry, about something.

"You're worried about the scent aren't you?" she asked.

"Yes," he whispered into her hair.

"What do you think it means?"

"We're being watched. But, the fact that the scent smells old indicates something entirely different than a vampire who is simply curious about what's happening between us."

Gwen turned to face him. His perfect features look distressed. "What do you think the vampire wants?"

"I wish I knew. I'll get to the bottom of it, though."

"What should I do?" Gwen asked.

"Nothing. Just live your life as you normally would," Connor said, while holding Gwen tightly in his arms.

"You make it sound so easy."

"Leave it to me, Gwen."

"I know you're all going to keep watch. I just hate feeling powerless. I'm so used to be the rock in my household."

Connor pulled Gwen even closer to him. She knew he was trying to comfort her, but he couldn't possibly understand what she was feeling. Gwen's strength and self-reliance were an important part of her persona. In fact, she took pride in her fierce independence. That, however, was before she knew that vampires existed. For a moment, she wondered what it would be like to return to a world where vampires were simply fictional characters in folklore, novels, and movies. If she chose to stay mortal, she'd go back to her blissful ignorance. Gwen contemplated that for a moment. She'd have her life back where she felt in control of the events that happened to her. The idea did appeal to her in a way that she couldn't deny. But, she'd be alone without Connor in that life, too. Gwen sighed, feeling the weight of the world on her shoulders knowing she would need to make up her mind soon.

"Are you hungry?" Connor asked, breaking the silence between them.

"Yes, actually I am."

"What would you like?" he inquired, stroking the back of her hair.

"I don't know I'm not picky. Anything is fine."

"I have a couple of steaks I could grill. I also have a salad ready to go. How does that sound?"

Gwen normally didn't eat a lot of red meat, but the thought really appealed to her right now. "Yeah, steak sounds fantastic. What kind?"

"Filet mignon."

Gwen's eyes lit up. "Can I help?"

"You can sit outside on the patio with me while I grill."

Gwen nodded and followed Connor into the kitchen while he grabbed what they'd need to grill the steaks. Evidently, he had marinated the steaks earlier, during the day while she slept. When Connor removed the plastic that covered the steaks, Gwen was overwhelmed with their scent. She felt an intense urge to pick one of the steaks up with her bare hands and bite into it raw. Her hand instinctively reached out to one of the plates, before she quickly came to her senses and withdrew it. Repulsed by her thoughts and actions, Gwen looked away from Connor and the plate of meat he was holding.

"Gwen, you ready to go out to the patio?"

For once, Gwen had wished Connor had read her thoughts. If Connor did sense what she was thinking, he didn't act like it. "Sure."

Gwen followed Connor through the sliding glass door that led from the kitchen to the pool area. Connor had a massive stainless steel grill that likely cost him thousands. Gwen stifled a giggle realizing it was just for appearances. The grill looked pristine.

"Is this the first time you've used this grill?" she asked.

"Second, actually. I held a small party for some of my neighbors when I moved in."

Gwen nodded. She knew Connor had held the party to show he was a typical friendly next-door neighbor. She could imagine several families enjoying Connor's amazing culinary skills blissfully unaware of his true identity. She wondered how many of them would sleep so well if they knew they were living next to a vampire.

"Let me guess. Hotdogs and hamburgers during the Fourth of July?" she asked grinning.

Connor smirked at her. "Close. It was shrimp and steak on the Fourth. Wouldn't want the neighbors to think I was cheap."

Gwen laughed. "Right, hotdogs and hamburgers would be more my neighborhood's speed."

"Immortality does have some advantages. Your money can grow to fairly large amounts when it sits in the market for over a hundred years."

"So I see," Gwen said, keeping her eye on the steaks as Connor turned them on the grill.

"How would you like them cooked?" he asked, his radiant eyes fixed on hers.

Gwen salivated watching the steaks sizzle. She saw the steaks were clearly pink in the center. Normally, she would always ask for her meat to be cooked well done, but right now rare was sounding too good to pass up.

"Rare please," she whispered, the pupils of her eyes dilating in anticipation.

Connor raised an eyebrow staring at Gwen. "Are you sure?"

"Yes, why?" she asked, a little defensively.

"Oh, nothing," he said, failing to suppress a chuckle.

"Is something funny?"

"No."

"Okay. Well I'll go get our drinks." Gwen went back into the kitchen to pour herself some water. She opened the temperature-controlled room containing Connor's bottles of blood. The bottle was warm to the touch and Gwen brought it out along with a dark glass so that the blood wouldn't be visible while he drank it. She put the beverages on the table outside the patio while Connor placed her steaks onto a plate in front of her. Gwen noticed the salad sitting by her plate, but pushed it aside. She didn't have much of a desire for vegetables right now. Connor spoke to Gwen, but she didn't hear a single word. All she could do was focus on the meat, watching the red blood pour down the plate as she cut into it before placing a piece in her mouth. The taste was phenomenal, but the best part was the red juice being squeezed out with each bite. Gwen was ravenous and devoured both pieces of meat in minutes. If it wasn't for the fact that it would be considered gross and socially unacceptable, she would have licked the plate clean as well. When she had finished she put her fork and knife down to look at Connor. He sat there in pure fascination, staring at her with his mouth wide open.

"What?" she whispered.

"Guess I had forgotten about the side effects."

"Side effects?"

"Of being a *familiar*. You will have heightened sensitivity to lights, odors, and tastes. It goes away with time, if you haven't been bitten for a while."

"How long?"

"A few weeks to a month. It's different with each human. Anyway, it's the reason why you will experience enhanced sensitivity and a desire to eat meat that is practically raw."

Gwen looked at him with her head cocked to the side. "You know, now that you mention it, I smell something else that is strong and kind of salty. I can't quite place it, is there something else on the grill?"

Connor looked a little uncomfortable. "No, there is nothing on the grill."

"Well, I smell something. It smells *really good*." Gwen got up looking around the table sniffing, trying to figure out where the delectable scent was coming from when she realized it was the liquid in Connor's dark glass. It was the smell of the blood he was drinking. Gwen couldn't help herself; she grabbed Connor's glass putting it close to her lips about to drink, when he abruptly pulled the glass from her hands.

"Gwen, that wouldn't be such a good idea. I don't want you drinking HIV infected blood."

Gwen recoiled from the glass, grimacing in disgust. "Oh my God, what was I thinking," she said. Her face flushed bright red.

"It's okay, Gwen. What you are experiencing is normal. It's part of the longing I was telling you about."

Gwen was embarrassed and didn't know what to say. "So is that what blood smells like to an immortal?"

"No. It smells even better. Your just getting a glimpse of what it's like for us."

Gwen didn't know what to say. Although horrified by her thoughts, she desperately wanted to drink the blood in Connor's glass more than anything else at this moment. The longing had begun.

Hours after dinner, Connor held Gwen close to him as they lay in bed. Neither of them was particularly tired at the moment, just relaxed. Connor lightly stroked Gwen's side as he stared out the window watching the cloud cover roll in off the Gulf.

"There are storms heading our way. I can hear the lightening off in the distance," he whispered.

"I hate rain. Something about a murky, gray sky leaves me feeling depressed and lousy. Not to mention it bothers my sinuses too," Gwen, said sighing as she rolled over to face Connor, her bare chest resting on his.

"You would have hated New England then."

"Lots of storms?"

"Loads. The worst were the bloody Nor'easters that would drench the area and flood the town."

"Well, Long Island had its fair share of storms, too. Of course, living here with the threat of hurricanes is a nightmare in and of itself."

"It rained the night I was changed. I can remember it like it was yesterday. It was a sticky, hot day in August. Elizabeth wasn't feeling well and decided, last minute, to stay with her mother, while I met my cousins and some other family members at an Inn in Salem. We were having a Cole family gathering. My mother and Lucinda's mother were both Coles by birth. The place was packed and we had a wonderful time. We all had so much to be thankful for. Aidan was planning to propose to Lilly, and Lucinda was dating a fellow she was smitten with, too. Derrick wasn't interested in marriage, but was happily making money in his business and doing well for himself. And—as for me, I was going to be a father in six months."

Connor briefly turned away from Gwen. She could see spots of red forming in his eyes. He was finally opening up to her about the traumatic events surrounding his becoming a vampire and the lost chance at fatherhood. It pained Gwen to watch him relive the experience, but she knew there was no turning back, now. He needed to communicate the horror of that night to her.

"Connor?"

"It's okay, Gwen. I want to tell you everything once and for all."

"Okay, I'm listening," she said, stroking the icy smooth skin of his hand.

"Elizabeth was nearing the end of the first trimester and she wasn't feeling well. She had a rough time with morning sickness, like many women, and opted to stay with her mother. In retrospect, I should have refused going to the reunion to stay with her, but she insisted. It had been planned for nearly a year and she wouldn't hear of my canceling. In any event, we were all having a great time at the party. By nightfall, several family members left to go home and some went to other relatives' houses that were close by. Only my cousins and I planned to stay at the Inn. That evening, when each of us retired to our respective rooms, Matthias attacked us one by one. He had been watching us during the day, noting how close we were and decided he wanted us to be a part of his coven."

Connor stopped talking, lost in thought for a moment. "Connor, what happened during the attack?" she asked, looking into his eyes, which seemed to be focused elsewhere.

"I was fast asleep in my bed, when something ice cold grabbed my hand and rolled me over with such force it I couldn't breathe. My strength as a young human man was no match for the old immortal that made me. I can still remember seeing Matthias' blood red eyes boring into mine. He told me not to be afraid, that I was going to receive the gift of everlasting life, but I was terrified and believed I was going to die. He bit into my neck with such intensity I heard bones crack. He vigorously sucked my blood nearly draining me. I felt my heart slow to a crawl and prepared myself for death. I saw images of Elizabeth, my family, people who mattered to me slipping away. I was dying when I felt something warm and salty pouring into my mouth. It was blood dripping from his wrist into my throat. At first I was repulsed, but then I realized the blood tasted good and he told me I'd die if I didn't drink. So I did, I drank until he forced my mouth off of his wrist. A few minutes later I felt my heart completely stop. Yet I was alive. I was no longer human, and overwhelmed with new senses and abilities I didn't understand."

"What about the others?" she asked.

"It was pretty much the same with the others. I was the first to be made, since Matthias would need the bulk of his strength to restrain me. Derrick was next, followed by Aidan, and finally, Lucinda. It went on all night, and by the morning, we fled with Matthias to a home he had purchased not far away from the Inn. We slept there during the day and by that night he began the process of teaching us how to control the thirst, how to hunt, and how to deal with the thoughts of humans we would be bombarded with. We were completely competent to be on our own within a month. Then, in secret over the course of the next year, we planned our revenge on Matthias and the other vampires in his coven."

"What happened to Elizabeth while you were away," Gwen asked.

"Matthias had sent messages to all our family members that we had been detained for medical reasons in another town and that we couldn't return to our homes until the illness was cured. In those days, they didn't know about bacteria and viruses. They just referred to illness in vague terms and people often died very young of diseases that are now easily treatable. Anyway, Elizabeth stayed with her mother. Only a week after the reunion, she suffered a miscarriage and lost the baby. If I had been there I could have comforted her and we could have tried for more children. But, as a vampire, I could no longer father children and so my only chance at fatherhood was taken from me along with my human life."

Gwen sighed at Connor's last comment. She grieved for the things he had lost when he was changed. Now she understood more clearly why he had reservations about changing her. "How did Elizabeth handle your homecoming?"

"She was frightened of me, because she knew the minute I walked in the door I wasn't the same man who had left for the reunion. She touched my pale cold skin and stared into my glowing eyes like I had the plague. I explained as calmly and carefully as I could what had happened. She wept when she found out and said she couldn't turn her back on me. Unlike Aidan, I was lucky with Elizabeth. Of course, that was to be short lived. You know the rest of the story."

"Connor, it's kind of a weird question, but didn't this happen around the same time as the Salem Witch trials?"

"Yes, it did. But, it wasn't witches in Salem causing mass hysteria and mayhem. Vampires had a lot to do with it."

"So vampires are to blame for the witch trials?" Gwen asked.

"Well, vampires played a major role in what happened."

"I don't understand. How did vampires have anything to do with the witch hunts?"

"Matthias and his vampires exploited the situation to their advantage. You see—the Puritans were a very strict and repressed religious group. Life revolved around work and prayer with little tolerance for anything else. A couple of young Puritan girls were bored and began listening to the amazing tales of voodoo and sorcery from a slave woman who had been brought to Salem from the West Indies. Soon the girls started accusing all kinds of innocent people, including, the slave woman, Tituba, herself, of bewitching them with spells and hallucinations. Of course, the girls were putting on a show for their families and other adults in the community who believed them. They usually accused people they didn't like or folks who had something they wanted such as money or power. Sadly, the whole thing turned into a giant circus and over twenty people died as a result. One man, Giles Corey, was even pressed to death by heavy stones. It was awful."

"Okay, but that still doesn't explain the vampires' involvement," Gwen said.

"Matthias sized up the situation and saw he could use it to his advantage. He and his vampires could easily gain access to the girls and townspeople to influence their emotions, thoughts, and anxieties. Specifically, he wanted to foment their fears. You see, our ability to erase memories and implant false ones can come in really handy when you want to confuse people into believing they've been the victims of a crime. It's also useful to relay this information to the judges who oversee the cases. So much of the hallucinations, bizarre sensory experiences, and hysteria were the result of vampires manipulating human thoughts and feelings. With the town's attention diverted to the witchcraft scandal, and not the unusual disappearance of some of their inhabitants, Matthias was free to grow his coven, while innocent mortals were framed and executed."

"God, that's awful. It must have been torturous for you and your cousins to see all those innocent people die."

"It was and consequently, we grew more cohesive and focused in our goal to annihilate Matthias and his coven. He had power to stop the witch-hunts, but instead indirectly promoted them for his own gain. More than a year after the witch trials, we killed nearly all of his followers, save a few "lucky" ones such as Ignacious and Varanos, who got away."

"What about Matthias? You mentioned before that you couldn't kill him. Any idea what happened to him?"

"No one really knows for sure what happened to him. We heard rumors that he tried rebuilding his coven a couple of times, but was unsuccessful in his choices. Most of those vampires defected to Josef's side once they figured out Matthias' plans."

"Connor did you ever find out who killed Elizabeth?"

"No, I detected an older scent, but it was impossible to determine her murderer at the time. Today I would be more adept at detecting the nuances of the scent as well as other clues, but I was too young in my transformation to figure it out back then. I suppose I'll never really know. But her death was meant to ruin my life and for nearly a century, it did. If I ever find out who killed her, I'll make it my mission to return the favor."

The sound of rumbling was noticeable outside. The storms would soon be upon them. Connor instinctively pulled Gwen closer to him, her head nestled near his.

"I'm curious, what color were your eyes before the change?" Gwen asked, slurring her words from fatigue that was quickly invading her consciousness.

"They were grayish-blue like yours."

"How come Matthias had scarlet-red eyes, while you have luminescent blue ones?"

"It has to do with vampire age. As vampires age their irises grow darker until they become either bright orange or red. It varies with the vampire."

"Would I be strong like you if I were to become immortal?"

"A vampire's strength is related to the age of his or her sire as well as the number of years the vampire lives as an immortal. Because an ancient sired me, I'm freakishly strong for a middle-aged vampire. You'd be fairly strong because of my age, but in comparison to me you would be weaker because your sire isn't ancient yet. It takes at least a thousand years to be considered ancient in the vampire world. I hope that makes sense. It can be a little confusing."

"So I won't be as strong as you. That's disappointing," she said.

Connor laughed a moment. "Sorry Love, I didn't make the rules. Besides you may find you are faster than I, or better at reading minds. We won't know your strengths unless you undergo the change so it's an empirical question at this point."

"Are there a lot of vampires your age and older?"

"Not really. A number of young vampires wind up being killed by older, stronger vampires for their acts of stupidity or lack of training. If a young vampire starts wreaking havoc and creating chaos, he or she risks exposing the rest of us. I suppose it's almost a form of Social Darwinism within the immortal community. I feel bad for young vampires, but I don't have the time to worry about training them when I have other things to deal with. Marcus was the one notable exception to the rule. His sire abandoned him fairly soon after he was made and had it not been for me, Marcus would have gotten himself killed. I took him under my wing and things went well for him. He was just a kid killed long before he hit his stride."

"How old was Marcus?" she asked, feeling sleepier by the second, her eyelids shut as she spoke.

"He was a year or so shy of a hundred."

"If you think he was a kid, what do you think of me?" she asked, curious.

"Hell, you're just a baby," he said, stroking her hair with his cold fingers.

"Most people in society wouldn't agree with you on that," Gwen said, failing to suppress laughter.

"Well when you've lived as long as I have, trust me, forty is nothing."

"I'm not forty! At least not yet."

Connor laughed. "You humans are so obsessed with age. It means nothing, really."

"It does when you have death to look forward to," Gwen said.

"Gwenevere, I know it may be hard for you to understand, but death isn't the worst outcome in life. I've experienced things that are more agonizing than death and would rather have taken the great dirt nap centuries ago than endure the pain of living. But, I know what you are trying to say."

Gwen tried to stifle a yawn, but was unsuccessful. "I don't think I can keep my head up anymore."

"It's okay, you need rest. Besides, the storm is going to be ugly and I'd just as soon you'd be asleep through it. Sweet dreams—"

Gwen grabbed Connor's arms draping them around her, before shutting her eyes for the night.

Chapter 16

Connor drove Gwen home late the following afternoon. Evidence of last night's storm was readily apparent in the city's streets, which were littered with tree limbs and branches. Gwen stared out her kitchen window looking at debris strewn about the yard lamenting the fact that the weekend was nearly over. Connor opened the front door and brought her suitcase into the living room. Gwen was so lost in thought she didn't notice him approach her.

"Gwen?" he said, gently taking her hand in his.

"Yes?" She turned to look at him.

"You okay?"

"Yes, I'm okay."

"You seem a little distracted today," he pressed.

"I guess it's just the enormity of what you told me last night," she whispered, as she glanced at him.

"Maybe I should have waited a little longer," regret in his tone.

"Don't be silly, I'm glad you told me. It means you're finally comfortable being yourself with me."

A beautiful smile spread across his sultry lips.

"Will you be staying with me tonight?" she asked.

"No, I'm needed at the club. Aidan will be here before I leave."

Gwen pursed her lips as she momentarily shifted her gaze away from Connor's eyes to the lawn outside the window.

"Gwen, if you'd rather I change my plans, I'll contact Aidan and call it off."

"No, that's unnecessary. You go and take care of things."

"You sure?"

"Yes."

"You know I'm only a call away."

"I know." She grinned at him, attempting to assuage his concerns.

A knock at the door interrupted their conversation. Connor strolled over to Gwen's front door examining the figure outside the stained glass window.

"It's Aidan," he said, before quickly opening the door allowing his cousin access. Aidan and Connor briefly exchanged glances before Aidan shifted his focus to Gwen.

"Gwen, how are you this afternoon?" Aidan asked.

"I'm good. How about you?" she asked, smiling at the stunning young vampire who could easily be confused for a marble statue of a Roman God.

"Great," he mumbled, flatly.

"Aidan, Lucinda told me you both detected an old scent on the porch and near Gwen's window. Do you have any idea who the scent belongs to?" Connor asked with his arms folded across his chest. Gwen noticed how rigid his body appeared, despite the relaxed expression on his face.

Aidan shook his head back and forth. "Unfortunately, I haven't a clue who the scent belongs to. It's definitely old, but I can't be of more help than that. Sorry to disappoint you."

"That's alright. Maybe Derrick will recognize it. When is he coming over?" Connor inquired.

"Tomorrow night," Aidan said.

"Good. Well, I'll go over to club now and take care of things for tonight. You're going to keep watch till the morning?"

"Yes, and Derrick has agreed to keep watch tomorrow night if you're busy," Aidan said, his eyes darting back and forth between Gwen and Connor.

"I'll be here in the morning before Gwen wakes up."

"Don't worry cousin, I've got it covered. Besides, I brought a couple of movies in case Gwen gets bored," Aidan said, with an impish grin.

Aidan and Connor stared at one another for a moment in silence, before Connor choked back a laugh, shaking his head.

"What?" Gwen asked, wondering what she was missing.

"Oh, nothing. Aidan has interesting taste in movies. Well, I'd better get going." Connor turned to Gwen pulling her in his arms before he kissed her forehead.

"Have a good night," she whispered

"You, too," Connor said, as he pulled away from her and swiftly exited the house.

For a few moments Gwen stood with a vacant stare on her face, wondering why she suddenly felt so lonely. She had just spent the weekend with Connor and knew logically that it was healthy to have her space apart from him. Yet, she missed him beyond words and she wondered why. Gwen wasn't one of those needy types and this feeling bothered her.

"Gwen?" Aidan asked, deliberately waving his hand back and forth in front of her eyes.

Gwen abruptly jerked her head. "Yes?"

"You were lost in thought there. You alright?"

"Yes— I don't know what's wrong with me. It's stupid really," she replied, blushing with embarrassment.

Aidan appraised Gwen carefully. He moved towards her and gently touched the wounds on her neck with his cold fingers. Gwen felt tiny impulses travel from the bite marks down her arms and torso. She reflexively shivered, before the sensation passed.

"Don't worry, Gwen, what you're experiencing is part of the longing. It's a normal reaction to the bite."

"It is?" she asked, wide-eyed.

"Yes, there's nothing wrong with you. Longing for him is all a part of it."

"Oh— good so I'm not losing it after all," Gwen said, relieved.

Aidan laughed for a few minutes. "Well, I don't know about that. But, missing him even when you've spent several days together is normal."

"So what causes the longing?"

"It's some sort of neurotoxin that is emitted when you are bitten. It's responsible for the feelings of euphoria you experience, as well as the other side effects. You see the bite is the first part of the process in the transformation into becoming an immortal."

"And this neurotoxin lingers in the body for days or weeks?" she asked.

"Yes. But, some mortals like you experience a stronger reaction. The time course varies among humans."

"Is there any link between a mortal's reaction to the neurotoxin and his or her response to the full transformation?" she asked, examining the brilliant color of his azure eyes in contrast to his alabaster skin.

"I don't know myself since I've never changed anyone, but I've heard stories of *familiars* with strong reactions to the neurotoxin later being unusually gifted vampires."

"What do you mean?" she said, her brows knitted in concentration.

"Well, there are stories of vampires with rare abilities that the majority don't possess. Like the ability to influence thoughts and memories without touch, prophetic dreams, that sort of thing."

"Have you ever met a vampire with those abilities?"

"No, not me personally. But, I have heard about them. Of course, it's possible that these are just tall tales. Anyway, I hope you feel better knowing the feelings you're experiencing are normal for *familiars*."

"Actually I do. Thanks."

"So you want to watch one of the movies I brought?" he asked, changing the topic.

"Sure, what did you have in mind?"

Aidan handed Gwen a stack of movies. Gwen scanned the titles of each noting they were all horror movies and most of them were about werewolves. She looked at him, with one eyebrow cocked to the side.

"What, you have something against werewolves?" Aidan asked.

Gwen shook her head in disbelief. "What is it with you and Connor and horror movies. How about a comedy for a change?"

"Nah, I don't like fiction that much."

Gwen stared at him unblinking. "You're not saying what I think you're saying?"

Aidan didn't speak; he simply winked at her.

Gwen sighed to herself a moment before picking up one of the movies and loading it into the DVD player. She decided not to press the issue, because on some level she didn't want to know.

A couple of hours later, after the movie ended Aidan sat on the loveseat with a far away look on his face.

"What are you thinking about if I might ask?" Gwen inquired.

"Nothing in particular. Just relaxed. I like spending time with you. You're such a kind person."

"Thanks Aidan." Gwen blushed a little. "Do you mind if I ask you a question?"

Aidan looked at Gwen. "No, go for it."

"I know you've worked with children as a mentor for many years. Do they figure out that you're a vampire?"

Aidan produced a half-smile. "Most do. Others just think I'm really *unique.*"

"Do the ones that figure it out become frightened of you?" she asked, her expression serious.

"Only once did a child become frightened of me until he realized after a few more visits that I would never harm him. The rest think of me as some sort of superhero, if you can believe it. I've learned that children quickly pick up the motives of people around them, and these kids knew I wanted to protect them and were more than willing to overlook my abilities."

"That's encouraging," Gwen said, with a heavy sigh.

"Your worried about Andy aren't you?"

"Yes."

Aidan smiled at Gwen. "Andy knows you love him, Gwen. That love won't change if you become immortal and Andy will pick up on that. And your being repulsed by his blood, will mean that he has nothing to fear from you."

"I just don't want him to fear me if I choose to become immortal?"

"Based on my vast experience with children, I'd say he'll be okay with you. You'd just have to show him that you're still you, and any fear he might fleetingly experience will vanish. I hope this helps."

"Yes, it helps a lot, actually. Thank you, Aidan."

"No thanks required. I'm going to go and hang out on your porch the rest of the night. Relax and get some rest. You look like you could use it," he said.

"You're right, I wiped out. Have a good night."

"You too."

Gwen collapsed in bed. A small smile of contentment spread across her face when she thought of the events of the weekend. Moments later she drifted off to sleep.

Towards the early morning, Gwen's peaceful slumber dissipated only to be replaced with a terrifying nightmare. She saw a man outside her house crouched below the windowpane of the kitchen. He was chalky white with crimson-colored eyes and a menacing smile. His nostrils visibly flared as he sniffed at the window; his lips thin and drawn back over his prominent teeth. His canines slowly descended into inch-long fangs that protruded outside of his mouth. He crept around the porch following the scent until he reached the window outside her bedroom. Reaching up with his gnarled hand, the vampire scratched at the glass with fingernails shaped like talons. The glass splintered into several small jagged lines that fanned out from the center like those of a spider's web. Under the pressure of his nails the glass continued to fracture into small shards that would eventually allow him access inside her room.

Gwen woke up screaming as loudly as her vocal chords would permit. Tears slid down her face in torrents and her sheets and body were sopping wet. In the dark, she clawed at the air trying to defend herself against the creature with scarlet eyes and daggers for nails. Something rock-solid and cold grabbed her, which made Gwen flinch even more hysterically. She fought against the entity trying to immobilize her, beating it with her fists.

"Gwen, it's me! Connor!" he yelled, trying to be heard over her frantic screams.

Gwen continued to shriek in panic, her efforts to evade Connor futile.

"Connor, turn on the lights, she still thinks she's dreaming," Aidan shouted from across the room.

Connor held Gwen with one hand and turned on the light by the bed with the other. She stopped screaming and fighting when she saw his face looking calmly into hers. Her heart, which was thunderously pounding in her chest, altered its rhythm, as did her respiration. Gwen's eyes darted around the room anxiously looking for any sign of the ancient immortal, but there was no evidence of his presence. She felt Connor gently release her arms. When she looked down at her wrists she noticed purple spots forming where she had tried to beat him. No doubt those spots would swell and become prominent bruises.

"Connor, did you see him?" she asked, her voice small and meek like a child's.

"Who, Gwenevere?" Connor's brilliant eyes focused on her cloudy bloodshot ones.

"The vampire with the scarlet eyes and talons for fingernails. He was clawing through the glass of my window to get into my room," she said, still trying to catch her breath.

"No, Love, there is no one here."

"Are you sure?" she asked, frightened.

"Yes, Aidan's been here all night and I just got in a few minutes ago. We both would have smelled an immortal and sensed his presence immediately."

"But—" she whispered, feeling slightly less anxious with each passing minute. Gwen looked over at the window seeing the glass was fully intact on both sides of the pane. Sunlight was barely visible above the tree line, suggesting dawn was near.

"Gwen, tell us about your nightmare?" Aidan asked, now closer to the bed where she sat with Connor whose arm was tightly wrapped around her waist.

"Aidan, I don't know if now is the time—," Connor said.

Gwen interrupted him. "No, it's okay, I want to tell you both while it's still fresh in my mind. I saw an ancient vampire with dark red eyes, inch long canine fangs, and sharp fingernails creep along the windows in the back of my house till he found my window. He used his nails to crack the glass trying to invade the house."

Aidan looked at Connor.

"What do you think it means?" Gwen asked, searching Connor's face for clues as to what he was thinking.

"Honestly, Gwenevere, I have no idea. I think it's just a dream and nothing more," Connor said, stroking the skin of Gwen's neck, sending soothing sensations down her skin and spine.

"I'm in agreement. There is nothing specific or unique about the immortal in your dream to suggest otherwise," Aidan stated.

Gwen sat on the bed mystified. She was sure the dream had meant something. Gwen heard Aidan say something to Connor about having to feed, but she didn't hear him leave. Gwen was still freaked out by the strange nightmare. She couldn't get the face of the ancient vampire out of her mind. Everything about him terrified her.

"Gwen, you're soaked. Why don't you take a shower and I'll change your sheets, okay?"

She searched Connor's striking face and delicate features. Gwen could see the compassion and concern in his glowing eyes. She nodded her head and climbed out of bed. Opening the door to the linen closet she pulled out clean sheets, which she handed to Connor before shutting the door to the bathroom. As she turned on the facet in the tub, images of the vampire flitted through her mind. Gwen saw the ominous look in his eyes, the razor sharp teeth jutting out from his lips, and the creepy way he moved. Tears welled up in her eyes and she peeled her wet nightgown off of her body, dropping it to the floor. Gwen climbed into the tub, reflexively grabbing a washcloth and bath gel. She quickly lathered her body scrubbing her skin to remove the sweat that had clung to her only moments earlier. She couldn't stop thinking about the dream, and she started to hyperventilate. Images of the ancient vampire frightened her. Gwen decided she needed Connor. She didn't yell out to him. Instead, she concentrated on sending her strongest thought of worry and need to him. Gwen closed her eyes a moment thinking her action foolish, but was pleasantly surprised to feel him suddenly step into the shower behind her. He pulled her body close to his, the coldness of his skin a stark contrast to the heat of the water, sending unusual heat sensations throughout her skin, a phenomenon she knew as psychological heat. Gwen sent out another mental signal wondering if he'd read it. Seconds later she had her answer when she felt him sink his teeth deep into the side of her neck. Familiar feelings of rapture came in waves until all images of the vampire in her dream were forgotten. Gwen watched in fascination as the clear water dripping down the drain suddenly turned red.

Connor surprised Gwen with a large breakfast late in the morning. Although she was weary from lack of sleep and blood loss, the coffee invigorated her and she decided to work a half-day at the university. Connor insisted on following Gwen to work. While she answered email and worked on slides for her classes, Connor hung out at the library. The library had an excellent view of the parking lot and was close to Gwen's office. Connor picked up a couple of periodicals he thought looked interesting and lightly perused them while he surreptitiously examined the human traffic that trekked by the door. Dressed in faded blue jeans and a t-shirt, Connor blended with his surroundings; he could easily be mistaken for a student. By mid-afternoon, Gwen dropped by the library to check in with him. She found Connor with his feet propped up on an ottoman reading an article on blood-borne pathogens and other blood-related disorders. A baseball cap and dark glasses did little to conceal his delicate features. Connor smiled when he saw her and put the article down on the table by his chair. Gwen sat down in an empty seat beside him.

"Getting a lot accomplished today?" he asked, removing the dark sunglasses that were meant to hide his luminous blue eyes.

"Yeah, for the most part. See anything interesting today?" she asked, watching a flock of students pass by.

"No immortals if that's what you mean. Just stressed college students working on projects due next week."

"I suppose that's good," she said, relieved.

"Well, for *you*, yes, but not for your poor students," he said, his devilish eyes sparkling.

Gwen laughed a moment.

"Are you feeling better now? You were pretty upset early this morning."

"A little," she confessed.

"Good, because I *will not* let anything happen to you," he whispered, lightly stroking her leg with his hand.

Gwen grinned at him while she adjusted the scarf she had tied around her neck, pulling it down over the bite marks. Its position had become dislodged with her movements. Connor's eyes briefly scanned the scarf around her neck. Gwen watched his smile slowly fade. She reached over to him, delicately sliding her finger down one of his icy cheeks.

"Connor, don't worry. I'm fine."

He took her hand in his. "Sorry, guess I'm feeling a little guilty about the shower this morning."

"Don't! It was *my* idea," she said emphatically.

Connor studied the outline of her face and doe-shaped eyes.

"So, are you going back to your office?"

"Yes, I've got a couple of things to finish. Oh, and Cindy called. She asked me to stop by and see her on my way home."

"Good, you should see your friend. When are you going?"

"In about an hour. I don't think you'll need to follow me. I should be okay; I'm just going for a brief visit," Gwen said, as she caressed the frigid skin of his palm with her index and middle fingers.

"I'm not crazy about your being out of my sights."

"I know, but I hate to think you feel obligated to watch me everywhere I go."

"It's wise to be vigilant at this point, Gwenevere."

"Hmm, I suppose you're right," she said, noting the sadness in her voice, the loss of freedom a reminder of her human weakness.

"I'll park across the street while you visit with Cindy, so you can have your privacy okay?"

"All right. Well, I'd better get back to my office and finish up."

"Meet me on your way out. I'll be here reading about blood flukes. They are revolting, but terribly fascinating at the same time." Connor smiled sardonically before putting his shades back on and turning his attention to the article in his hands. Gwen shook her head back and forth giggling as she walked away.

When Gwen returned to her office, she noticed the light on her phone was flashing indicating she had messages. She briefly listened to her voicemail before returning the calls. One call in particular, interested her. A colleague in the Criminology department asked if she'd be willing to give a brief talk on psychopaths that Friday in the auditorium. She would be one of four speakers discussing various forms of criminal psychopathology and the talk would be open to the public. Gwen returned her colleague's call accepting his invitation to be a guest speaker. Following that, she finished her projects for the day and left the office. She walked by the library waving to Connor who was already close to the door prepared to leave. They didn't speak as they walked out of the building, just exchanged a brief glance before she got into her Infiniti and he into his Porsche. Within twenty minutes, Gwen pulled into the parking lot of Cindy's school. She looked in the rear view mirror noting the black Porsche parked across the street. Gwen got out of her car and quickly ran to the entrance of the building, where Cindy was waiting with the door wide open.

"Hi, Gwen, come on in," Cindy said, a smile spread across her beautiful face.

Gwen gave Cindy a bear hug before she spoke. "Hey Cindy, it seems like a year since we all went out to dinner. What's new?"

"God, where do I begin? We've added new equipment in the playground, as well as, hired three new teachers to work with the kids. Come take a look at our recreational area, you'll love it," Cindy said, practically skipping toward the back of the school where the playground was situated.

Months earlier, the school's playground had been outdated and sparsely equipped. Gwen remembered it had only contained one swing set and was rather dilapidated. Now, three shiny, new swing sets were installed, including one designed to support the weight of older children. Since the kids in Cindy's school had autism and related developmental disabilities, this new playground would be useful to train play skills as well as provide a nicer recreation area for them to congregate.

"Cindy this is fantastic! Those swing sets are perfect and I'll bet the kids love them."

"Oh, they do! And, I'm also so excited about the new teachers we've hired. Things have really improved here. I might even hire another behavior analyst to oversee things," she said.

"These are big ticket items', did that additional funding from the state finally come through?" Gwen asked.

"No— the state still hasn't given us word on our project yet. The funding for our playground project and staff hiring came from an anonymous donor. Can you believe it? I got a letter a week ago saying a benefactor has decided to give us three hundred thousand dollars. Gosh, I really wish I knew who was behind it. In the very least, I'd like to thank him or her for the generosity."

Gwen's expression was one of surprise mixed with disbelief. "Wow—that's incredible, Cindy! I— don't know what to say," Gwen stammered.

"Yeah, I know. It's just amazing! When I first opened the letter I was sure it was some kind of a joke or prank. But then I saw the check made out to the school and I realized it was serious. It couldn't have come at a better time, too. Our budget was tight and I was worried I was going to have to let a few people go. It's like a miracle!" Cindy cried, with a gleam in her eyes.

"That's wonderful Cindy! And— you really have no idea who gave you the money?"

Cindy shook her head. "Not a clue."

Gwen was fairly certain she knew who had given Cindy the funds for the school. She listened as Cindy talked about the other projects the school was conducting as well as how things were going with her husband and their kids. Gwen was sure the topic of Connor would eventually come up and Cindy didn't disappoint.

"So how are things with Connor?"

Gwen sighed a bit. She desperately wanted to tell Cindy everything that was happening in her life. But, she knew it was impossible. For a moment Gwen thought about what it would be like to be perfectly candid with Cindy about her situation. She could almost imagine what she'd say in her head. *Hi, Cindy I'm in love with a vampire who happens to be over three hundred years old and I'm weighing the pros and cons of becoming a member of "the undead" myself. Oh, and I'm also being stalked by an ancient vampire, who in all probability, wants to kill me.* Gwen suppressed a giggle as she thought about how absurd this would sound from her lips, though she knew it to be true. There was no getting around it; Gwen would have to filter what she would say about Connor. Although Gwen hated lying to people, if she chose to stay with Connor and become a vampire, she'd have to become comfortable with being less than forthcoming about the events and circumstances in her life. Gwen thought that everything in life comes with a trade-off; this one might become hers. "We're great!"

Cindy studied Gwen's expression. "Is it serious?"

Gwen smiled because she could answer this particular question honestly. "Yes, very much so. We spend most of our free time together and we're happy."

"That's fantastic. So has he met Andy, yet?" Cindy asked as she crossed her arms over her chest and sat down at one of the picnic tables on the playground.

"No, but he will in less than two weeks. I'm kind of nervous about the whole thing. I just want it to go well," Gwen said, pulling up a folding chair so that she could sit near Cindy.

"Well, I'm sure it will." Cindy replied.

"I hope so. I'm probably just being hyper-anxious as usual," Gwen said with a sigh.

"No, Gwen, you're just being a cautious parent. Don't worry; it's going to go well. I have a good feeling about it."

"You do?" Gwen asked.

"Yes," Cindy said, reassuringly.

"Well, I suppose you're right. Anyway, we'll soon find out won't we?" Gwen grinned at Cindy.

"Yep, we will."

Just then a mosquito landed on Gwen's leg and she reflexively leaned over to smack her shin. Her effort was rewarded as she saw remnants of dead mosquito when she pulled her hand away from her skin. Unfortunately, when Gwen looked over at Cindy she immediately noticed the worried expression on her friend's face.

"Gwen, did something bite you?" Cindy's brows were knitted.

"What?" Gwen said, alarmed. She pulled the scarf down that had clearly moved when she leaned over to swat the insect on her leg.

"Your neck— you have two small wounds. They look like—bite marks."

"Oh— *those*! They're nothing. I have a couple of bug bites from when I was out the other night," Gwen said, trying to act nonchalant hoping Cindy would buy her lame explanation.

"They look painful."

"No, they don't hurt. They're healing pretty fast."

"You also look a trifle pale. Are you feeling alright?"

"Yes, I'm okay. In fact—I hate to be rude, but I have to get going. I have some things I have to do before the evening is over. Sorry to have to run so soon," Gwen said, carefully pulling her hands close to her sides, so that Cindy wouldn't see the bruises that had formed on her wrists from the morning's battle with the imaginary vampire. It was bad enough that Cindy had noticed Gwen's bite marks; she didn't want her seeing the bruises too. It looked like Gwen had been forcibly restrained and she didn't want Cindy to think Connor was physically harming her. Gwen knew it would be extremely difficult to come up with a rational non-violent explanation for the bruises, given their location.

"Shoot, I wish you could stay longer, we haven't talked alone for a long time."

"I know, I miss that too. Let's have dinner soon. How does that sound?" Gwen asked, getting up from the bench and grabbing her purse. She purposely grabbed the sides of her sundress with her hands, in an effort to partially conceal the purple skin of her wrists.

"Yeah, that would be nice. I'm just so glad I got to see you. Give me a call in a week or so. I know you have a lot going on with Andy coming home, so I won't press you, but when you can, let's get together," Cindy said, in her calm and serene voice.

"Okay, will do. I love you Sweetie," Gwen said, as she hugged Cindy one last time.

"Love you too."

Gwen walked through the school with Cindy to the front door and then quickly ran to her car. She smiled at Cindy one last time before she jumped into the G and fled down the road to her house. Gwen didn't mean to rush out of the school, but she was concerned Cindy would get the wrong impression if she noticed the bruises on Gwen's wrists.

Chapter 17

When Gwen pulled onto the street near her home she spotted a slick black exotic sports car in her driveway. The car was parked sideways making it impossible for her to park next to it. Gwen uttered several obscenities as she parked her car by the curve in front of her house instead of her usual parking place in the driveway. Connor's Porsche followed suit parking just in front of her.

"What's that about a jackass I heard?" Connor quipped as he walked towards her failing to suppress a smile.

"What kind of a jerk parks in your driveway taking up both spaces?" she said.

"The kind of jerk who's been asked to look out for you," Derrick said, strutting towards them. For a moment, he reminded Gwen of a peacock fanning out his feathers.

"I didn't see you there, Derrick," she remarked, turning red. "I'm not trying to be ungrateful, but do you mind telling me why you needed to take up both spaces in my driveway?"

Connor laughed as he eyed Derrick, waiting for his response.

"It's a *Ferrari*, it deserves more than one parking place," Derrick retorted, shaking his blond medium-length mane like a proud lion parading in front of his pride.

"I don't care if it's one of the Presidential limousines. It shouldn't be parked that way in my driveway," Gwen huffed.

"Testy — testy," Derrick said, flashing a pretentious smile.

"Derrick, some things never change. You still think the sun revolves around you," Connor said, shaking his head in disgust.

"That's such a cliché, Lad," Derrick said. "You disappoint me, I would have expected something more creative out of you."

"Doesn't make it any less true." Connor glared at Derrick.

"Not everyone shares your opinion," Derrick said, with a smirk.

"How is Jasmine these days? Still a part of your harem?" Connor asked his eyes narrowed.

Derrick ignored Connor's question, choosing to glower back at him instead.

"Boys, let's not do this. People are beginning to stare," Gwen warned. Although Gwen lived at the end of a quiet cul-de-sac, Derrick's exotic car, as well as the standoff between the two men, was attracting unwanted attention from her neighbors. Some had come out of their homes to gawk.

"Gwen's right, this isn't the time or place for this. Let's go inside and discuss the important issue of the vampire's scent," Connor demanded.

"Fine, but we'll have it out later, cousin, when it's just you and me," Derrick said, through clenched teeth.

"I look forward to it," Connor retorted.

Gwen walked past the black Ferrari quietly admiring its beauty and elegance. She loved sports cars, but didn't feel the need to compliment Derrick on his choice of vehicles; she didn't want to feed his already over-inflated ego. Of course, for a vampire, a Ferrari was a lousy choice for a car since it drew attention to the driver. But, that mattered little to Derrick. Although Gwen wasn't in the habit of diagnosing, she'd say Derrick's was simple; he was what the psychiatric community referred to as a Narcissist Personality Disorder. He seemed to care only for his own needs and little for the needs of others, which included his own family members. He had a malignant sense of entitlement and need for adulation that was insatiable. Initially, his charisma, wit, and intellect made him attractive to mortals and vampires alike, but once they got to know him, his allure quickly wore off. Simply put, Gwen didn't like him. In so many ways, Derrick reminded Gwen of her ex-husband and she didn't feel comfortable being around him.

Connor and Derrick quietly followed Gwen inside the house. Misty and Panda commenced hissing as soon as Derrick crossed the threshold. He mumbled something unpleasant under his breath that Gwen couldn't hear, but Connor glanced at him with a stern expression. Derrick sat on the loveseat opposite the couch where Connor and Gwen seated themselves. Connor snapped his fingers and Panda quickly padded across the wooden floor to greet him. The kitten vigorously rubbed his head against Connor's cold pale fingers. Moments later, Panda gracefully jumped up onto Connor's lap, and plopped down closing his eyes, his purr in full swing about as subtle as small jet engine. Derrick stared at the whole event with little emotion; save for an over-exaggerated eye roll.

"So I assume we're not going to just sit here and watch you play with kittens all day," Derrick said, annoyed.

Connor clenched his fists and his body became rigid. His facial expression was tense and his lips formed a tight rigid line. Gwen lightly touched his arm, as a reminder for him to keep his anger in check. She didn't want to see the two of them get into a brawl; she was pretty sure they'd destroy her house in the process. Connor cleared his throat before speaking. Tactfully, he chose to ignore Derrick's earlier snide remark. "Have you checked the back porch and the windows for the vampire's scent?"

"Yes," Derrick said.

"What do you think?" Connor asked.

"It's ancient and I suspect it's one of Josef's first born immortals. The scent is quite old, nearly as old as Josef himself. Of course, I have been known to be wrong from time to time," he added half-sarcastically.

Connor sat appraising Derrick's thoughts. He looked visibly shaken for a moment, before regaining his composure. "I see. Well, then under the circumstances it would be in all of our best interests if we

204

shut down *The Immortal*."

"Last time I checked, I was still the leader of our coven," Derrick scoffed.

"Derrick, this isn't about you and me, this is about the safety of our coven and the people we—care for. For once, be sensible. We can shut the club down now before anyone else gets hurt."

"You'd like that wouldn't you? You know how important the club is to me. It's not like I have the assets you do with your company," Derrick said, seething with resentment.

Connor shook his head in frustration. "Derrick, I don't know how to respond to that. I have no interest in infringing on your territory; my motives are driven only by concern for our security and welfare. Why must you make this personal?"

"We're not shutting down *The Immortal*. End of story," Derrick said.

"Fine—then any deaths that occur are on your head. It's probably best if you leave now," Connor stated, with steely eyes.

Derrick, oozing animosity, glowered at Connor while he quietly got up and walked out of the house.

"Well, that went well," Gwen, said sarcastically as she listened to the Ferrari's engine spring to life and flee her driveway.

Connor sighed as he leaned back against the couch, his body collapsing into the pillows. "You were right— he is a jackass."

They both broke out in nervous laugher.

"He's so damn jealous of you, it's unbelievable. What is his problem?"

"I don't know. We used to be best friends, Gwenevere. I loved Derrick like he was my brother. Somehow, through the years he's grown bitter and resentful. I don't understand it; I have always looked after him. He's so ungrateful."

"Did Derrick need your help to get the club started?"

"Sort of—" Connor whispered.

Gwen studied his radiant eyes, which momentarily looked lost in thought. "He needed your money didn't he?"

"Yes, he did. I really don't want his business to fail, I just think we're in trouble now and it concerns me."

"Connor have you ever thought about resuming your role as coven leader?" she asked, using her fingers to remove an eyelash that was stuck near the corner of her eye.

"Unfortunately, I have, but Aidan would simply side with Derrick and Lucinda with me. I'd face an uphill battle convincing everyone why I should regain control over the coven after all these years. I think something truly egregious would have to occur for me to usurp Derrick's authority."

"It does sound rather unpleasant."

"It would be and I'd have Aidan ticked off at me for years. Not to mention, Derrick might abandon the coven all together. Of course, on second thought that might not be such a bad thing."

"What would happen if the coven split up?" Gwen asked.

"I don't know. I guess Lucinda would go with me and Aidan would stick with Derrick. Either way, splitting up would weaken us."

"What if it's five of us?" she asked.

Connor smiled at her, stroking the soft skin of her hand. "We'd be an impressive coven with five immortals. Are you trying to tell me something?"

"Not yet, but I'm getting closer to making a decision," she said, grinning at him.

"Whatever, you decide I'll be okay with it you know," he whispered.

"I know." Gwen changed the topic a bit. "Connor, why are you so worried about Derrick's thoughts regarding the immortal outside my house? He said he could be wrong."

Connor pulled Gwen close to him. He gently stroked the ivory skin of her face with his icy fingertips. She felt lightheaded, but tranquil. "Derrick is rarely wrong about these things. Although it's possible, I suppose. Anyway, the older the vampires, the stronger and more powerful they become. A vampire close to Josef's age would be quite formidable to fight."

"But—not impossible right?" she asked, her grayish-blue eyes searching his.

"No—not impossible, just improbable. It would take several of us, together, to subdue and kill an ancient immortal."

Gwen frowned turning her head away from his. She didn't want him to notice her apprehension. Connor touched her chin gently angling her face towards his.

"Gwenevere, don't worry."

"That's kind of — difficult for me. Even, under normal circumstances." Nervous laughter escaped her lips.

"I haven't told the others, but if it becomes absolutely clear this vampire is coming for you, we'll flee the area."

"Connor, what about Andy? And — what would I tell the university?" she asked, concerned.

"Gwenevere, I have money. Real money. We'd leave until things calmed down here. As for Andy I'd hire a teacher to attend to his educational needs so he wouldn't miss anything at school. You'd take a leave of absence from the university citing a family emergency. You could pick where you'd want to live. I'd leave that up to you."

"You've thought it all through haven't you?"

"Yes. I'm not going to play with your life or Andy's." Connor purposely stroked her arm alleviating her anxieties.

Gwen cuddled up next to him, placing her head on his chest. Connor played with her hair lightly caressing her scalp. A sigh escaped Gwen's lips as she felt her body relax collapsing onto his. "Are you sure you're real?" she whispered.

Connor's chest rumbled with laughter. "Yes, as real as a member of the undead can be."

Gwen remembered her earlier conversation with Cindy. "Hey, how come you didn't tell me you gave money to Cindy's school?"

"Well, you didn't ask."

Gwen looked up from his chest into his delicately sculpted face. He was grinning and his gleaming white teeth were nearly blinding in the light.

"Thank you for doing that," she whispered.

"You're more than welcome." Connor moved his hands across Gwen's back pulling her upwards to his face where their lips met.

The rest of the week Connor followed Gwen into work, camping out in the library while she worked. He'd managed to read every volume on blood disorders and infectious diseases, and was starting to work his way through parasitic diseases. Most evenings he'd cook some amazing dinner while he recounted some of the bizarre diseases or parasites he'd read about that day. On the nights Connor couldn't stay, Aidan or Lucinda was by her side. She had grown quite close to the two cousins in the past couple of weeks. Gwen also spoke with Pam and Bridget on several occasions making sure she kept them abreast of activities. She didn't want them to unnecessarily worry about her. Unfortunately, the image of the ancient vampire creeping outside her house haunted her in dreams much of the week. Inexplicably, the dreams became more intense with each passing day. Although Connor and his cousins weren't concerned, Gwen couldn't suppress the feeling that time was running out for all of them. She simply hoped she was wrong.

Friday morning Gwen worked on last minute touches to her presentation on psychopaths. The topic had fascinated her for years, but she was particularly interested in the evidence of neurological dysfunction in psychopaths compared to typical individuals. Among the findings, psychopaths showed significantly less frontal lobe activity compared to individuals without the diagnosis. This under-activity could, in part, explain the impulsivity, impaired judgment, and poor emotion regulation in psychopaths. She had encountered a couple of psychopathic individuals and the experience, had been chilling. These people could lie to your face and yet, seem like some of the most honest and trustworthy people one had ever met. Often quite charming and likeable, one could easily be sucked into their psychopathology until it was too late. Gwen saved the file onto her flash drive as well as emailed herself a copy in case something went wrong with the drive during her presentation. Before leaving her office for the day Gwen gathered a printed copy of her talk and other materials she'd review before giving her presentation that evening. Connor was waiting for her by the door when she reached the library. Like so many days before, they walked in silence until they were out of the building and into the parking lot. She had opted to drive with him to the university that morning so they both got into his black Porsche.

"You nervous about tonight?" Connor asked, as he shifted the gear into reverse and backed out of the parking space.

"Is it that obvious?"

"Well—you didn't say much this morning and that's unlike you. You're normally a chatterbox when you wake up."

"Gee *thanks*," she quipped.

Connor backpedaled. "I didn't mean it in a bad way. I mean you're just more vocal than I am. It makes it easy for me. I don't have a lot of pressure to fill any awkward moments of silence with you."

Gwen regarded him with narrowed eyes aware of her irritation, a two on a scale of one to ten.

"So, am I in the doghouse?" he asked a few minutes into their drive down Twenty-Third Street.

"You better believe it," she said, suppressing a smile that was tugging at the corner of her lips. Gwen's anger with Connor was always short lived. He was simply too amazing a person for her to stay angry with for long. But she couldn't completely drop her angry facade; Gwen didn't think he deserved total clemency right away.

They drove in silence most of the ride home. Gwen stole a few sideward glances in his direction and noted he had a slight smile. She figured he had tapped into her thoughts and knew she wasn't really that upset with him. Of course, Gwen didn't like his prying, but she knew it must have been difficult for him to refrain at times. They pulled into her driveway and Connor fast-forwarded to her side of the car to open the door for her.

"Connor, you used immortal time, what if someone had seen you?"

"I checked it out before we got here. Most of the mortals on your street are at work and the few that are home are preoccupied. We're good," he said, grinning from ear to ear. "Besides, I have to make it up to you right?"

"Well, now that you put it like that, how can I argue?" Gwen giggled.

They walked into Gwen's house and she put her papers on the table. She noticed her answering machine had a message, its bright red light flashing like a beacon. She hit the button to listen to the message and Dan's annoying voice filled the room. He informed Gwen he'd be bringing Andy home the next day. A work emergency had come up and he'd have to fly out to San Francisco within days. He would be dropping Andy off in the early afternoon. Gwen sighed.

"Poor Andy, he's going to be so depressed his dad is cutting his visitation short," she said.

"I'll call Aidan and Lucinda to let them know we'll have to change our plans for Andy's earlier arrival home. Be right back." Connor pulled his cell phone out of the back pocket of his jeans, as he opened the door to the back porch. Gwen heard him speak in muffled tones outside. She scanned the living room observing the mess from weeks of her bustling in and out of the house. Connor opened the door and strolled into the living room where Gwen was sweeping the floor. Her brows were furrowed and she looked deep in thought.

"Gwen, I spoke with my family. Everyone is on board with Andy's homecoming. I'll have to go into the club tonight, but Derrick will be at the symposium keeping watch. Aidan said he'd be ready to tail Andy when he comes home so you needn't worry about your son."

"Thanks," she said her expression one of frustration and concern.

"Gwenevere, what is it?" Connor asked his shimmering eyes focused on her.

"I just feel so overwhelmed, right now. I have this big talk to give in mere hours, the house is a mess, we don't know what this ancient vampire wants, and I still haven't decided what I'm going to do." Gwen dropped her head and combed her fingers nervously through her hair.

Connor walked over to her, taking her in his arms. He whispered in her hair, "Gwenevere, it will all be okay. I'll have some of the club employees stop by and tidy up in here. As for the talk, you're going to be fantastic, and we'll get to the bottom of this immortal's intention soon. Remember what I told you, we could leave at any time. Okay?"

She leaned against Connor, the coolness of his body feeling pleasant against her warm sweaty skin. "Alright. I can do this."

"Yes, you can. Now, why don't you go into your office and look over your notes while I get a maintenance crew to come over?" he said, stroking her back.

Gwen smiled and nodded as she grabbed her notes off the table and walked down the hallway to her office. Connor was right; she would just have to focus on one task at a time. She sat down in her office chair reading over the main points of her talk. Gwen tried to anticipate questions members of the audience might ask and how she'd respond. At one point she heard several people enter the house before she heard the vacuum cleaner running. By the time Gwen finished looked over all the notes for her talk she was amazed to find the house was spotless.

A few members of the cleaning crew were packing up their gear and leaving when she came out of the office.

At four, Gwen showered and changed. She chose one of her nicest suits and hoped she wouldn't sweat too much in it before she made it to the auditorium. Connor had dinner ready to go when Gwen came out of the bedroom and she managed to eat a small portion of it before pushing the plate away from her. Connor briefly glanced at the generous portion of food still left on Gwen's plate before shifting his attention towards her. She had a vacant stare on her face. He moved his chair closer to hers and lightly stroked her back, the rigidity of her posture easing under his touch.

"I wish you could be there." She smiled at him.

"Me too. Trust me, I'd rather be there than at the club. Is anyone taping it? Maybe I can get a copy."

"Actually, yes, I believe the criminology department is taping it," she said.

"Excellent. Then I'll have something to look forward to," he replied smiling.

"Well, I guess I'd better be going. It's already five-thirty and the talk is in an hour. I want to have time to find a decent parking place and to set up my talk. I'm actually the last speaker, but I still want to have everything ready to go when it's time. Will Derrick be at the auditorium when I get there?" she asked.

"I've told him to be there by six so he can meet up with you and let you know where in the audience he'll be seated."

"Okay, I'll I look for the Ferrari, then."

"I'm not sure if he'll be in the Ferrari tonight. It might be the Lambo. You won't be able to miss it. It's a bright metallic orange color. Custom painted of course; only Derrick would be so brash."

"The Lambo?" she asked, confused.

"Lamborghini. He has a thing for exotic Italian cars."

"Why am I not surprised!" she said.

"You know Derrick. He has to announce his presence to the world."

"Did Derrick's personality change after he was made a vampire?" Gwen asked.

"No. He was like that as a mortal man. Always showing off for the ladies while doing his best to intimidate the men. Vampirism simply enhanced his predilections. But, enough talking, you've got a presentation to give and I have a club to manage."

Connor walked Gwen to her car. He kissed her lips softly before opening her car door. Gwen got situated and turned to face him.

"I'll call you later. Knock them dead, okay?" he whispered in his silky voice.

"I will. See you tonight," she said, before closing the door and driving off.

The parking lot was already half-full when Gwen pulled up to the university. She spotted the orange Lamborghini in the back of the faculty lot. She didn't see Derrick by the car, but noticed him standing near the doors of the auditorium. He was impeccably dressed in an expensive custom designed dark gray suit with a garnet colored shirt and silk tie to match. His hair was spiked out in various directions from his head giving him a very modern and sophisticated look. Derrick was obscenely attractive and you could tell he enjoyed all the female attention. Some of the women who walked by him were furtive in their glances, while others were obvious. Gwen winced. If these women knew the kind of man he really was they wouldn't pay him any attention. Then again, there were some women who wouldn't mind. Gwen walked over to him and noticed several women gave her dirty looks as they passed by.

"Hello, Derrick. You look very nice tonight," Gwen said, trying hard not to choke on her words. She wanted things between them to be more pleasant than the last occasion in which they spoke at her house.

"Gwen, you look stunning as usual. How is your spoiled sport of a boyfriend?" Derrick said, the corners of his lips forming into a grin showcasing his sharp white teeth.

Gwen ignored the insult. It wouldn't do her any good to allow Derrick to ensnare her into his pathetic mind games. "He's fine. He said to say hello and that he would check with you later."

Derrick stared at her unblinking a moment. Gwen's playing it cool had caught him off-guard. "Well then, shall we go in?" He opened up his arm with the elbow out, an invitation for her to take his arm so that he could escort her inside the building.

"Let's." Gwen wrapped her arm around his cold rock-hard one. They walked into the auditorium to find most of the seats already filled. Gwen walked with Derrick down to the second row that had been blocked off for speakers and their family members and friends. Her colleague, Matt Wilson, came over to her and introduced himself to Derrick. To Gwen's surprise Derrick was quite cordial during the process. Derrick could be a real jerk, but he did have social graces and could navigate social situations quite well. Derrick took his seat in the second row next to Gwen. Matt quickly approached Gwen asking for her flash drive so that he could load up her presentation into the computer. She pulled the drive out of her purse, handing it to Matt. Gwen scanned the audience; there were only a few vacant seats left. She noticed people continuing to stream in the doors and it wouldn't be long before the symposium was standing room only. The turnout was phenomenal particularly when you considered it was a Friday night in the middle of the summer. A few minutes later, the lights dimmed and the hum of the crowd died.

The Dean of the university made a few opening remarks and handed the microphone over to Gwen's colleague, Matt. Matt welcomed faculty and the public for coming to the symposium on the criminal mind and criminal psychopathology before he made a few jokes designed to lighten the mood of the audience and warm them up for a series of talks. Gwen listened to the first two talks with rapt attention. The third talk was just beginning when Derrick tapped her shoulder.

"Gwen, Jasmine's out front, I'll be back in a moment." Gwen quickly nodded her head and turned her attention back to the guest speaker who was discussing the genetics of criminal psychopathology, specifically as it related to conduct disorder and antisocial personality disorder. Several minutes went by with no sign of Derrick, and Gwen was scheduled to speak next. Gwen heard her name called from the microphone; it was Matt introducing her as the night's last speaker. As he announced the title of her talk, Gwen got out of her seat and strolled towards the podium. She felt her legs become rubbery as she walked and took a deep breath to calm her nerves. She stood behind the podium and said hello to the audience from the microphone in front of her. Matt brought up her slide presentation and handed Gwen the remote control.

Gwen began her talk as she had rehearsed it defining psychopathy, followed by a description of the typical pattern of a person with the disorder, and finally ending with several slides on the neurological and autonomic nervous system data obtained on psychopaths. The anxiety Gwen had experienced prior to the talk had completely dissipated as she became engrossed in discussing the subject. Audience members seemed to be particularly interested in a number of her main points and this positive feedback encouraged her as she continued. She was nearly done with her talk when she inexplicably felt an unusual sensation. It was like a fog had suddenly seized control of her mind and body. Gwen powered her way through the presentation, but her confidence was slightly shaken. The sensation eased and Gwen viewed the audience to see if anyone noticed a brief change in her demeanor, but was relieved to see that there weren't any odd expressions aimed her way. At least not from the people she could see closely. A few members of the audience asked her questions. She was in the middle of answering one of the questions when she felt the weird and uncomfortable sensation take hold of her again. As before she was able to answer the person's question, but it wasn't without a struggle. Applause followed the question and answer period.

Gwen joined the rest of the speaker panel at a table in the center of the room. She looked for Derrick, but he still hadn't returned to his seat. Gwen nervously fidgeted in her chair and her hands were clenched tight into fists by her side. The speaker sitting next to her was answering a question from a member in the audience when suddenly Gwen couldn't hear him or anything else in the room. Frantically, she looked around the auditorium seeing people's mouths moving and gestures that indicated the audience members were laughing. But, for Gwen there was total silence. For a second she thought she might be having a stroke since she couldn't think of another explanation for her sudden deafness. Then she heard him say her name, in her thoughts. *Gwenevere.* His voice had a deep resonance to it that she found strangely appealing. She nervously bit her lip; looking at various sections of the audience for the immortal who was speaking to her until she spotted a man with sunglasses. The pallid figure was sitting in the third row from the back of the room and wore a dark blue baseball cap, a long sleeve shirt, and dark pants. It was the fact that the man wore dark sunglasses in an auditorium at night that struck her as odd. When her eyes finally rested on his face, he slowly removed the spectacles revealing a pair of piercing scarlet-red eyes that were fixed on her, his mouth twisting into the menacing sneer she'd seen in her nightmares. Gwen was transfixed and unable to look away. Yet, she was absolutely terrified and could feel the full ferocity of her heart as it raced inside her body. She wanted desperately to glance away from the vampire, but he seemed to exude a hypnotic power over her that she struggled to defy. It was obvious to Gwen that he wanted her, but to what end and why was unclear. Unblinking, she stared at him hearing him whisper words to her in a language she didn't comprehend. Although Gwen wanted to run, her limbs simply wouldn't cooperate. A surge of fatigue enveloped her like a shroud, rendering her helpless before everything went black.

Chapter 18

Frantic voices surrounded Gwen, jarring her into awareness. Even before she opened her eyes she heard them repeatedly shouting her name. She felt something squeeze her upper arm and a cold hard object pressed deeply into the delicate skin of her limb. Gwen winced in pain from the cuff that was constricting her blood flow. Her eyes fluttered open and she noticed several individuals hovered over her body; concern in their facial expressions. The two paramedics that kneeled on the floor beside her were discussing her blood pressure readings and other vital signs. The men were young, both in their mid-twenties and they smiled reassuringly when she looked in their direction.

"Dr. Ryan, you fainted, but your vitals appear normal. Are you feeling okay?" One of the paramedics asked. Gwen noticed the name, *Tom*, sewn into the man's starched blue shirt.

Gwen stared at Tom for a moment, trying to figure out where she was. When she noticed Matt Wilson, a fellow faculty member standing close by, as well as the Dean and several other familiar faces, Gwen realized she was at the university, but she couldn't remember why? Then she spied the wooden podium in the background and everything came flooding back. Gwen's eyes darted from face to face, searching for Derrick's. She was frightened, but she knew the best tactic for her at this moment was to remain calm so that she could leave the university to find Connor. "Yes — I feel fine, just a little tired I guess. I don't know what happened, must have been my nerves." To Gwen's surprise, the paramedics bought her ridiculous explanation; she'd been certain they were going to question her about taking medication or allergic reactions. Tom helped Gwen sit up, to the relief of her colleagues and the Dean. The Dean briefly mentioned to Gwen that she should consider taking some more time off before the semester began, while Matt congratulated her on giving a great presentation. Gwen smiled and thanked the men for their support, as she scanned the room for Derrick or the ancient immortal, but saw neither of them.

Something frigid and stiff unexpectedly grabbed Gwen's hand in hers, startling her. Gwen looked up to see Derrick kneeling beside her, his expression apologetic and forlorn. She glanced at the individuals around her searching their faces for signs or other indications that they had seen Derrick move at an unnaturally rapid pace, but they seemed oblivious to his sudden presence. Derrick moved closer to Gwen, whispering in her ear. "Gwen I'm taking you to Connor's. He's left the club and is on his way home. Can you walk?"

"Yes, but please stay close. I don't completely trust my legs at this point," she said, softly while clutching onto his arm. Emotions she didn't completely understand welled up inside of her and she feared an outburst in public. "Derrick, get me out of here," she pleaded.

Derrick quickly hoisted Gwen up as if she weighed only ten pounds and assisted her out the door of the auditorium. Gwen thanked Matt for the opportunity to present the talk as well as said goodnight to the rest of the panel and the Dean before leaving. Once safely outside of the building, tears streamed down Gwen's face as Derrick walked her to his car. Gwen continued to cry as Derrick drove towards the beach, the gravity of the ancient vampire's bold actions finally hitting her.

"Gwen, I'm so sorry. You have to believe me; I didn't detect anything unusual until I came back into the auditorium when I saw you had fainted."

"Oh, my God, all those people saw what happened to me?" she said, mortified.

"Other than fainting, I doubt they saw anything."

"You didn't see the immortal?" she asked, incredulous.

"No, I didn't see anything or detect his scent until after he'd fled," Derrick replied, with a sigh. "Again, I'm so sorry. I went out to speak with Jasmine for what seemed like a few minutes and the next thing I knew you had blacked out."

Gwen bit her tongue to hold back the anger she felt towards Derrick. He had abandoned her when he was supposed to be protecting her inside the auditorium. Gwen wanted to lash out at him, but she knew Derrick had it coming from Connor and she refrained from saying what she was thinking. It was likely Derrick knew, anyway, from the obsequious manner in which he was currently treating her. The Lamborghini pulled into Connor's driveway. Connor was waiting for them and quickly rushed to Gwen's door opening it and helping her get out of the car. She pulled Connor close to her, draping her arms around his icy torso while her head rested near his chest. They hugged for a few moments before walking inside the house, Derrick trailing behind them. Wide-eyed with worry, Connor stared into Gwen's red-rimmed bloodshot eyes; the lashes still wet from her tears.

"What happened, Gwenevere?" Connor asked, in a whisper.

"Derrick didn't tell you?" she asked, surprise in her tone.

Connor's eyes shifted from Gwen's face to Derrick's eyes. "No, I just received a voicemail that I was to meet you back at the house right away. What's going on?"

Gwen explained, in detail, the series of events that had occurred during her talk. As she recounted her story she noticed that Connor's posture and expression became more rigid with each new detail. When she mentioned the part where she couldn't hear anything, he stared at her transfixed for a few moments, his mouth gaping open.

"Let me get this straight, you were deaf?" Connor asked, his eyebrows rose as he stared at her in disbelief.

"Yes, there was absolute silence. I observed people laughing and talking, but not a sound came out of their lips. Then I heard *him* talk to me," she said, examining the details of Connor's angelic face.

"What did he say?" Connor asked.

"He said my name clearly in English, but the rest of his words were in a foreign language. It sounded Slavic, but I can't be sure of its origin. He looked beautiful like you and your cousins, but his eyes were almost ruby red and his mouth formed a demented grotesque smile that terrified me." Gwen reflexively shuddered and Connor pulled her close to him.

"Where were you while this happened, Derrick?" Connor eyes formed narrow slits.

Derrick's gaze shifted from Connor to the floor. "I went outside to speak with Jasmine. I was only gone a few minutes, I assure you. When I came back into the auditorium, Gwen had fainted and was on the floor surrounded by university personnel and paramedics."

Connor's pupils flared and he stood up from the couch, in a semi-crouching position. He spoke through clenched teeth. "You left Gwenevere alone, when I specifically asked you to keep her in your sight?"

Derrick began backing away towards the front door. "Connor, I feel terrible about it, but everything worked out okay. You see? Gwenevere is in one piece. Come on, Lad; let's not get into a fray."

"You arrogant self-serving bastard, it's too late for your useless apologies. She could have been killed," Connor snarled. With that he lunged for Derrick's throat with his hands knocking Derrick into the wall that separated the living room from the dining room. The sheetrock easily shattered under the weight of the vampires. Connor's fangs were fully extended and he brutally bit into Derrick's shoulder ripping flesh in the process. Derrick growled and managed to force Connor off him, flinging him across the room. Connor's head slammed into the heavy oak dining room table splitting the wood in several places; blanketing the floor with wooden splinters. Connor got up and resumed a crouching position creeping towards Derrick, his eyes filled with rage. Derrick snarled at him in an inhuman voice warning Connor to back off, but it was futile. Connor was livid and unwilling to comply. Connor was fast and Gwen barely noticed as he tackled Derrick to the ground, forcing him into a headlock. Gwen panicked; it looked like Connor was going to snap Derrick's neck. As angry as Gwen was with

Derrick she didn't want him dead, and she knew Connor would never forgive himself once it was over.

"Connor! No!" she screamed.

Suddenly, Gwen noticed two flashes of movement that descended upon Connor and Derrick. The movements were barely perceptible to Gwen. When the movement stopped, she noticed Aidan and Lucinda were standing at the end of the room with Connor pinned against the wall. He was snarling and trying desperately to get past them to Derrick, who was sitting on the floor bleeding and badly wounded. White powder from the sheetrock coated the wooden floor as well as Derrick's dark gray suit. Derrick stood up staring at Connor, his mouth agape.

"What happened here?" Lucinda demanded, her eyes shifting back and forth between Connor and Derrick.

There was silence as they communicated telepathically among each other.

"You son of a bitch! How you could leave her alone like that?" Aidan shouted at Derrick. "You disgust me!" Gwen was surprised to hear Aidan turn on his brother. She had a soft spot for Aidan and it appeared the feeling was mutual.

"Derrick, what the hell were you thinking?" Lucinda asked.

"Lucinda, as usual, he wasn't thinking about anyone except himself," Connor retorted in a more human-sounding voice. Although it was clear that Connor was furious with Derrick, his fight with Derrick was over for the moment and Aidan and Lucinda released their hold on him.

"I really didn't mean to be so careless. I underestimated the ancient's motives. I'm so sorry, you have no idea how much I regret my actions." Derrick bowed his head at Connor, Gwen, and the others. His apology seemed genuine and he looked humiliated.

The room fell silent a few moments before Lucinda spoke. "Connor, what are we going to do?" To Gwen, it appeared that Derrick's position as coven leader was in jeopardy.

Connor sighed as he surveyed the massive damage in his house. "We need at least two of us to be with Gwenevere at all times now. I don't think any of us could kill this immortal alone. He has abilities we lack and it's best if Gwenevere and I make plans to leave the area.

Gwenevere, do you agree?" Connor asked, as he approached her. She was sitting in the corner of the sofa with a blanket wrapped tightly around her. She nervously swept strands of hair away from her face as she looked at him.

"Yes, but what about Andy? He doesn't know you and he won't understand why we're leaving the area. I wish we could leave tomorrow, but I think we'll need a little time to prepare," Gwen said, looking intently at Connor.

"You're right. We have a lot to consider before we leave. Andy comes home tomorrow and we'll be waiting for him. Aidan and Lucinda, I need to know your schedules so there will always be two of us with Gwen and Andy. Of course, Andy won't know what to make of us, so we have to keep him entertained as well as safe."

"I'll take care of Andy. You know kids love me." Aidan smiled confidently, before winking at Gwen who produced a small smile of gratitude in return.

"When will you leave?" Lucinda asked.

"By the end of the week, at the latest. I'll have to get my finances in order and make arrangements. Gwenevere and I will discuss where we'll relocate and how to handle the administration at her workplace," Connor replied.

"Connor, I want to help," Derrick said.

"I think you've done enough." Connor glanced away angrily from Derrick towards Gwen.

"Connor, give him a break. He's contrite. It won't happen again," Aidan huffed.

"Why should I trust him, Aidan?" Connor asked, folding his arms across his chest.

"Because he's blood and our coven leader, that's why," Aidan answered, sarcasm in his tone.

"He's not our original coven leader. I think Connor should take over the coven," Lucinda said, standing defiantly by Connor's side.

"This isn't the time to discuss family business. Aidan, I'm sorry, but I cannot put my trust in Derrick to protect Gwenevere and her son. Derrick, you can help, but only if Lucinda or Aidan are also present."

"Fine. Well, if I'm not currently needed here, I'm leaving," Derrick scowled as he marched out of the house slamming the door behind him.

Aidan gave Connor a nasty look, but walked over to Gwen, and lightly touched her shoulder. She looked up at him smiling briefly before leaning her head back against the couch. Aidan quickly fled, likely following his brother home.

"Connor I'm going to stay in your guest room tonight. That way we're both here with Gwen. I suggest you call a general contractor about the house damage tomorrow. It looks like a small tornado touched down in your living room. Good night, Gwen," Lucinda said, before gracefully walking out of the room.

Connor laughed a moment in response to Lucinda's remark. The damage was significant and even Connor had to acknowledge he'd lost control. Connor held out his hand to Gwen who was sitting on the couch pensively. She placed her hand in his and they ambled to his bedroom where Gwen climbed into bed. Connor slid under the covers moving close behind her; wrapping his arms around her body. Gwen replayed the events of the night over and over searching for any missing clue or piece of information that might be helpful, but nothing came of it. Instead she lay there sleepless consumed by anger. The more she thought about the ancient vampire's deliberate attempt to frighten and disarm her the more furious she became. Gwen welcomed the anger. Another emotion Gwen failed to identify began gnawing at her. Connor, wide-awake and aware of Gwen's thoughts, rubbed her shoulders for several minutes until her heart rate slowed and her muscles slackened. Gwen turned to face him.

"Connor, I think I've made my decision." She looked into his eyes wondering if he knew what she was thinking. He smiled tenderly at her.

"You need to be certain," he whispered.

"When will I know for sure?"

"You know I can't answer that, Gwenevere. Only you will know," he whispered, as he caressed her hair, lightly tugging on some of the strands.

"I have worked many years to gain my independence and strength and I'm not willing to relinquish that to this immortal, or anyone," she said with conviction.

Connor smiled briefly. "That's my girl."

As Gwen lay there next to him she examined the vibrant blue color of Connor's veins near his wrist. Gwen had never really noticed them before. She lightly compressed the skin over his wrist with her fingers, watching changes in the appearance of the blood flow. A pleasant salty odor wafted off of his skin. Reflexively, she started to kiss the delicate skin near his wrists, inhaling the powerful scent. Gwen felt this undeniable urge to taste the blood in his veins. While she engaged in an internal monologue arguing every logical reason why she shouldn't drink his blood, her actions were not dissuaded. Instinctively, Gwen opened her mouth and bit down with her canines into Connor's wrist, but her teeth weren't sharp enough to pierce his hard skin. Gwen recoiled from him mortified by her actions. To her relief Connor didn't laugh or pull away from her. Rather, he surprised her by biting into his wrist ripping the skin and veins, allowing the blood to flow freely down his hand. He then placed his wrist in front of her mouth. Gwen wasn't sure what she should do. She glanced into his eyes for answers, but soon could only focus on the fragrant scent of the warm red liquid dripping in front of her. Hesitant at first, she slowly pulled Connor's wrist to her lips and tasted a small drop of blood. To her amazement she realized she really enjoyed the taste of his blood and reflexively sucked on his veins for more. Gwen wondered why she didn't feel repulsed by her actions. Then it occurred to her that the emotion she had struggled to identify earlier wasn't an emotion at all, but a *need*. *Hunger*! Her longing for the change was growing and she felt a renewed sense of strength and power from drinking Connor's blood. After several minutes, Connor gently removed his wrist from Gwen's hungry mouth and pulled her close to him. He lightly unbuttoned her blouse exposing her chest before he sank his fangs deep into a vein above one of her breasts.

The next day Connor and Gwen arrived at her house early afternoon to prepare for Andy's homecoming. They had stopped at the store earlier to pick up some groceries along with a few new electronics that Andy would enjoy. Connor wasn't sure what Andy would like so he bought him the most expensive and versatile video gaming system the store had stocked, along with all the accompanying games that went with the system. Gwen was stunned when she saw the bill, but

Connor didn't seem the least bit concerned. He simply grinned and continued shopping. Gwen assumed that he was a bit nervous about meeting Andy and wanted to make a good impression. Connor hadn't said much that morning and she wondered if it had anything to do with what happened the previous night.

Gwen heard a knock at the front door and quickly sprang from the couch to answer it. Glancing through the stained glass window she instantly recognized the woman with the beautiful heart-shaped face and long brown curls. Gwen opened the door and hugged the young woman who had become an unlikely friend.

"Lucinda, thanks for coming," Gwen said.

Lucinda's pupils enlarged as she focused on the details of Gwen's face. Silently she reached out with an icy cold finger to trace the delicate bones of Gwen's neck, cheeks, and lips. Gwen felt the encounter a bit too intimate to be comfortable and was slightly unnerved. Gwen stared at Lucinda bewildered by the vampire's actions. She also wondered why Lucinda's skin didn't feel quite as cold as it normally did. Just then, Connor walked down the hallway and into the foyer where Gwen and Lucinda were standing. His eyes rested on Lucinda's before she addressed him. "When?" Lucinda asked.

"Last night," he said, his eyes downcast, with a hint of guilt.

"Then you've made your choice?" Lucinda asked, smiling as she gazed into Gwen's eyes.

"I — don't know yet. I'm still not quite sure what I want to do."

"Oh—," Lucinda said, a soft lilt in her voice.

"Lucinda, it just happened. The longing appears to be greater in Gwen than I've seen in other mortals," Connor said.

"Indeed, if she drank from you, the longing will only grow stronger," Lucinda warned.

"It will?" Gwen asked, surprised. "I don't understand."

"Gwen, why did you drink Connor's blood last night?" Lucinda asked.

"I don't know. I wish I could give you a logical explanation, but I can't. We were lying close together and I noticed a powerful and inviting scent coming from his skin. I realized the scent was coming from the veins near his wrist. Soon, it was all I could think about and I wanted to know what it tasted like. When I finally did drink the blood I felt physically and mentally stronger than ever before."

Lucinda glanced at Connor. "Gwen's true nature is revealing itself, cousin."

"Gwen's not a killer, Lucinda."

"No, not yet. But, she has the instincts, Connor. On some level you've always known it," Lucinda replied.

"Well, what does that mean? Am I becoming a vampire?" Gwen asked, concerned, as she still wasn't certain she wanted immortality.

"Gwenevere, until I've nearly drained you and then had you drink our blood merged together the transformation won't be complete. You can still stay mortal, if you choose, at this point. You haven't crossed over, yet."

"That's true. But, each time you drink blood your body will undergo more changes making you less human in the process. Have you noticed you look different today?" Lucinda asked.

"What changes? I don't see anything different in my body today that wasn't there yesterday." Gwen cocked her head to the side looking at Lucinda like she was delusional.

"Your skin is cooler to the touch and your eyes are a brighter shade of gray," Lucinda remarked. "If you don't believe me, look for yourself."

Gwen walked over to the mirror and observed her reflection. She was much paler today than yesterday and her eyes had definitely lightened in color. They were almost blue, instead of her usual dark gray. Gwen walked down the hallway to her bathroom where she grabbed a thermometer from underneath the sink that she placed in her mouth. She rejoined Connor and Lucinda in the foyer while she patiently waited for the thermometer's digital tone to signal when her temperature had been calculated. Gwen handed the thermometer to Connor for him to read it.

Connor cleared his throat as if reported the reading. "Ninety-five degrees."

Gwen was stunned. "That can't be right! I'm always a solid ninety-eight point six degrees, unless I'm sick."

"You want to check it again?" Lucinda asked.

"Yes," Gwen huffed as if she didn't believe the reading.

A few moments later the thermometer signaled it had a new reading and she looked down at the digital number it displayed in dark red numerals. Ninety-five degrees just like the first measurement. "My core body temperature is colder. I can't believe it," she said in disbelief.

"Gwenevere, you are not a vampire. At least not yet," Connor said.

"But, I'm not completely human, either, am I?" Gwen asked.

"No, you're in a hybrid stage," Connor said, guilt in his expression. "I should never have let you drink from me last night."

"You said I could still stay mortal. How?" Gwen asked, her voice inflections rising sharply.

"As long as the transformation is never completed, eventually the longing will fade and your body will return to normal. There isn't enough of the neurotoxin in your system to override your human cells," Lucinda explained.

Gwen sighed with relief. Yet, she knew she couldn't remain indecisive for much longer. "Well, hopefully Andy won't notice anything."

"We're the ones that he'll find strange Gwen. You have nothing to worry about," Connor stated.

An hour later, there was a knock at the door. This time it was Andy with Dan. As soon as Gwen opened the door Andy rushed into her arms.

"Hi Mom! Are you glad to see me?" Andy asked, with a large smile that spread across his angelic face.

"Of course, Baby. I'm very happy to have you home." Gwen wrapped her arms tightly around Andy as a smile spread across her face. She loved how wonderful he smelled and the soft feel of his skin near hers.

"Mom, you're crushing me. Not so tight. Did you grow muscles while I was away?" Andy asked, giggling.

Gwen flashed him a mischievous grin. "Could be! Want to arm wrestle?"

"Nah, I don't want to injure you," Andy said with a grin.

Gwen laughed for a moment before she stood up. Connor and Lucinda walked over to greet Andy, while Dan stood silent in the background appraising them.

"Andy, I'd like you meet two of my new friends. This is Mr. Connor

Blake and Ms. Lucinda Blackmore."

"Pleased to meet you, both," Andy said, smiling in their direction.

Lucinda's eyes sparkled as she stared at the little boy, while Connor walked over and shook Andy's hand.

"I've heard great things about you Andy. I hope we can be friends." Gwen could tell that Connor had used his ability to ease any misgivings Andy might have had, as the little boy appeared absolutely calm. "Andy, your Mom says you love video games. Would you like to play with the one she bought for you?" Connor asked, winking at Gwen.

"Yeah, that would be great!" Andy blurted-out, excitedly rushing to the television set where Connor had already hooked up the gaming console.

Connor briefly shifted his attention to Dan whose eyes were narrowed into slits as he surveyed Connor and Lucinda with a look of suspicion.

"Hello, I'm Connor," Connor said as he walked over to Dan and produced his hand for Dan to shake, but Dan simply nodded and kept his hands by his side.

Connor ignored Dan's snub glancing briefly at Gwen before assisting Andy in setting up a two-player game. Lucinda simply smiled at Gwen's ex-husband and strolled out the back porch to the patio. Gwen observed Lucinda putting birdseed into the feeders through the kitchen window.

Dan's brows were knitted. "How are you, Gwen? You look different. You feeling okay?"

"I'm fine. Why?" Gwen returned Dan's gaze with a blank stare. She was playing things cool and knew Connor and Lucinda were listening to their interaction as well as Dan's thoughts.

Dan pulled Gwen aside to speak with her away from Connor and Andy, who were currently ensconced in a video game. Andy appeared to be winning, but Gwen knew Connor was purposely letting him.

"Well, you look very pale. And how well do you really know these people? They seem *different*. I don't know if I feel comfortable leaving *my* son here with them in this house."

"*Your* son," she said, heat rising in her cheeks. "You spend a few weeks out of the entire year with Andy and suddenly you think you have ownership over him? What happens the rest of the time when I'm on my own with him while you have complete freedom to do whatever you want? You have no right to tell me who I can interact with in my home." Gwen couldn't believe Dan's gall.

"I do if my son's in danger." Dan announced, in his typically smug voice.

It was ironic that the people Dan accused of being dangerous would actually die to protect Andy. Gwen pursed her lips. For a moment, she envisioned how it would feel to reach out and swipe his face with her hand, knocking him to the ground. Years of suppressed rage momentarily threatened to break free. Gwen knew she was in trouble when she fixated on the pulsing action of Dan's carotid artery. She could smell his blood and wanted to tear his skin open to get to it. Gwen realized she needed to smooth things over with Dan so he wouldn't give her any trouble and would stop meddling in her life, but she was still struggling with repressed anger. Lucinda must have read her thoughts, because she was suddenly by Dan's side, her pallid cold hand firmly placed on his.

"Hi, I don't believe we've met yet. I'm Lucinda. Would you like to take a brief walk in Gwen's garden? It's quite lovely out there," Lucinda said.

Dan's face went blank and he robotically followed Lucinda outside the back porch to the flower garden. Connor looked over his shoulder at Gwen and winked. For the first time, Gwen could hear his thoughts. *Don't worry Gwen; Lucinda will implant a false memory that Dan spent the day with us having a barbeque before returning to Atlanta. He won't pose any more problems for us.* Gwen was relieved and to her amazement watched Dan walk back into the house, give Andy a hug goodbye, and leave without another word. Gwen was in awe. The power that vampires could exert over their victims was immense and deserving of respect. No wonder they were the deadliest predators among humans.

"Mr. Blake, I've beat you three times so far, I think you need some practice killing zombies in this game," Andy said in a serious tone.

"I guess I do, Andy. Will you teach me the tricks?" Connor said, as he surreptitiously grinned at Gwen when Andy wasn't looking.

Gwen smiled back at him. Things seemed to be going well with Andy and Connor. Gwen went into the kitchen for a couple of hours to prepare chicken potpie, one of Andy's favorite dishes, while Connor played more video games with Andy. Lucinda was out in the yard, pruning the bushes and weeding the flower garden. When dinner had finished baking, Gwen put out four plates with generous portions for her and Andy and small portions for Connor and Lucinda. Gwen wasn't sure how they'd handle the food situation, but it would look strange for her to exclude Lucinda and Connor from the dinner table.

When the four of them sat down to dinner, Gwen watched Andy practically inhale his food. Connor and Lucinda smiled at Andy who seemed genuinely happy to be home. Gwen was in the middle of chewing when she heard Lucinda speak to her telepathically. Nearly choking on her food, Gwen nervously drank water from her glass before she regained her composure and stared at Lucinda. It was odd hearing someone speak to her without sounds being produced by their vocal chords. *Gwen, I'll get up and wipe my plate clean before Andy notices. A few moments afterwards, Connor will follow suit.* While Andy chomped down on another piece of piecrust, Lucinda swished past Gwen cleaning off her plate and returning to her seat like nothing had ever happened. Lucinda had her fork raised to her mouth like she had just finished the last bite of food. "Clever," Gwen thought, but then again, Lucinda had over three centuries of practice, faking food consumption. Andy didn't seem to notice anything. He continued eating his dinner while Connor flashed past Andy removing the contents of his plate into a plastic container on the table Gwen would use for leftovers. After dinner, Lucinda excused herself and acted as if she was leaving for the night. Of course, Gwen and Connor knew she'd be outside until Andy was asleep. Connor played a couple more games with Andy before he, too, exited Gwen's house.

Gwen informed Andy it was time for a bath before his bedtime. Andy grumbled a bit under his breath as he grabbed a towel out of the bathroom linen closet and ran the water in the tub.

"Do you need anything from me, Andy?" Gwen asked with the bathroom door slightly ajar.

"I'm good, Mom. Just need pajamas from my room."

"Which ones?"

"The ones with the racecars would be cool," Andy said.

"Okay, anything else?"

"Nope, that's good."

Gwen went into Andy's room and retrieved his pajamas from his bureau. She walked back towards the bathroom door and knocked on it.

"Yes, Mom?"

"I've got your pajamas, Sweetie. I'm going to put them on top of the hamper."

"Thanks."

"Come say goodnight before you go to bed," Gwen said.

Gwen cleaned up the kitchen and waved to Lucinda who was sitting in the backyard on one of Gwen's lawn chairs, her pale perfect features barely visible in the dark. Cloud cover from storms rolling in across the Gulf were obstructing the moon's light, leaving the outside darker than usual. Gwen looked for Connor, but didn't see him outside. She briefly leaned down to retrieve a toy car from the kitchen floor and jumped when she saw Connor standing next to her. Gwen hadn't heard him come inside the house.

"Sorry, didn't mean to startle you. Just wanted to see how you're doing." He pulled her close to him and lightly kissed her lips.

"What if Andy comes in?" she asked, looking into his magnificent eyes.

"He's a sharp kid, he's already figured it out."

"He knows?" Gwen asked wide-eyed.

"He was thinking about it during dinner."

"How does he feel about us?" she asked, as she pulled her long hair back into a ponytail.

"He knows you're happy and he seems to think I'm a nice guy. He realizes there is something different about Lucinda and me, but he's certain it's nothing dangerous."

"I didn't think a ten year-old thought about these things," she admitted.

"Well, kids will surprise you Gwen. Dan has a girlfriend you haven't heard about that Andy doesn't like, so he's happy that at least his mother has a boyfriend he does approve of," Connor said, smiling.

Gwen giggled a bit. "Well, that's a relief."

"Wait till he meets Aidan. He'll be in heaven. Oh,— here Andy comes." Connor fled the room, retreating to Gwen's bedroom safe from Andy's view.

Andy wandered into the living room, wearing his red racecar pajamas, his hair combed straight back. "Mom, I really like Mr. Blake. He's cool for an adult."

Gwen managed to suppress a laugh. "Well, I'm glad you like him. I think he's a pretty great, too."

"It's nice to see you have a friend now. I know you've been kind of lonely."

"You're pretty smart, you know that?" Gwen said, as she pulled Andy close for a hug.

"I try".

"Do you like Ms. Lucinda too?" Gwen asked.

Andy smiled. "She's really pretty Mom. And, I've never met people with eyes that color before. It's a beautiful shade of blue."

"So you feel comfortable around Mommy's friends?"

"Yeah, they're really nice. But, what I like the most is how much they care about you."

"You figured that out?" Gwen asked.

"Mom, please give me some credit. Just because I'm a kid doesn't mean I clueless. I can tell when people are being phony. Dad's girlfriend only pretended to be nice to me when Dad was around. When Dad wasn't looking, I saw her give me dirty looks. These people seem to really care about us."

Gwen pulled Andy close to her hugging him tight before she released him to look into his little gray eyes. "What would you like to do tomorrow?" Gwen asked as she stroked his light brown hair.

"Can we go to the zoo?"

"Sure."

"Will Mr. Blake come with us?" Andy asked, hopeful.

Gwen grinned at Andy's question. "I think we can convince him to come with us."

"Cool." Andy wrapped his arms around Gwen's waist for a big hug.

"Well, you'd better to get to sleep. You've had a long day and I have too," Gwen whispered, as she stroked his back.

"Okay, good night, Mom."

"Good night, Andy. Love you."

"Love you, too." Andy leaned up to give Gwen a kiss before he walked down the hallway into his bedroom. A few minutes later, Gwen opened his door to see he was fast asleep with his favorite lion wrapped under his arm.

Chapter 19

The phone rang shortly after midnight, waking both Gwen and Connor. She rolled over to grab the phone noticing the club's number was listed under the caller ID.

"Connor, it's someone from the club calling." Gwen handed him the receiver.

"Hello?" he said, before sitting in silence for several minutes. "Aidan, I can't leave now and I need Lucinda here for obvious reasons. Are you sure Alexei and Julia are missing?" There was more silence as Connor listened. "Aidan, don't panic. I'm sure there's a rational explanation for their absence from work tonight. Don't assume the worst, okay? All right. Let me know if they turn up. Talk with you tomorrow. Goodnight." Connor handed the phone back to Gwen.

Connor sat up in bed with his arms folded across his broad chest, his lips drawn up tight. The rigidity of his posture as well as his obvious anxiety worried Gwen.

"Who are Alexei and Julia?"

He turned to face Gwen, his luminescent blue eyes focused on hers;

his jaw clenched. "Two club employees. Neither of them showed up to work this evening."

"They're vampires, aren't they?" she asked, taking his hand in hers, the icy coolness sending small chills down the delicate skin of her hand.

"Yes, they are, and neither one of them has ever missed a day of work. My family has employed them in one form or another for nearly two centuries. Aidan's anxiety is warranted."

"Do you think this has to do with the ancient vampire who's been stalking me?"

"Not sure — but the events of the past two days seem like more than a coincidence. Maybe Derrick's right. This ancient immortal is likely one of Josef's vampire hunters sent here to destroy us. I just don't understand why he's been stalking you when it's clearly my *family* he wants," Connor said, looking particularly distressed by his own comment. "In any event, if Alexei and Julia don't show up by tomorrow, I'll need to investigate their disappearance."

"Andy has his heart set on going to the zoo tomorrow. Do you think we can still go or should I cancel?" Connor pulled Gwen towards him. She laid her head on his chest, while he wrapped his arms around her.

"I don't know. We'll have to see how things unfold tomorrow. Sorry I can't be more definitive at this point," he stated.

"I understand."

"Gwenevere, we haven't talked about it, but you'll need to let me know where you want to go by the end of this week. I have to start making arrangements."

"I would like to leave the country. Maybe we could go to Spain? What do you think?" she asked as she lightly kissed the cold hard skin of his chest.

"Josef's got many confidants and clan members in Europe and Asia. We're better off staying in the Americas. Think of somewhere in that range you'd like to go for a few weeks till things calm down here." Connor's hands caressed Gwen's shoulders and back.

"Okay, I'll mull it over and let you know." Connor's distinctively sweet scent filled her nostrils reflexively eliciting hunger for his blood. She wanted to taste him.

"Gwen, each time you drink from me, your longing will increase in intensity."

"It's getting harder to resist, Connor."

"I know, that's why I think you should refrain until you know for sure what you want," he said, holding her close to him.

Gwen sighed heavily. "You're probably right."

"However, that doesn't mean I can't taste you," he whispered, before he unexpectedly pulled her to him and bit into her chest.

Gwen woke to the sound of light tapping at her bedroom door. She rolled over and noticed Connor's side of the bed was empty. Gwen groaned a few minutes, still fatigued from last night. "Andy?"

"Gwen, it's Lucinda. I need to speak with you right away."

Gwen sat up, pulling her nightgown over her head concealing the fresh bite marks on her left breast. "Come in, Lucinda," Gwen muttered. Lucinda walked into Gwen's bedroom sitting down on the bed next to her. "Gwen, Alexei and Julia are still missing. No one from *The Immortal* has seen or heard from them since Friday night. Aidan and Derrick are outside on the porch talking with Connor."

"Is Andy up yet?" Gwen asked.

"No, but he's stirring. He'll probably be up soon. You may want to come out and join us before he does."

"Okay, that sounds like a good idea. Just give me a few minutes."

"See you outside," Lucinda said before she slipped out Gwen's bedroom door.

Gwen washed her face and quickly dressed. When she existed the bedroom the four cousins were sitting on the back porch deep in discussion. Storm clouds had stalled over the region flooding the area and heavy rain continued to hit the ground and surrounding terrain. Thunder and lightening were off in the distance and the sky had a grayish hue to it. The gloomy weather seemed to mimic the facial expressions of the four immortals sitting on the lanai. Connor walked over to hug Gwen as soon as she joined his family.

"Lucinda's filled you in on the situation right?" Connor asked.

Gwen nodded. "So, what do we do now?"

"We don't have any proof the ancient immortal has done anything yet so for now we're going to continue to act normally and keep a low profile. You and I are going to make plans to leave by Friday. In the meantime, Aidan and Lucinda will alternate staying with us, while Derrick runs things at the club."

Gwen surveyed the dismal landscape with a sigh. "Guess I've got my answer about taking Andy to the zoo today. "

"Don't worry, Gwen. We'll keep him entertained. Lucinda and I were thinking we could all go out together and take him to a movie," Aidan suggested with a smile.

"Well, that would be great! I just want him to feel like things are normal. He's a pretty perceptive kid, and he'll pick up on my anxieties if I'm not careful," she said.

"Well, leave that to me, Gwen. I am quite good at assuaging your worries, among other things." Connor smirked at Gwen. Gwen noticed Aidan and Derrick rolling their eyes, while Lucinda looked the other way. Gwen was red with embarrassment as she gave Connor a look of admonishment. Connor simply shrugged his shoulders and grinned at her.

Gwen knew Connor was trying to lighten her mood, but she couldn't suppress her concerns. She was convinced that the ancient immortal had murdered the two missing vampires, and that Connor and his family suspected that, as well.

When he awoke, Gwen had a big breakfast waiting for Andy. He was disappointed when he saw the lousy weather conditions, knowing the zoo trip was cancelled, but bounced back to his usual cheerful mood when he heard they were going to the movies that afternoon. Aidan had left Gwen's to run some errands before Andy got up and returned with several gift boxes of toys and other video gaming accessories. Andy was ecstatic playing with the toys and Aidan. Aidan had been right; kids did gravitate towards him and Gwen wondered, of the two of them, who was actually having more fun. As far as she was concerned, it was a tie. Gwen, Connor, Lucinda, Aidan, and Andy piled into Aidan's Nissan Xterra to see a kid's movie about dinosaurs at the local Cineplex. Connor bought Andy a large popcorn and drink, along with some chocolate covered raisins, which kept Andy happily entertained during the movie.

Most of the time Gwen was able to focus on the movie, but occasionally one of the vampires' thoughts would invade her consciousness throwing her concentration off. She couldn't follow the entire conversation; she just received bits and pieces like the bleed-through of one radio station into the frequency of another. She surmised that the intermittent ability to hear them telepathically had to do with her hybrid mortal status. They were all more apprehensive about the situation with the missing vampires than they let on. After the movie was over, the group took Andy out for dinner at an Italian restaurant. Connor, Lucinda, and Aidan told Andy they weren't hungry, and he bought it. Gwen ate only a small bit of her food, as her mind was focused elsewhere. Following dinner, the group drove back to Gwen's house where Aidan and Connor took turns playing with Andy on the gaming console, while Gwen and Lucinda spoke about superficial topics in the background to keep up appearances for Andy. Connor's cell phone rang and everyone froze in position.

"I'll take it outside," Connor said, immediately exiting the house.

Aidan continued playing with Andy, keeping him occupied while Lucinda and Gwen joined Connor on the porch.

Connor nodded his head a few times before he hung up. His expression was grave and he sighed heavily. "They're dead. One of the bouncer's found their bodies with the heads severed in a dumpster not far from the club. "

Gwen felt nauseous, clutching her mouth with her hand; while Lucinda burst into tears, blood streaming down her perfectly sculpted face.

"Are you sure it's not some horrible mistake?" Lucinda cried, her face a red wet mess.

"Yes, Derrick positively identified them," Connor said, his eyes downcast. "There's more —another employee is missing. Kendra left the club late last night and never made it to her apartment."

"We've got to shut down the club and get out of here." Lucinda said, wide-eyed and panicked "Josef's coming for us, Connor. I can feel it!"

Connor grabbed Lucinda's face with each hand firmly placed on each cheek. "Lucinda, I need you to calm down and focus right now. Quietly go into Andy's bedroom and pack a suitcase with some of his belongings. Okay?"

Lucinda slowly nodded her head and walked into the house wiping her face clean.

"Gwenevere, I also want you to quickly pack a bag of your basic necessities along with a few clothes. We'll leave within the hour and convoy to my house in Destin. We're going to be fine, we just need to act," Connor said, with a forced calmness that was meant to reassure her.

Gwen could sense the urgency of the situation, she went into her bedroom, and immediately threw some clothing and toiletries into an overnight bag. While Gwen and Lucinda packed suitcases, Connor telepathically briefed Aidan on the murders and plans to evacuate Gwen's house. Thankfully, Andy was blissfully unaware of what was happening. Connor told Andy they were going to Connor's house on the beach, so Andy was happy to help Gwen pack his suitcase into Gwen's car. Just before they left, Connor placed Panda and Misty into a cat carrier and into the Porsche. Gwen followed Connor fairly closely, breaking every speed limit from Bay to Walton Counties. It took under an hour to get to his Cape Cod home on the bluff in Destin. In silence, Connor, Aidan, and Lucinda quickly unpacked the cars and escorted Gwen, Andy, and the cats inside the house. Andy was sleepy from the day's busy activities and climbed into Connor's guest bed with little hesitation, while Panda and Misty found a comfortable section of the couch to curl up on in Connor's living room. Gwen petted Panda nervously wondering what she should do next. Connor sat down next to her and Lucinda joined them on the accompanying loveseat.

"Aidan's going back to the club. He and Derrick are going to shut things down and set the club on fire. We need Josef to see we're backing down from our actions and that we've got his message. It's probably too late to save Kendra," Connor said, rubbing his temples with his index finger and thumb.

"What about us?" Lucinda asked, her eyes weary and heavy-lidded.

"We'll stay here tonight, and leave in the morning. Gwen, where do you want to go?" he asked, massaging her hand in his.

"San Diego. Andy loves zoos. We'll have plenty to keep him busy until we can return home," she said.

Connor smiled at her. "San Diego it is. You should leave a voicemail with your Dean that you have a family emergency to attend to and will be out of town for a month. You have about that much time till school starts right?" he asked.

"Yes. I'll go make the call now."

"Good," Connor remarked.

Gwen left messages for the Dean and his assistants regarding her family emergency. She then called her parents and told them she was taking Andy to San Diego for an impromptu vacation. Initially, her mother sounded alarmed, but when Gwen mentioned that it was a surprise trip courtesy of her millionaire boyfriend, her mother was more receptive to the idea. Gwen hated lying to her mother, but the alternative was even less appealing. By the time she finished with her phone calls and returned to the living room, Connor was alone. Lucinda wasn't sleeping, but had retired to one of Connor's bedrooms to lie down. Gwen sat down next to Connor.

"What now?" she asked.

Connor smiled pulling Gwen close to him. He began stroking her face and hair, sending pleasurable sensations throughout her body. She felt her body slacken and go limp.

"Tomorrow is going to be a busy day and it's best if we get some rest," he said, as he escorted her to his bedroom where the two were asleep within moments of getting into bed.

Chapter 20

Gwen stumbled onto the sand of the beach, while being pulled by frigid hands that tightly gripped her arm. Her body felt heavy, uncoordinated, and she could barely open her eyes. Gwen called out Connor's name, but what came out of her mouth sounded incoherent. For a moment she thought she was dreaming, until she dropped to the ground and felt the sand scrap against her legs. Gwen heard a wicked laugh that had a resonance to it she'd heard once before. With effort she forced her eyes open to face the vampire who would most likely end her life. The ancient immortal stood before her, his long brown stringy hair swirling in multiple directions like serpents undulating in the wind. His face was angelic, but his blood-red eyes and prominent razor-sharp teeth that protruded over his thin cracked lips undermined his beautiful features. Gwen noticed his nails resembled talons like she'd observed in her nightmares. He came towards her and she recoiled, shrinking even closer to the ground. A raspy laugh escaped his throat, sending chills down Gwen's body. Another immortal, standing nearby, grabbed Gwen and forced her to her feet so that she was standing near the ancient vampire.

"Hello, Gwenevere I've been waiting a long time to meet you," the ancient immortal said, sneering.

"What do you want?" she asked, amazed she could speak.

"Isn't it obvious?" he inquired, running his icy cold finger down the side of her face. His fingernail, sharp and jagged, lightly pierced the skin of her cheek causing a single blood drop to slide down her face.

"You want to kill Connor and his family," she said, terrified.

"Oh, yes, I definitely want to kill Connor and his family. But, not before I've had my revenge, first. Oh, I do love the taste of AB positive blood." The vampire moved closer; his teeth millimeters away from her cheek. His long pointed tongue licked the single blood drop off of her face. Gwen watched in horror as the vampire closed his eyes and inhaled her scent as if he were savoring a delicacy.

"Where's Connor?" Gwen cried.

"Anxious to get started, are we? He's over there along with that female cousin of his," the ancient vampire said, pointing to four vampires who were holding Connor and Lucinda hostage. It was a full moon and Gwen could see the fury in Connor's luminescent eyes. Lucinda looked terrified.

"Let's join them, shall we?" the vampire said, as he seemed to glide over to where Connor and Lucinda were being held. Gwen barely noticed the ancient vampire's feet touching the ground. "Oh, by the way, I haven't formally introduced myself. I'm Varanos, the first sire of Matthias and keeper of his clan."

"Your not one of Josef's vampire hunters?" Gwen asked, incredulous.

"Don't insult me, human, I have nothing to do with Josef. In fact, he knows nothing of *The Immortal*, or should I say, what's left of it?" Varanos laughed pulling Gwen close to him, while Connor strained against the two immortals immobilizing him.

"Varanos, you can have me, but let Gwen go. She means nothing to you," Connor pleaded.

"Connor, I've been waiting for over three hundred years for the moment when I could destroy you. Killing you will be the last thing I do tonight. I want you to suffer the way I did when you murdered most of our clan and sent our leader into exile. You almost finished me off.

Matthias, on the other hand, went mad after the massacre in Salem. I've kept what's left of our clan together all these years."

"Gwenevere's never done anything to you. She's an innocent!" Connor screamed.

"Connor, you disappoint me. Isn't it obvious what's happening here? Gwenevere and her son mean everything to you. That's why I intend to drain their bodies dry while you watch. Afterwards, I'll burn you and the rest of your family alive," Varanos said, before he broke out into maniacal laughter.

Connor screamed as his hand broke free of one of the immortals, clawing at the air. "I'll kill you, Varanos, you hear me!"

Varanos lightly stroked Gwen's hair with a look of sadistic pleasure. "I don't blame you Connor. She is rather lovely, but then again so was your precious Elizabeth. I remember how she pleaded for her life just before I sucked her bone-dry. It wasn't quite the revenge I had hoped for; you see, I should have done it in front of you. Three centuries have given me a lot of time to plan your real punishment." Varanos looked at Connor's fury filled eyes. "Oh, you didn't know it was me did you?"

"I will enjoy every moment of killing you, you sick demented bastard," Connor seethed, hatred twisting his face.

Even though Gwen realized it was likely she was going to die, she couldn't bear the thought of her son dying, too. In that moment her decision became clear, although it might be too late. Gwen knew she couldn't fight Varanos, but if she was going to die it wasn't going to be in vain. She needed to distract Varanos and the other vampires, so that Connor could break free of them and get Andy to safety. Gwen listened as Varanos antagonized Connor with a description of her impending death, the way a cat bats prey around with its paws before it kills it. She scanned the area for anything that could be used as a weapon against Varanos when she saw several flashes of movement in her peripheral vision. Varanos had seen the movement as well. He stopped talking, orienting to the flurry of motion surrounding him, allowing Gwen her chance to break free of his hold. Gwen took off running towards the house to get to Andy. If nothing else, it would divert Varanos' and the other immortals' attention away from Connor. If she weren't successful at getting to Andy, Connor would be. Unfortunately, Gwen underestimated Varanos' desire for revenge, as he tackled her to the ground twisting her arm and immobilizing her. Varanos ripped open her blouse and bit into her neck.

"Gwenevere, no!" Connor shouted.

Varanos' bloodlust was great and he hungrily siphoned the blood from her body. The flurry of activity Gwen had witnessed earlier was Derrick, and Aidan. Gwen noted that Aidan looked very weak and badly burned. Lucinda, released from the vampire that had been restraining her was now fighting with the immortals that belonged to Varanos' clan, while Derrick and Connor rushed to Gwen's side. Together they ripped Varanos off of her, but not before he managed to dislocate Gwen's arm in the process. The pain Gwen felt was excruciating. She cried out in agony as she watched Connor and Derrick fight Varanos.

Connor crouched low and lunged at Varanos knocking him into one of the sand dunes. The two thrashed about, rolling back and forth. Gwen heard Connor scream and using her good arm managed to push herself upright so that she could see what was happening. She saw Varanos sink his teeth deep into Connor's shoulder; Connor's eyelids fluttered and he looked like he was going to lose consciousness.

"Derrick, help me," Connor pleaded in a weak voice.

Derrick came from behind and managed to dislodge Varanos from Connor's body, pulling the ancient immortal off of him. Derrick held Varanos' arms pinned behind his back while the ancient immortal thrashed about trying to pry himself loose of Derrick's grip.

"He won't be vulnerable for long, Lad, bite him now!" Derrick yelled.

"With pleasure, Derrick!" Connor exclaimed, forcing Varanos' head to the side. Connor's fangs extended from his mouth and he thrust them deep into Varanos' neck. For a few minutes Varanos fought against Connor and Derrick, but soon his limbs went limp and he collapsed against Derrick. Connor didn't pull away from Varanos until he'd completely drained the ancient vampire. Wiping his mouth off with the back of his arm, Connor placed his hands on other side of Varanos's head and snapped it off, severing it from his body. Gwen sighed with relief before she remembered her injury and the searing pain that went along with it. Connor was the first by her side. He looked down at

Gwen; anguish in his facial expression. He surveyed Gwen's injuries. In the background, Gwen heard several cracks as Derrick and Lucinda snapped off the heads of Varanos' followers.

"Gwenevere, you will live. We can get you to a hospital to have them reset your arm. You'll be anemic for awhile but Varanos didn't take enough blood to kill you," Connor said, gently holding Gwen's injured hand in his.

"No, Connor. I've made my choice. It's to become immortal," Gwen whispered, her body racked with pain.

"Gwenevere, you don't have to do that. You and Andy are safe now," he pressed.

"Connor, I will never be able to protect my son as a mortal woman the way I can as a vampire. And—there may be others like Varanos, out there, waiting for us. I know what I want and it's to be by your side as an equal," she whispered, looking into his blood-covered face.

Connor nodded and pulled Gwen to him. She winced in pain as he unintentionally nudged her dislocated limb. He kissed her lightly on the lips, before he gently moved her head to the side and sank his fangs deep into her carotid artery. Gwen felt the agonizing pain recede along with all the other unpleasant sensations she'd experienced that night. Thoughts of Varanos and his battle with Connor dissipated from her awareness. Gwen felt weightless; like she was floating and the slow and hypnotic sound caught her attention. She knew it was the rhythm of her heartbeat slowing its pace. Gwen felt a sense of peace she had never known and she noticed it was harder for her to breath. She started struggling to get air, but something cold and hard stroked the side of her face, easing her respiration efforts. Darkness surrounded Gwen from all sides and she thought of Connor and Andy before she felt her heart beat for the last time.

Something pried Gwen's mouth open forcing salty liquid down her parched throat. To anyone on the outside there was no visible response from Gwen's nearly lifeless body. The warm liquid felt good to the burning tissues in her esophagus. As more of the warm viscous liquid invaded her throat, Gwen's body responded. She heard voices around her.

"I drank too much. She's not going to make it. What have I done?

What am I going to do if she doesn't change?" Connor said, anguish in his voice.

"She's going to make it. Gwen's a fighter," Derrick said.

"Please Gwen, don't leave us," Aidan whispered, coughing.

"Derrick, you've got to help Aidan. It will take weeks for his burns to heal," Lucinda remarked. "Connor, Gwen will make it."

"I took too much, Lucinda, I've never changed anyone before. How do you know she's going to survive?" Connor asked, panicking.

"You're forgetting something important, Connor. It's not just your blood co-mingled with Gwen's that you've fed her. It's the ancient's blood too. Gwen will make it and she'll be more powerful than most of us can even imagine," Lucinda said, with reverence.

"Lad, she's right. Gwen will have gifts most of us can only dream about," Derrick said.

"All I want is for her to survive. I never got the chance to tell her, how I really feel about her," Connor said. "I've given her all the blood I can. Now all I can do is hope. I need a few minutes to myself cousins. I'll be back shortly."

Connor walked down the beach until he was well out of their sight. He didn't want them to see him lose control of his emotions. He wept like a child, wondering how he was going to explain Gwen's death to Andy. He looked up at the moon overlooking the Gulf and thought of the first night they spent here. He remembered carrying her across the sand and holding her in his arms while she slept. He whispered out loud, "I love you, Gwenevere."

I love you too, Connor.

Connor glanced around looking for the silky voice that he had heard in his head. He ran down the beach towards his cousins and that's when he saw her. She stood on the beach facing the surf. The long locks of her blonde hair framed her pale perfect skin and delicately chiseled features. She turned to face him, smiling and holding her hand out to him. The last thing Connor noticed before he pulled her in his arms was that her doe-shaped eyes were no longer dark gray, but a brilliant shade of light blue.